Mayhem on the Michigamme

Six Murder Mysteries

Bill Blewett

Mayhem on the Michigamme
Six Murder Mysteries

Bill Blewett

Editor: Tyler Tichelaar

Medical Advisor: Charlene Blewett R.N.

Copyright © 2017 Bill Blewett

This book is a work of fiction. Names, characters, places, and incidents either are products of the author's imagination or are used fictitiously. Any resemblance to actual persons, living or dead, events, or locales is entirely coincidental. No part of this book may be reproduced without the expressed written consent of the author.

ISBN: 978-0-692-824221

Printed in the United States of America
First Printing, 2017

Globe Printing, Inc.
200 W. Division St. Ishpeming, MI 49849
www.globeprinting.net

I dedicate this book to my three children Beth, Jeff, and Joe.

Acknowledgments

    I would like to take this opportunity to thank everyone who helped write these stories. Many thanks to my family, friends, editor, and book publisher, for without all of you, this endeavor would not have been possible.

Table of Contents

Part 1 - The Murders on the Michigamme 11

Part II - The Fall of Maderis. 81

Part III - The Mayor's Murder 123

Part IV - The Moose Shed Murders 173

Part V - The Revenge of ISIL 207

Part VI - The Lion of Michigamme 237

Introduction

Lake Michigamme is a pristine lake that reaches a depth of over 70 feet and covers 4,300 acres most of it lying in Mesabi County, Michigan.

The lake runs about seven miles east to west, with a southern arm extending about another mile and a dam separating the Michigamme River from the main body of the lake at the end of the southern arm. The Spurr River flows into the lake's west end and the Peshekee River flows into the lake in the northeast. Game fish include smallmouth bass, northern pike, and walleye. The name Michigamme is derived from the Ojibwa language meaning "large lake."

Following are the cast of characters.

The amateur-detectives who appear in all of the stories:
  Bill Bennett, Retired Sheriff, Husband to Barb
  John Baldwin, Retired Military Police Officer
  Mark Kestila, Retired Military Police Officer
  Ben Myers, Retired Victorious Police Officer
  Tyler Baldwin, Current Needleton Police Officer
  Jenni Durant, Aspiring Police Officer
  Kelly Sanderson, Aspiring Police Officer

Law Enforcement:
  Andy Roads, Mesabi County Sheriff's Deputy
  Carolyn Raft, Mesabi County Medical Examiner
  Connie Stevenson, NYPD Advisor
  Strom Remington, Mesabi County Sheriff

Characters according to the stories they appear in.

Characters in "The Murders on the Michigamme"
  Brawn Dilfour, Poacher
  Kate Cather, Kent Hendricks' Mistress
  Kent Hendricks, Retired Baseball Player
  Sheila Hendricks, Wife of Kent Hendricks
  Pam Meadows, Wife of Dr. Meadows
  Peter Meadows, Son of Dr. and Pam Meadows
  Samantha Perkins, Friend of Kate Cather

Characters in "The Fall of Maderis"
  Cindy Morgan, Personal Assistant to Maderis
  Connor Simpson, Former Boyfriend of Stella Stevinski
  Eddy Lavens, Bartender
  Floyd Dilfour, Poacher
  John Rudolf, New York Playboy
    and Kate Cather's Jilted Lover
  Maderis (Stella Stevinski), Starlet
  Maggie Grenville, Public Rations Director to Maderis
  Rogue Garrison, Hollywood Director

Characters in "The Mayor's Murders"
  Dr. Frank Goodney, Committee Member
  Fred Wilder, EPA Administrator
  Glen Magnum, ATV Store Owner
  Helen Michaels, Committee Member
  Henry Brennen, Committee Member
    and Pharmaceutical Salesman
  Lars Larson, Cascadia Logger
  Pete Runnels, County Commissioner
  Sara Goodney, Committee Member
  Sam Waters, Glen Magnum's Employee

Characters in "The Moose Shed Murders"
Brawn Dilfour, Poacher
Charley Rollins, Murdered CO
Jack Carver, Brother of Lindsey Haynes
Lindsey Haynes, Charley Rollins' Mistress
Chris Rollins, Widow of Charley Rollins
Donnie Rollins, Charley Rollins' Son
Floyd Dilfour, Poacher
Jack Carver, Lyndsey Haynes' Brother
Tom Renfrow, Chris Rollins' Brother

Characters in "The Revenge of ISIL"
Abu al, Krik, ISIL Terrorist in America
Amreen Malek, Mohid's Sister
Captain Kormel, Clay Bennett's Commander
Donna Bennett, Wife of Clay Bennett
Mohid Malek, Clay Bennett's Friend
Zawihi al-Badr, ISIL Leader in Andahar Province

Characters in "The Lion of Michigamme"
Carlos Gomez, Daredevil Rider in the Circus
Consuelo Garcia, Maria Garcia's Cousin
Dr. Feel Good (Josh McQueen), Cascadia Drug Dealer
Emil, Animal Trainer
Henry Bartle, Circus Owner
Javier Garcia, Brother of Maria Garcia
Jeb Stalworth, Circus Ringmaster
John Crane, Private Detective
Maria Garcia, Aerial Star of the Circus
Tomas Gomez, Daredevil Rider in the Circus

Part 1

The Murders on the Michigamme

Chapter One

The warmth penetrated your bones and the foliage was lush with the wildlife enjoying the most beautiful time of year. Summer in the Superior Peninsula of Michigan is unlike any season in any other place in the world. Tourists flock to Mesabi County to enjoy our natural beauty only to return to a world of blacktop capped off by skyscrapers. We leave our doors unlocked at night and windows open.

A nearby village, Cascadia, is located a few miles away from Victorious. Cascadia is a small community of approximately three hundred inhabitants who reside on the western end of Lake Michigamme. Founded in 1871 by miners who dug iron ore though strip mining, it is a quiet town that only comes alive once a year, the Fourth of July. This year, Cascadia store owners were ecstatic. Ever since it had been announced that local hero Kent Hendricks was going to be the parade marshal, the community had been flooded.

Tourists came by the thousands, all hoping to see former baseball great, Kent Hendricks. Hendricks had built a sizeable home on the north shore of Cascadia and had become a local hero to the townspeople. Having pitched for several major league baseball teams, he was seen moving about the community on a regular basis. The locals had become used to him in the stores, but the out-of-towners couldn't believe a retired professional baseball player would call Cascadia home. Hendricks would live to regret that.

Truth be told, it wasn't the draw of a small town community that Hendricks enjoyed. The real attraction was that he had fallen in love with a local girl, Kate Cather, when his wife was out of town. He had a chance to enjoy life to the fullest, and he felt he deserved a reward. One evening, he had stopped in The Timbers Bar for a beer, and after a few cold ones, he worked up the nerve to ask Kate for a date. "How about seeing me after you finish your shift?"

"I don't know you. Can I trust you to be a gentleman?" Kate asked.

Kent answered, "You can trust me to do whatever you want me to."

"My shift ends at midnight. Can you wait that long?" Kate asked.

"I will wait forever if it means seeing you," he replied.

Later that evening, Kate removed her apron and shouted, "Good night, Eddy," to the other bartender as she prepared to leave. She was pleasantly surprised to see Hendricks sitting on a stool near the door. "Aren't you the patient one," she said.

"I told you I would wait forever just to see you," Hendricks replied. He had used the line dozens of times, and it always worked. Women were thrilled to be with him, so he was obliged to meet their expectations. Kate knew it was wrong; she knew he was married, but she couldn't resist the excitement of being with him. After all, he was a celebrity in the community. That date led to more evening romances over the next few weeks, and Kent invited her over to his home for romantic rendezvouses. His wife, Sheila, was none-the-wiser since she didn't care to spend time in Cascadia, or as she called it, "a mosquito-infested dump." While the cat's away, the mouse will play.

Sheila liked the bright lights of New York and all it had to offer. One of those offerings was a handsome young man whom she met while presenting her fashion designs at a style show. John Rudolf, who worked for an established fashion designer, Jasmine, helped her set up her display and even volunteered to assist dismantling it after the show was over. Sheila felt obligated to buy him a drink in the hotel bar, which led to a sexual encounter in her room. Her husband was as dumb as a post and would be none the wiser. It was her way of coping with an unhappy marriage that left her unfulfilled. Every time she visited New York, she made it a point to call John up and engage in a night of immoral passion.

Chapter Two

Sheila was arriving on the American Airline flight at one o'clock. Kent Hendricks knew he had to be at Mesabi International Airport. It was too dangerous to try to meet Kate that day and still be at the airport in time for his wife's flight.

Kent Hendricks' cell phone rang. Opening one eye he moaned "Yeah."

"I want to see you this morning," Kate pleaded over the phone. Kent said, "I can't. I have to pick up my wife at the airport. It's clear across the county. I'll call you tomorrow when things get back to normal."

"I need to see you right now. It's very important. Now get over here, now!" she screamed and slammed her phone down.

"Bitch," Kent said. He had not expected this kind of behavior from her. Now he would have to deal with this. He had thought he had Kate in his back pocket.

Kent drove to the airport and waited dutifully for his wife's plane to touch down. They embraced in the terminal and migrated to the luggage carrousel. Sheila's luggage filled up an entire luggage caddy.

"What do you have in here?" Kent asked.

"I had to take a lot of drawings for the show," Sheila said. With little fanfare, they proceeded to their vehicle and started to drive home. As they were driving, Kent turned the local news on and caught the end of a broadcast. The announcer was finishing an especially tragic story, "She was twenty-seven years old, brown hair, brown eyes, 5' 4" tall and weighs approximately one hundred and twenty pounds."

"I wonder who that could be," said Sheila.

Kent stated, "I don't know many people in Cascadia."

They continued driving in silence. They didn't know what was coming.

As they pulled into their driveway, several sheriff's deputy cruisers were waiting. As they stepped out, one of the deputies introduced himself. "I am Deputy Roads and this is Deputy Wilson." Deputy Roads continued, "Are you Kent Hendricks?"

"Yes, I am," Kent replied. "What's the matter?"

Deputy Roads said, "We would like you to come with us. We have some questions for you."

Hendricks said, "I haven't done anything. I am not going with you until you tell me what this is about."

Deputy Roads said, "A young woman was found in Lake Michigamme and we have been told by friends of hers that you knew her well."

"Who are you talking about?" Sheila interrupted.

"I'd rather not say right now," Deputy Roads said.

Hendricks, suspecting the worst, did not want his wife to find out about his romantic fling, so he said, "All right, but I want my lawyer."

"You can call her from the Mesabi County Sheriff's Department," Deputy Roads said.

The deputy opened the backseat of his cruiser and Hendricks stepped in. Sheila had a quizzical look on her face as they left. She didn't know what to do. She entered her house and called their lawyer, Sandy Sundell.

"Hello, Preston and Sundell," said the receptionist.

"I want to speak with Ms. Sundell," said Sheila.

"May I say who is calling?" asked the receptionist.

"Sheila Hendricks."

"One moment, please," replied the receptionist.

"Hello, this is Sandy Sundell. May I help you?" Sheila Hendricks said, "Yes, my husband has been picked up by sheriff deputies and brought to their headquarters for questioning. I just don't like the looks of this. Can you meet him there?"

"Yes, I can be there when he is questioned," replied Sandy Sundell.

~~~

Kent and the deputies entered the Sheriff's Department and were led into an interrogation room.

Upon entering, Kent was surprised to see a group of law enforcement officers already seated.

"Hello, I am Sheriff Remington," the older man began. "Thank you for coming down. We're trying to unravel a mystery. We have a young lady's body and no witnesses. The locals have told us you were particularly close to Ms. Cather. People even saw you leave The Timbers with her many times over the last few months." The sheriff paused for a reaction. Receiving none, he continued, "Some kids found the body near an old hunting camp that is only a quarter of a mile from your place. Are you able to account for your whereabouts over the last twenty-four hours?"

"What are you talking about?" Hendricks asked.

"Don't play games with us. Many people in The Timbers have identified you as leaving with Miss Cather several times. Now were you with her last night?" Sheriff Remington asked.

Hendricks said, "Yes, I saw her last night. She called me this morning and wanted me to come over. I told her I had to pick up my wife at the airport."

Just then, the door swung open. Sandy Sundell stepped in and said, "Don't say another word. This meeting is over unless you are going to charge my client with something."

The door opened again and Deputy Roads entered and walked over to Sheriff Remington. After Roads whispered into Remington's ear, Remington stood and said, "Well, Ms. Sundell, you are going to get your wish. We are charging your client with murder. The M.E. just confirmed the body is Kate Cather's."

"What grounds do you have to arrest my client?" asked Sandy Sundell.

"For now, we have motive and timing. He was the last person to see Kate Cather alive, and he has a motive. He didn't want his wife to find out he was seeing Ms. Cather. Read him his rights and lock him up."

"Don't worry, Mr. Hendricks. I will have you out by tonight," Sandy Sundell said.

"I don't think so," Sheriff Remington replied. "The court is closed, so Hendricks will have to spend the night as a guest of the county. You can bail him out in the morning."

Chapter Three

Early the next morning, my phone rang. Being a retired sheriff, my phone didn't ring very early anymore except if it was John Baldwin calling to go for a mountain bike ride.

"Hello," I moaned.

"Mr. Bennett?" the voice asked.

"It depends. If you're selling something, or you want him to take a survey, he just left," I said.

"Mr. Bennet, this is serious. This is Sandy Sundell, and I have been retained to represent Kent Hendricks in a murder investigation. I would like to hire your pseudo-detectives and yourself to help defend my client."

"I really don't hire out for detective work," I replied. "My friends and I only help out when someone is really desperate. There are a lot of good detectives in the phone book. Now, if you don't mind, I would like to go back to sleep."

"Wait a minute. Let me explain. Mr. Hendricks has been accused of murdering his mistress. His wife was out of town and he has no alibi. Money is no object. Can you help him?" She supplied me with the rest of the details of the murder. She continued, "Could you meet me in my office tomorrow morning?"

"I will have to check with the others and see what they say. I can't promise anything," I said as I disconnected.

"Who was that?" my wife Barb asked.

"Apparently, Kent Hendricks has been charged in the murder of his mistress, Kate Cather. I don't know any more than that."

"You owe it to Hendricks to at least talk it over with your friends," Barb said.

I have been fortunate to remain friends with some great senior gentlemen who were once unequaled in their respective detective fields. My best friend is John Baldwin, who had twenty years as a military detective under his belt and was now retired. His son, Tyler, is a police sergeant in a nearby community, Needleton. Tyler's fiancée, Carolyn Raft, has also become a regular. She is a great medical examiner and has helped us solve numerous crimes. Along with Deputy Roads, she had endured a terrible helicopter crash last winter and by rights should not have survived. My old duck hunting partner, Mark Kestila, had earned his detective stripes while serving in the Army in Europe during his younger years. Ben Myers is a retired police officer from my hometown, Victorious. Ben has almost single-handedly closed many meth labs in Victorious. Although my friends and I helped solve a lot of crimes in Mesabi County the last few years, now I thought we could just enjoy our golden years. "I'll call them and see if they want to tackle this murder," I said.

~~~

That evening, the pseudo-detectives convened at Geno's Pizzeria. As usual, Rick Bonnetelli was behind the bar, wearing a grin and pointing to a booth in the back. He knew a good thing when he saw it.

"What do we have?" asked Mark Kestila once he sat down.

"We have a baseball celebrity accused of murder," I said.

"What evidence does the prosecuting attorney have?" asked Ben Myers.

"Very circumstantial," I said. "He was the last person to talk to her, but the most incriminating evidence of all was his wife who was out of town when he was seeing Kate Cather. It's safe to say that he wouldn't want his wife, Sheila, to get wind of his wandering escapades."

"I think it's too convenient," said Tyler Baldwin.

"I agree; it looks like he is being set up," Carolyn Raft added.

"Are we all in agreement? We will look into the case with no guarantees. Is that satisfactory?" I asked. They all nodded their heads and we got down to the task of enjoying a few cold drinks and some pizza.

The next morning, I arrived at Sandy Sundell's office with a feeling of apprehension. The receptionist showed me into Sandy's office.

"How are you, and will you take the case?" Sandy greeted me.

"I'm fine, and I'll get right to the chase. Last night, I talked with my friends. We will look into the case, but no guarantee that we will continue. If we think he is guilty, we will drop out. Is that agreed?"

After a moment of reflection, she said, "That works for me." We shook on the agreement.

Chapter Four

July 4th was the most exciting day in Cascadia. For a small town, it had a wonderful parade and family-friendly activities in the afternoon. In the town square, a local band, Black Rock, led by lead singer Phil McPhail, performed into the evening before the day was climaxed with a wonderful fireworks display honoring America.

Since our children were out of the area for the Fourth of July, I asked Barb to come with me to visit Cascadia and try to glean an insight into the locals' opinions. The parade started, and I watched the veterans pass with "Old Glory" unfurled. Cars full of beauty contestants and fire trucks followed. It wasn't as enormous as big city parades, but it was obvious that the people of Cascadia had put their hearts into making it a true celebration of our nation's Independence Day.

During the parade, I had the opportunity to listen to people's true feelings regarding Hendricks' innocence.

"Embarrassing, simply embarrassing," one disgruntled parade viewer mumbled. She continued, "We have one parade a year with a chance to make some money and celebrate our Independence Day and the grand marshal is under suspicion for murder."

I tried to act nonchalant, but it was impossible to ignore. While the floats and firetrucks passed, it was obvious everyone was very disappointed with the outcome. Kent Hendricks was out on bail, but nowhere to be seen. Undoubtedly, he had decided it was best to stay out of the public spotlight with the impending trial. I moved stealthily among the parade viewers and tried to listen to anything that might help me make up my mind.

"He must have done it," one person quipped.

"I agree. His wife was out of town and he took advantage of it. You know how those professional athletes are. They think they are above the law," extolled one anguished parade viewer.

"I hope he gets what he deserves. She was a nice girl and didn't deserve to end up stabbed and mutilated," another parade viewer chimed in.

It was pretty obvious this crowd already had Hendricks tried and convicted on circumstantial evidence. It made me feel that I had to take the case to appease my inner sense of justice. As a long-term police officer, I had learned things aren't always what they seem. Hendricks might be a scum-bag, but he deserved a fair trial.

I felt a tap on my shoulder, and as I turned around, I saw a distinguished-looking, middle-aged gentleman. He held out his hand and said, "Hi, I'm Dr. Meadows. I'm the local pediatrician, obstetrician, podiatrist, internist, and nurse. I recognized you from the newspapers, Mr. Bennett; you have quite a reputation and it's well-deserved. I even remember when you were Sheriff of Mesabi County. Are you enjoying the festivities?"

"Yes, I am. This is my wife, Barb," I said, introducing them to each other.

"What brings you to our fair community? I am sure Victorious has a bigger parade," he said.

"I just wanted to get an insight into the locals' feelings on Hendricks," I replied. "I have been asked to assist in the case."

"Well, I wish you good luck, but I don't think you will find any sympathy for Hendricks in Cascadia," Dr. Meadows said. We shook hands and departed.

"Well, do we go home, or do we wait for the fireworks tonight?" asked Barb.

"Let's pay a visit to that hunting cabin where they found Kate Cather," I said.

I followed the directions Sandy Sundell had given me yesterday.

We drove past the Cascadia boat launch and the cemetery; eventually, the Red Road narrowed with a thick canopy of

Part I - The Murders on the Michigamme

maples blocking out the sunlight. As we neared Cardinal Point, I said, "I think that's it," spotting an old dilapidated cabin in the distance.

"I can't believe this was the scene of the crime," Barb said. "Nobody would even go near that wreck."

"I know, and that's why I want to take a better look at the building and figure out why the murder may have occurred there."

We stepped out of our car and walked through the thick underbrush up to the ramshackle building.

"If you don't mind, I'll stay outside," Barb said.

"That's fine. The police have been through this building many times, but I just can't understand why her body was found here," I stated.

I entered the cabin precariously, stepping as lightly as I could so as not to put too much weight on either foot in case I went through the floor boards. It was a small, twelve-foot square room, probably built by hunters or trappers in the early twentieth century. There was only a small window from which to view the lake. When I leaned down to peer out the window, I suddenly fell through the outside wall. Falling into the water, I was able to make my way to shore. In my thrashing, I felt something under the water. It was an old fishing net, probably used by trappers over a century ago to catch their daily meals. Just to be sure, I decided to find someone who would know more about this type of net. After all, it was the closest thing to any sort of suspicious evidence I could find.

Chapter Five

Ben and Mark decided to pay our client a visit. They drove to Cascadia, exited their car, and knocked on his door.

Hendricks' wife, Sheila, opened the door.

"Hello, my name is Ben Myers and this is Mark Kestila. We're working with Sandy Sundell to help your husband."

"I'll see if he's around. I think he's in the backyard mowing the lawn. I'll get him," she said. "Won't you come in?" She departed out the back door. Shortly after, Kent Hendricks entered the room, wiping the sweat from his brow. Sheila closed the door from the outside.

"Hello," Kent said. "I understand you have been retained by Sandy Sundell to help defend me. I appreciate it."

Ben and Mark re-introduced themselves, and then Mark said, "We need to know more about Kate Cather. What can you tell us?"

"I only know she worked at The Timbers Bar in Cascadia. I met her a few weeks ago and we hit it off. My wife and I are trying to work through this, but it's difficult," Hendricks said.

"Did she have any relatives in the area?" Ben asked.

"Yes, she did," Ken replied. "She had a brother who worked at the lumberyard. I think both their parents are deceased."

"Did she have any old boyfriends, or anyone who might want to hurt her?" Ben pushed the interrogation.

"I'm sure she did, but I didn't know them. We only got together a few times. We didn't talk much," Hendricks said as he looked out the back window to make sure Sheila was out of earshot.

"If we're going to help you, we need to know everything about her," Mark stated.

"I know she liked the lake. After we had intercourse, she liked to walk down by the lake and just sit and stare," Hendricks said.

"We'll stop at The Timbers and see if anyone knows anything," Mark said.

"Good luck working this out with your wife," Ben said as they stood and left.

On the way home, they stopped at The Timbers Bar. After they entered and sat down, the bartender approached them and asked, "What'll you have?"

"How about some information?" Ben asked.

"That depends on your questions," the bartender responded.

"First of all, what's your name?" Mark asked.

"I'm Eddy Lavens."

"We're looking into the Cather murder. What can you tell us about her?" Mark asked.

"Are you with the police?" the bartender asked.

"No, we're working for the defense," Ben said.

Eddy Lavens said, "I'll tell you what I know. Kate and Black Rock's lead singer, Phil McPhail, used to be a regular item, but since Kent Hendricks entered the picture, he's yesterdays newspaper."

Eddy seemed to recoil when he heard this. Lavens thought for a moment and said, "I liked her a lot and we got along well. I am pretty sure Hendricks killed her because he liked to pick her up after she finished her shift and leave right away. I don't know of anyone else who would have wanted her dead."

"We understand she had a brother. Does he come in very often?" Ben asked.

The bartender seemed a little surprised with the question.

"That's him over in the corner," Eddy said.

"What's his first name?" Mark asked.

"His real name is Larry, but he likes to be called 'Big L.'" Mark and Ben could see why he liked to be called Big L. He was over six feet tall and weighed over four hundred pounds.

Ben and Mark stood and walked over to Big L.

"My name is Ben Myers, and this is Mark Kestila," said Ben. "We're sorry about your sister. We're looking into her murder.

Can we ask you some questions? Can you help us in any way?"

"I want Hendricks dead. I know he killed her, and I won't rest until he is dead," Big L said.

"We need you to tell us as much as you can. We don't know if Hendricks killed her or not. If he did, we'll help put him away. Right now, we're just gathering information," Ben said.

"What can you tell us?" Mark asked, repeating the question.

"I know she left almost every night with that scum, Hendricks. He didn't care about my sister. He just wanted to bang her while his wife was out of town."

"Did she have a friend she might have confided in?" Ben asked.

"There was one girl," Big L said. "Her name is Samantha Perkins. They shared an apartment in Cascadia, but Samantha works at Rocky's Bar in Needleton."

"We'll talk to her," Mark said. "Thanks again, we're sorry for your loss."

Mark and Ben left the bar and returned to Victorious.

Two scruffy-looking men had been sitting at the bar and trying to eavesdrop during Mark and Ben's conversation with Big L. Both men were in their forties and had seen better times.

"Did you hear any of the conversation those two old duffers said while they were talking to Big L?" asked one to the other.

"No, but I don't think anyone has a clue as to what really happened to that Cather broad," the other one answered.

"We just better keep quiet and not tell anyone, or we're going away forever. Do you understand, Floyd?"

"Yes, I know you're my big brother and you always look out for me," Brawn said.

"That's right, now order us another beer," Floyd said.

As they were returning to Victorious, Ben said, "We should probably check out Samantha Perkins at Rocky's Bar tomorrow."

"Okay, I'll call Tyler. He can check with Samantha Perkins at Rocky's Bar on his rounds," Mark said.

Chapter Six

The next day along with my wife, Barb, I drove into the parking lot of the DNR and carrying the fishing net, I entered the office, scanning the room until I saw an officer sitting at a desk. Looking up, he asked, "Can I help you?"

"I hope so. I found this net in Lake Michigamme. Could you tell me approximately how old it is?" I asked.

"Let's see," he said. He took the net from me and thought for a while. He said, "This is from a Trammel Net. It has three walls and when a fish swims into it, the walls collapse."

"You mean to tell me this is relatively new?" I asked.

"Yes, it is probably only a few years old. Where did you get it?" the DNR officer responded.

"I found it in Lake Michigamme near the crime scene. I have been hired to help defend the accused," I said, then thanked him and left.

I now had the answer I was looking for. The net didn't belong to some old trapper from a century ago. It was being used illegally to catch fish, probably at night.

Barb, who was waiting in the car patiently when I returned, asked, "Did you find out what you wanted?"

"Yes, I discovered this net is only a few years old, so it couldn't have been used by early trappers a hundred years ago. I have to assume it was left by poachers who didn't want to get caught. Would they have been desperate enough to take a life to protect their illegal actions?"

"You never know," Barb replied.

I had to find out the truth. While driving Barb home, I called John Baldwin and asked him to meet me at The Timbers Bar. If anyone could find trouble it was him—he had a nose for it.

∼∼∼

John and I met outside the bar and entered together, sitting at a booth that allowed us to survey the entire room. The bartender came over and asked, "What'll it be, guys?"

"Two beers, Eddy," I said, reading his name tag. "Do you know anyone who uses gill nets on the lake?" I asked.

"Are you cops? That question can get you into a heap of trouble around here, guys," he said.

"No, we're not, but I found a piece of Trammel Netting near the spot where Kate Cather's body was found. I think there's a connection. Do you agree?"

He thought for a few minutes and then said, "Kate and I were good friends, but I don't want trouble. Do you see those two grisly-looking guys over there?" He pointed to a couple of men who looked down on their luck. "They're the Dilfour brothers, Floyd and Brawn. They're not the sociable type; they keep to themselves, and they're not above poaching. I don't trust them as far as I could throw them. I will get you the two beers, but we never had this conversation. Understand!" Eddy said.

"Got it," I said.

After Eddy delivered our beers, we decided to pay the Dilfour brothers a visit. John and I walked over, sat down at the table, and started a polite conversation.

"Nice weather we're having," I began.

"Kiss my ass. Do we know you?" Floyd Dilfour asked.

"No, but I think we have something in common," I said.

"What's that?" Floyd asked.

"I found a piece of Trammel Netting where Kate Cather's body was found. Do you fellows know anything about that?" I asked.

The bigger one started to stand up, but John was right with him, staring him down, and posturing for a fight.

"Brawn, sit down. Look guys, we don't know anything about any Trammel Netting, and we don't want trouble. Leave us alone," Floyd Dilfour said.

"We're helping to investigate the murder of Kate Cather, and so far the trail leads right to you. I'd say you're in the hot seat. You can help us, or talk to Big L. I'm sure he would be very interested in knowing I found a piece of Trammel Netting near his sister's body. It's your choice."

We took advantage of the situation, but we didn't kill anyone," Floyd Dilfour said.

"Out with it. What do you know?" I ordered.

"We found Cather's body the other night caught in our net," Floyd Dilfour replied. "We didn't like the way it looked, so we ditched her body in that dumpy cabin and left. We felt we might be blamed for the murder."

"You got that right," John said.

John and I nodded toward them, stood, and left the bar.

Black Rock was setting up on stage for the evening performance. I saw Phil McPhail staring at John and me as we left the bar.

Once outside, John asked, "Do you believe them?"

"Don't know," I said, getting in our vehicle. "At least we know how Kate Cather's body got inside the cabin."

We returned to Victorious to see whether Tyler had any luck searching for Samantha Perkins.

Chapter Seven

In Needleton, Connie Timmerman was rinsing out glasses behind the bar. She had recovered from a horrific attack last year at the hands of a kidnapper. She had inherited Rocky's Bar when her husband was killed in a shootout over drugs relating to the same crime. She could be accused of being too kind, and she always tried to help the downtrodden, no matter how much they took advantage of her.

When Tyler Baldwin entered the bar, he walked over to Connie.

"How are you, Connie?" he asked.

"I'm getting better every day. Thanks for asking. What's up?" she asked.

"I'm looking for one of your waitresses, Samantha Perkins. Is she working tonight?" Tyler asked.

"Yes, she's over there waiting on those men. Has she done anything wrong?" Connie asked.

"No, I just want to ask her some questions," Tyler responded.

He walked over to Samantha and asked, "Do you have a minute?" Samantha looked around as all eyes fell on her.

"I'm pretty busy," she said. "Will it take long?"

"No. It's about Kate Cather," Sergeant Baldwin said, continuing, "We heard you were good friends with her. What can you tell me about her last few weeks?"

"As you probably know, she hooked up with that scumbag, Hendricks. He only used her for sex," Samantha said.

"We know that. What else can you tell us?" Sergeant Baldwin persisted.

"I think she was seeing someone else before Hendricks, but I don't know who it was," she said. "He must have been pretty important because she wouldn't tell me anything about him. It was very mysterious. He dropped a few hints, saying he was married and was the pillar of the community."

"Thanks. If you think of anything else, give me a call," Tyler said, turning and walking toward the door. He nodded to Connie as he left.

Chapter Eight

The next day, Sheila Hendricks entered the antique store, browsing and pretending to be interested in some knickknacks.

"How much is this ceramic bear?" Sheila asked the sales clerk.

"Let me see," said the clerk, turning the bear upside down. "I believe it's $49.95."

Sheila put it back on the rack and pretended to be interested in other trinkets as she looked out the window and checked her watch. Her appointment said he would be here on the hour. *He'd better come*, she thought to herself.

Kling. A distinctive bell sounded, announcing that someone was entering the shop. In stepped a distinguished-looking gentleman.

"Good evening, Dr. Meadows," the clerk said.

"Good evening to you," Dr. Meadows responded. "I understand you have some new pieces of merchandise. Can you tell me where I might find them?" he asked.

"They're back in the corner near the maps," the clerk said.

"Thank you. I am looking for something to fill a small space on my bookshelf. I hope you have it." He moved toward the back corner. Sheila Hendricks casually followed, while pretending to be gazing at the knickknacks on the shelves.

When she got close to Dr. Meadows and didn't think the clerk could hear her, she said, "I had to see you. I'm going nuts playing the dutiful wife to that idiot Cro-Magnon. I can't stand the sight of that fool."

"Be patient, dear; it will all be over soon. That Cro-Magnon is our ticket to nirvana. If he is found guilty of murdering that slut, we will be home-free. But I'm concerned that his attorney has hired a group of senior detectives from Victorious. We have to be careful, or they might happen upon something. Keep a low profile and keep acting like you love that buffoon. Do you understand?" Dr. Meadows said.

"I guess so, but I have to get out of town for a while. I think I might go back to New York just to get away from the pressure of the impending trial," Sheila said.

"That's fine, but be careful not to get photographed having a good time. Remember you are the innocent wife who didn't know anything about her husband's marital infidelities," Dr. Meadows cautioned.

"I'll be careful. Take care of yourself until I get back." She reached over to give him a peck on the cheek, but he quickly pulled back. "Not here," he said.

Sheila turned and walked out of the antique store.

In the back of the store, her exit was viewed by an eavesdropper, Phil McPhail.

~~~

When Sheila got home, she asked Kent, "Do you mind if I go to New York for a few days? I have some business to take care of. Jasmine is working on the fall layout, and they want me to help."

"I suppose it would be okay. I have to meet with Sandy Sundell tomorrow, but I guess I can go to her office alone," he said.

"Great, I mean, thank you. I'll take my own car, and leave it at the airport. I'll call you when I get there. We'll probably be working long hours, so don't try phoning me; I'll be in meetings late every night," Sheila said. "I can catch the early flight out of Mesabi Airport tomorrow."

~~~

The next morning, Sheila had showered and dressed before Kent woke up. She stealthily opened the front door, picked up her suitcase, and quietly exited. She had no idea that would be the last time she would be in that house.

Several hours later, Sheila's plane touched down, and after being chauffeured to the Ritz, she called her lover boy, John Rudolf, and summoned him for a romantic tryst. Punctually, he showed up at her room within the hour.

"I'm really glad you called me," John Rudolf said.

"This is the best part of the whole trip," Sheila replied. "I have a lot of stress at home. This is the one place I can relax and enjoy myself."

They enjoyed carnal bliss until they finally fell into a deep sleep. After awakening later that evening, Rudolf looked out the window and could see nighttime descending on the city. He still had time to catch his friends at the new after-hour nightclub, Riskee. He dressed and quietly slipped out of the hotel room door, not paying any attention to Sheila.

As Rudolf was leaving, a maître d' was about to knock on their door. The man said, "The Madame ordered champagne. Would you like some?"

Remembering his friends were waiting, John Rudolf said, "No, thanks, but I am sure the lady would like some. Just set it inside." Rudolf then walked down the hall.

The maître d' entered the room and momentarily watched Sheila. Then he picked up a pillow. The assassin placed it on Sheila's face and pressed. Sheila struggled for air, but soon there was none.

After Sheila stopped struggling, her body became limp. The maître d' removed the pillow and smiled. After it was over, the murderer said, "You thought you could fool me, you tramp." Tossing the pillow on the bed, the murderer pushed the cart into the hallway. The executioner closed the door and then wheeled his cart to the elevator and pushed its button. Once the doors opened, the killer pushed the cart onto the elevator and pressed the "up" button without entering the elevator himself. With that completed, the murderer maneuvered down the back stairway and deposited the jacket in a waste container before ambling out the front door. He walked several blocks before hailing a cab. As the cab pulled up to the curb, the driver asked, "Where to?" The murderer responded, "JFK."

~~~

John Rudolf was halfway to his rendezvous with his friends

when he felt in his pockets for his cell phone. He had forgotten it at the hotel room. Should he go back, or just get it tomorrow from Sheila at the fashion meetings? He decided on the latter, which would create a fatal problem.

Chapter Nine

In Victorious, the pseudo-detectives and I were having breakfast at a local eatery, Millie's. Tyler entered last with a look of concern. He said, "You will never guess."

"What's up?" I asked.

"We were just notified that Kent Hendricks' wife was found dead in her hotel room in New York City," Tyler replied. "They're calling it a homicide because of its suspicious nature. We won't know for sure until the autopsy comes back, which will take a few days."

"That certainly turns things around," Mark said.

"I guess we can cross her off as the murderer," Ben remarked.

"Not so fast," I replied. "Tyler, could you probe into Samantha Perkins' background a little more? I will make some calls to the New York Police to see what I can find out. Right now, those are our only leads."

Tyler nodded in confirmation.

~~~

Later that day, I made a phone call to an old friend I had worked with years ago. Connie Stevenson had been a state trooper and now worked as an advisor to the NYPD.

Having checked her caller ID, she said, "Hello, Bill. How are you?"

"Connie, hello; I'm fine. How are you?" I asked.

"I'm good. How can I help you?" Connie asked.

"I'm working on a murder case in Mesabi County. I'm actually helping an attorney defend a retired baseball player. Maybe you know him. His name is Kent Hendricks."

"Of course I remember him. He beat my Yankees in the World Series with a lead-off home run in the ninth inning."

"He's been accused of murdering his mistress and now his wife has just turned up dead in your city. Can you help me discover anything about the wife's murder?" I asked.

"What's her full name?" Connie Stevenson asked.

"Her name was Sheila Hendricks, and she was staying at the Ritz-Carlton," I said.

"Give me a day and let me see what I can do," Connie said.

After thanking Connie, I hung up, wondering what the wife's murder would lead to.

~~~

Meanwhile, back in Needleton, Tyler was continuing to query Samantha at Rocky's Bar on her knowledge of Kate Cather.

"Samantha, any luck remembering anything more regarding Kate Cather's last few weeks?" Tyler asked.

"I went through her possessions after talking to you. I didn't find anything, but about a month ago, she used my iPhone to send a text message to her mystery man. I have it right here. Samantha called it up on the screen. She continued, "I had forgotten about the email until I was checking mine and saw this." She held the screen so Tyler could see it. It read:

"P, not tonight, but I can see you Friday night if that works for you," :) K.

Samantha said, "The caller used a throwaway cell phone with no return email, leaving me to believe he was very careful who he communicated with."

"Thanks," said Tyler. "At least it's something to go on. Let me know if you come across anything else." Tyler shook her hand and left the bar.

Chapter Ten

In Detroit, Dr. Marshall detrained from Amtrak. His wife, Pam, and their neurosurgeon to-be son, Peter, were waiting for the family patriarch. "How did the medical convention go?" Pam asked her husband.

Peter jumped in before his father could say a word, "Are there any new procedures or drugs that are on the market? What about the da Vinci Surgical System? I can't wait to ask you what new Laser Spine non-invasive procedures are available. Just thinking that we will be able to repair the spine and the patient could go home the next day pain-free is fantastic."

"All in due time, son. First, I want to have a hot meal and sleep in my own bed tonight."

They headed for the parking lot to return to Cascadia. As they walked through the railroad station, Peter couldn't resist saying, "I wish you would get over your fear of flying, Dad. I don't know why you'd want to take the slower Amtrak when you could take American Airlines directly to Mesabi Airport?"

"I enjoy taking the train and getting off along the route in the communities to shop."

Peter just shook his head as he walked to their car.

Unknown to the family, their rendezvous was viewed by Phil McPhail, who had followed Pam Meadows and her son to Detroit and was staying out of sight while making a note which train Dr. Meadows disembarked from.

Once they were on their way north, Pam asked," Did you hear about the murder of Sheila Hendricks in New York? Apparently, somebody snuck into her hotel room and smothered her?"

"No, I didn't hear anything about it. I was out of contact with the news for a few days while I was at the convention," Dr. Meadows said.

~~~

Back in Victorious, I was sitting on my deck at my summer cottage enjoying a cold beverage when my phone rang. I picked it up, checked caller ID, and said, "Hello, Connie. Have you discovered anything regarding the Sheila Hendricks murder?"

"Hello, to you. Yes, the NYPD detectives assigned to the case found a cell phone. It belonged to a fashion designer employee, John Rudolf. They're trying to locate him."

"Thanks for the update. Let me know if you hear anything else. Best regards to your family."

As I disconnected, my mind really started to roam. Did John Rudolf have anything to do with Sheila Hendricks' murder? He must have known something.

It was time to pay a visit to my favorite medical examiner, Carolyn Raft.

~~~

I entered the Mesabi County Sheriff's Department and proceeded down the back stairs. As I entered her lab, I said, "Hello, Carolyn."

"Hello, right back," she said, rising from her desk, and proceeded to the file cabinet. "I bet I know why you're here. Where's that good-looking Needleton sergeant? He's usually around trying to get into trouble."

"I left him back at Millie's Restaurant." She nodded as she opened the top drawer and removed a medical report. She said, "I can get into big trouble with Sheriff Remington if he finds out I am giving you classified information."

"I promise I won't breathe a word of it to anyone." I crossed my fingers behind my back.

Carolyn said, "Ms. Cather's injury was at the fifth vertebrae. It was severed and she died from asphyxiation. There were multiple contusions on her wrists, indicating she was held against her will. It was definitely a homicide."

"Thanks, Carolyn. I am going to call John and see if he wants to take a trip to New York," I said.

"Any special reason?" she asked.

"Yes, there's a suspect in Sheila Hendricks' murder, and I think we should look into it," I said.

As I left the sheriff's office, I called John Baldwin. I said, "Hello, John, what do you think about taking a flight to New York?"

"I'd rather have a colonoscopy. What's up?" John asked.

"There's a suspect in the Sheila Hendricks murder, and I think we should pursue it. Do you want to join me?"

"I suppose so. I don't like big cities. I'll take this place anytime."

"I know, but we have to follow a lead," I said.

"Let me know what time the wheels are up. I'll pack a travel bag and be ready," he replied.

The plane touched down at JFK the next day. We tried not to act overwhelmed as we made our way out of the terminal. We hailed a cab and I gave the driver the address for Connie Stephenson's office.

Connie's office was on the third floor of the NYPD One Plaza. We entered and tried to act nonchalant. We were both overwhelmed with the size of the city. We approached her secretary and introduced ourselves. The receptionist said, "Ms. Stephenson is in a meeting, but she should be through momentarily." Shortly after, Connie's door opened and some high ranking NYPD commanders exited. We waited for her to acknowledge us, and then she motioned for us to follow her.

We shook hands and I introduced her to John Baldwin. She said, "I'm pretty sure I know why you're here." She looked at her receptionist and said, "Three black coffees." We entered her office and sat down.

Connie started the conversation, "I bet you're here to find John Rudolf, aren't you?"

"You always were a good detective," I replied. "Do you know where we can find him?"

The receptionist entered, placing the coffee and treats in front of us, exited, and closed the door behind her. The cookies were so fancy we were too embarrassed to ask what they were.

Connie stated the obvious, "You do know you have no official capacity in the case. If Rudolf refuses to talk to you, you cannot pursue it."

"Yes, I understand," I replied.

"He is quite the gigolo," Connie said. "According to the detectives who caught the case, he had many addresses he used. He works for a large fashion designer called Jasmine. You might start there. All the top designers are there now getting ready for a show tomorrow night. Maybe one of them will know where he is." She gave me the address and I slipped it into my pocket. The idea of John Baldwin and me entering a fashion design show was ironic to say the least. Leaving NYPD One Plaza, we hailed a cab, gave the driver the address, and entered his cab. On the way to the fashion show, John and I were enthralled with the size of the city.

The driver asked in passable English, "Fist dem in Nu Yok?"

I responded, "Is it that obvious?"

The driver continued, "Eh kno where yu can hav good dem tunight."

John said, "We're here on business, but thanks anyway." We exited the cab and walked into the Fashion Show. Again, it was overwhelming. People were scurrying around, directors were shouting orders, and the end result was complete chaos. We entered and tried to blend in.

We finally saw a young lady who wasn't running in place. I asked, "Do you know John Rudolf?"

She nodded her head and said, "He's in the back helping the models try on their outfits."

"Thanks, I said. We moved toward the back of the theater and scanned the bedlam. John pointed to a well-dressed slender man with a well-manicured beard. We approached him and I asked, "Are you John Rudolf?"

"Depends; who's asking?"

"I'm Bill Bennett and this is John Baldwin. We're from

Michigan, and we're trying to find out who killed Kent Hendricks' wife? Could you give us some information regarding her murder?"

"I told the police everything I know. I'm very busy right now," Rudolf replied.

"How about if we meet tonight when you have more time?" I asked.

"I guess so. Be at the Riskee nightclub tonight about nine o'clock," he said.

"We'll see you then," I said.

As we left, John said, "If you think I'm going into a young bar, you're crazy."

I called Connie to get the address of The Riskee Bar. She laughed and said," My, aren't you moving up in the world."

"Just give me the address, please," I replied. I could hear her giggling all the while she looked for the address, located it, and then Connie told me where the bar was. She finished by saying, "Don't tell Barb how you're spending your time in New York."

I said, "Never mind. Goodbye."

We had some time to wait before we put our dancing shoes on, so we decided to see whether we could make any headway at NYPD Plaza One. We used Connie Stephenson's name to gain access to the detective offices. We approached a middle-aged man whom life had passed by. We introduced ourselves. I said, "Excuse me. My name is Bill Bennett and this is John Baldwin."

"I'm Detective Wilder," he replied. "I heard you were in town."

"Is there any way we could see the surveillance tape for the night Sheila Hendricks was murdered at the Ritz?" I asked.

"No way," he said. "We would break protocol and the chain of evidence. A good defense lawyer could get the whole case thrown out. I do have a few pictures of a maître d' passing John Rudolph in the doorway to Sheila Hendricks' room. They were taken from the hotel security camera. You can see those."

Wilder handed the photos to us, and John and I perused them. They were a little grainy. John and I examined them closely, but we were unable to identify the maître d'.

"Is there any way we could have duplicates of these?" I asked.

"I guess I can do that," Wilder replied.

~~~

That evening, we took another cab to The Riskee Bar. As we stepped out, it didn't look like much. It was located in a dark alley with no signs of identification on the outside. I turned to double-check with the cabbie, but he was quickly driving away.

"Well, here we are, John," I said.

"Do you have your dancing shoes on?" John asked.

We both smiled as we approached the door. There was a large man who instructed us to move to the back of the line. "No, you don't understand," I said. "We're looking for someone inside."

John looked at me and said, "Okay, Bill, take a round out of him and I'll hold your coat."

I looked up at the human skyscraper and said, "Maybe, next time. Right now we just want to talk to someone."

"That's what everyone says. Now move to the back of the line, or I will have to hurt you," the behemoth said.

"Do you want a fleet of patrol cars here in a few minutes?" I asked.

He gave me a dirty look but said, "You got five minutes."

"Agreed," I said.

As we walked toward the door, John said, "We'll have to dance fast."

The Neanderthal took a step toward us but I said, "Five minutes."

We stepped into the bar. After paying the cover charge, I said, "I'll take this side, and you check the other side."

John and I moved in opposite directions searching for our prey. In the middle of the dance floor, I spotted our subject. Rudolf was dancing with a woman who was scantily clad. When I moved toward him, he motioned for me to wait for the dance to end. I didn't realize how long current songs last. I wondered if I was getting old. Finally, he finished his gyrations with the young lady. He gave her a hug and walked toward us. Halfway to us, he suddenly collapsed into a heap. We couldn't tell what was transpiring. Everyone was running away from Rudolf as we were trying to make our way to him. He was gasping and trying to say something. I leaned over, but all I could hear was, "M...br...champagne." When I rolled him over, to my horror, I saw a knife in his back. There was a turquoise earring under him, which must have come off during the assault. Picking it up while being careful not to leave fingerprints on it, I glanced at the woman Rudolf had been dancing with, but she was wearing cheap imitation diamond earrings. The floor was cleared of people, and many of them likely left to avoid any contact with law enforcement. John and I took a seat at the bar. When I showed the earring to John, he nodded.

The police and the EMTs arrived, but there was nothing they could do. I handed the turquoise earring to the first detective I saw. He placed it in an evidence bag and joined the other officers, who started to take the remaining revelers' statements, which I knew would be fruitless. When John and I gave our statements, they naturally aroused the police's curiosity. One officer said, "You'll have to come down to headquarters for further questioning."

The police drove us to their station. Upon entering, I approached the officer of the day. I started to tell our story, but he seemed uninterested.

"You'll have to wait until a detective gets here," he said.

We took a seat and waited, knowing one lead had gone cold, literally.

Later that evening, a tired-looking man in a worn-out suit entered. I recognized him as Detective Wilder. He talked to the officer of the day and then looked at us. As he approached us, he said, "I see you're enjoying our hospitality. I understand you were eyewitnesses to the murder."

"I saw him go down," I said, "but I didn't see who stabbed him. Did you, John?"

John shook his head.

Detective Wilder asked more probing questions, but John and

I weren't any help. Finally, he asked, "Where are you staying?"

After we told him, he said to stay in town in case they needed us for further questioning. John and I agreed.

The next morning, we entered Connie Stephenson's office loaded with lots of questions.

"Come in. I understand you had an interesting night last night," she said.

"You could say that. We found John Rudolf, but as we were about to start talking to him, he was stabbed in the back. By the time I got to him, he was only able to mumble something about champagne."

"I wonder if it has anything to do with the champagne found in Sheila Hendricks' room," said Connie. "It wasn't even a brand the hotel carries. Someone delivered it either before or during the murder."

"What about John Rudolf's cell phone?" I asked.

"There were several calls to Sheila Hendricks' cell phone, and there were several throwaway phone calls also that we couldn't trace."

"What about Mrs. Hendricks' autopsy?" I asked.

"She died from asphyxiation. No doubt it was murder," Connie said.

"I think we have done all we can do here. I'd like to head back home, but the detective told us to stay close," I said.

"I can fix it with the NYPD," Connie replied. "Don't worry; if they need you, they'll call you."

"I guess it's time to head back to Mesabi County then," I said. "If you come across anything let me know."

I stood and shook Connie's hand and John did likewise.

Chapter Eleven

As John and I deplaned at Mesabi International Airport, I said, "I think we should have a meeting at Geno's Pizzeria. Let's get together at eight tonight. We can recap and see where the case leads. John said he would contact the other members."

That night, the pseudo-detectives filed in and we began our discussion. I handed out the hotel security camera photos to see if any of them could identify the maître d' in the picture, but they shook their heads. The owner of Geno's Pizzeria, Rick Bonnetelli, brought over two pitchers of beer and said, "The pizzas are in the oven."

With that inspiration, we began to dissect the case. John Baldwin started. "Bill and I were in New York to follow up on Sheila Hendricks' murder. While we were there, the only possible witness, a gigolo named John Rudolf, was murdered. He was stabbed in the back at an after-hours bar."

Tyler Baldwin added, "I talked to Samantha Perkins. Samantha told me Kate Cather used her phone once to reply to an email. She referred to the person as 'P.' Assuming that 'P' stood for the first letter in the person's first name, it could be any of the three Meadows."

I said, "The poachers, Floyd and Brawn Dilfour, moved Kate's body, but I don't think they were involved. They were just stupid. They could have been implicated in the murder."

John Baldwin added, "Since John Rudolf was murdered in New York, he was probably silenced in case he could make identification. The murderer must have been outside of Sheila's hotel room."

I said, "How about taking a second look at the photos." We were still unable to discern any positive ID from them.

Carolyn Raft said, "Okay, I can take a hint. I can bring them to our forensics lab. Maybe they can enlarge the pictures and ID a face."

"Show them to Sheriff Remington," I said, "and bring him up to speed on the murder of John Rudolf in New York. I hate to go behind the good sheriff's back." I think I heard John Baldwin choke on his beer.

Mark Kestila said, "Ben and I can pay a visit to The Timbers Bar and ask around. Maybe, someone saw something the night of the murder."

"I'll follow up on Samantha Perkins," Tyler said. "I think I can squeeze more information out of her. Who knows, maybe, she was involved somehow?"

We adjourned and agreed to meet the following week.

Back in Cascadia, the good doctor was reading *The New York Times*, which he valued for keeping him in touch with the real world. On page five was a short paragraph about a murder in an after-hours bar, Riskee. He leaned forward with piqued interest. There were no leads and no witnesses relating to the murder. He sat back in his easy chair and smiled. *That should close out that saga*, he thought to himself. He put the newspaper down, leaving the room as his wife, Pam, entered. Likewise, she enjoyed reading about the world outside of Cascadia. She scanned the pages, coming across the murder of a young man in an after-hours bar. She looked in the direction of her husband and mused, *what do I have to do to protect that idiot?*

In Needleton, Tyler Baldwin entered the bar and asked whether Samantha Perkins was working.

The owner, Connie Timmerman, said, "No, she is off tonight. Can I help?"

"Did Samantha ever socialize here before or after work?" Tyler asked.

"A few times," Connie said, "usually with the locals, but occasionally with an older well-dressed man."

That description aroused Tyler's interest. "Could you describe him?" he asked.

Connie gave him a brief, but accurate description of the occasional visitor.

~~~

In Cascadia, Mark and Ben entered the Timbers Bar. They scanned the room, took a place at the bar, and pretended to watch the game on the big screen TV.

The bartender approached them and asked, "What'll it be, guys?"

"How about some information?" said Ben. "Our buddies were in here a few days ago and you told them about the poachers. I suspect you know a lot about what happens here in Cascadia."

"I don't know much. Why don't you leave?' Eddy Lavens replied.

"Unfortunately," said Mark, "we're talking about a man's life. We feel we have to do everything we can to prove Kent Hendricks' innocence or guilt. In fact, I understand Big L doesn't know that you know a lot more than you're telling. What do you say? How about telling us everything you know and we will go away. We're not the police, so everything you tell us stays with us."

Eddy thought for a moment, then leaned over and whispered, "Kiss my ass. I have to live in this community. I don't want to end up like Kate. She knew too much and look where it got her. Goodbye." He walked down to the other end of the bar and took some orders.

Phil McPhail smiled as he watched the heated argument play out and the two would-be detectives exit the bar.

Once outside of the bar, Ben said, "Well, I guess, that didn't go well."

"Yeah, but we rattled his chain," said Mark. "I think we can keep working on him. I think we should wait for the bar to close to continue this conversation."

"And with no witnesses," Ben added.

With a nip in the air, the two pseudo-detectives returned to their vehicle and waited for the bar to close.

Eventually, the bar's lights went off and the last customer drove away, leaving the parking lot empty except for Mark and Ben. They stepped out of their vehicle, removed the jumper cables, and they hooked one end of the cables to the car battery. Eddy Lavens came out and made his way to his vehicle. Ben approached him and said, "We're going to continue this conversation under less-than-ideal circumstances. We asked you earlier if you knew anything, but you weren't very nice, so Mark is going to tie you to that light pole, and I'm going to ask you again what you know about Kate Cather's murder. Do you get the picture?"

Ben slipped on some rubber gloves, and after a struggle, Mark handcuffed Eddy to the light pole.

"Now, Eddy," said Ben, "this is going to hurt, so you can scream as loud as you want."

"You wouldn't dare," Eddy replied.

"That's a chance you're going to have to take," said Mark. "Are you willing?"

Ben approached Eddy with the jumper cables and leaned into him. "Wait; I'll tell you what you want to know," said Eddy. "Kate and her friend, Samantha Perkins, were running interference for Dr. Meadows. She was helping round up young girls and they took them to New York. Kate would persuade them she knew a Broadway producer who would help them break into the theatre. She said she could hook them up with Dr. Meadows, who was going on vacation anyway, and he would drive them to Detroit and then they would all take the Amtrak to New York. Everyone trusted Dr. Meadows. But once they got there the girls, were never heard from again."

Ben disconnected the jumper cables and closed the hood. He said, "Now wasn't that easy?" Mark took the handcuffs off Eddy Lavens, then looked on the ground under Eddy and said, "I think you need a toilet." Mark and Ben stepped into their car, driving away. Eddy Lavens stepped into his vehicle and started to drive toward Cascadia.

Meanwhile, a dark figure emerged from behind the bar and ran toward Eddy Laven's truck, opened the passenger door and he dove inside the truck.

"I couldn't take a chance," said Phil McPhail.

"Some friend you are," said Eddy Lavens as he drove into the darkness. "Why didn't you help me?"

~~~

While Driving back to Victorious, Mark looked at Ben and asked, "Would you have shocked him?"

"No. I was just trying to cut through the red tape."

~~~

Samantha Perkins' cell phone rang. She picked it up and said, "Hello."

"The cat's out of the bag," Eddy Lavens told her.

"Who did you tell?" Samantha asked.

"I think they were two of those private detectives that were hired to help defend Kent Hendricks," said Eddy.

"If I were you," Samantha replied, "I would get out of town permanently and not look back."

"I will. I just wanted to tip you off before I disappear," said Eddy.

Samantha disconnected and called Dr. Meadows.

After Dr. Meadows answered, Samantha said, "Eddy Lavens just told two of those detectives everything. Lavens is going to leave town and I am likewise. The game is over. I'm not going to prison for something I didn't do."

"Calm down," said Dr. Meadows. "They don't have any evidence. If Lavens leaves town, they have no proof. Just carry on as if nothing happened. They have enough evidence on Kent Hendricks to put him away for the rest of his life. Just hang in there and stay calm."

Chapter Twelve

I was home watching television when my cell phone rang. I checked the caller ID and then I answered.

"Hello, Carolyn. What do you have for me regarding the enlarged pictures?"

"You won't believe it," said Carolyn. "I had the forensic guys blow the pictures up, and you'll never guess who the maître d' is?"

"Well, tell me before I get any older."

"It's Pam Meadows. We did a facial recognition test and she—"

"Where did you get her picture from?" I asked, cutting her off. "I'm sure she doesn't have a criminal record."

"As I was saying before I was interrupted," Carolyn replied, "we got her picture from her driver's license. We compared the pixels and the angle of the nose to the rest of her face. Even though she was disguised, she couldn't hide her facial recognition."

"Great job," I said. "We have the murderer of Sheila Hendricks. We can relay the information to New York, and Sheriff Remington can hold her until they come for her. Now all we have to uncover is who murdered Kate Cather. Mark and Ben are pursuing clues in Cascadia, and Tyler is checking on Samantha Perkins at Rocky's Bar. We only have to find out why Kate was murdered and, of course, who killed John Rudolph in New York."

~~~

The next morning, the pseudo-detectives reconvened at Millie's Restaurant to compare notes.

Mark started the discussion. "We were able to ascertain some key information from Eddy Lavens. Under a little duress, he told us that Dr. Meadows has been running a kidnapping ring out of

Cascadia. He uses young women like Kate Cather and Samantha Perkins to cruise Mesabi County and gain the confidence of girls down on their luck, promising them lucrative careers on Broadway. Dr. Meadows transports them to New York, and then nobody hears from the girls again."

"I know I am going to regret asking this," I replied, "but what little duress did you use?"

"I just hooked up the jumper cables to our car and Mark handcuffed him to a pole," said Ben. "He was more than willing to tell us everything he knew."

"Are you crazy?" I asked. "We can't use that in court because it was obtained under duress."

Carolyn Raft joined in, "we did a facial recognition of the maître d' at the Ritz, and it's Pam Meadows."

"We have Pam Meadows with legal evidence," I replied, "but the testimony of Eddy Lavens certainly wouldn't be admissible in court. We have to pursue Pam, or her son, to see if one of them will give up the good doctor. She's going down, and I'm assuming she killed Sheila Hendricks for personal reasons."

~~~

That night, the Meadows were sitting down for their evening dinner. Suddenly, sirens and lights filled their driveway. Neighbors came out by the score to see the excitement.

Sheriff Remington approached the house, he knocked on the front door, and shouted, "Pam Meadows, we have a warrant for your arrest for the murder of Sheila Hendricks in New York."

Dr. Meadows opened the door and stared at Sheriff Remington before he said, "There must be some mistake. Certainly you can't accuse my wife of a felony."

"Get out of the way," Sheriff Remington bellowed, "or I'll arrest you for obstruction of justice."

Dr. Meadows turned and said to his wife, "Go along with them, honey. There must be a huge misunderstanding."

"You fool," she replied to him. "I've spent my entire life protecting you from yourself. Why did you have to have an affair with every tramp that came down the road?"

"Stop talking," Dr. Meadows replied. "You don't know what you're saying. You're incriminating yourself. I haven't done anything wrong. We'll work through this."

"There's nothing to work through," said Pam. "I've known for a long time that you were having affairs with every slut in Mesabi County. I even followed you once to Needleton and saw with my own eyes you talking with that Cather woman."

Dr. Meadows, trying to regain his composure, replied, "Darling, I was just giving her some medical advice."

"Save your lies for somebody else," Pam retorted.

Peter was listening to the confrontation and now said, "I agree with Mother. I've known all along how you manipulate everyone around you. I pretended your trips to New York were legitimate, but I checked and none of them were. There were no medical conventions occurring when you went to New York. It was such a charade of us picking you up in Detroit at the Amtrak station. I kept quiet to protect Mother, but now it's all out." Then looking directly at his father, he added, "I hope you rot in Hell." Peter turned and exited the house through the back door.

Sheriff Remington looked at Deputy Roads and said, "Make sure you Mirandize her carefully. I don't want her getting off on a technicality."

"Put your hands behind your back," Deputy Roads told Pam, and then he proceeded to read her rights while he handcuffed her.

Pam glared at her husband until the police led her to the squad car.

After the police drove away, Dr. Meadows returned to the dinner table and finished his wine.

~~~

The next morning, the news was all over Cascadia. Every antique shop and restaurant was buzzing with the arrest of their beloved doctor's wife.

Channel 7 sent newsperson Lana Kanton to get a feel for the community's pulse.

"It must be a mistake," stated one local to Lana Kanton.

"I know Pam and she is no murderer," added another.

"I can't believe she would travel all the way to New York and commit the murder," added a third Cascadian before asking for a refill on his coffee.

John and I decided to visit Pam Meadows, who was locked up in the Mesabi County Jail. After signing in, we were ushered to an interview room. While we waited for Pam to arrive, we discussed how we would approach her. We thought the best avenue would be to convince her that by her talking to us, it would help her defense.

We were a little taken aback when Pam Meadows was shown into the interview room with us. She looked absolutely dazed. I decided to start gently by asking her, "How are you holding up?"

"Not very good," she replied. "I talked to my lawyer this morning. They're having a bail hearing later today, but I told my attorney I didn't want bail. I don't care what happens to me. I confessed the whole murder to the sheriff's detectives and I deserve what I get."

"You must have been pushed to the limits," said John, "for you to travel to New York to murder Sheila Hendricks."

"Yes," said Pam. "I have listened to my husband's lies for years. Somehow he'd get to Detroit and take Amtrak to New York. Several times, I flew out of Mesabi Airport, easily getting there ahead of him. I knew from our online bank account that he was staying at the Ritz-Carlton. I bribed a bellhop and found out that he always stayed in the same room. The last time I followed him to Hendricks' room. That night, I disguised myself as a maître d' and waited for the door to open. One of Hendricks' gigolos came out, and I fooled my way past that kid. I smothered Hendricks with a pillow and left. I was just sick of my husband's infidelities. If he only could have been faithful, I never would have had to kill that woman."

"What about the murder at Riskee?" I asked. "Did you do that also?"

"No, I have no idea who murdered that playboy," Pam replied, "but he got what he deserved. I'm not sorry for his murder."

John and I had plenty of experience coaxing a confession out of people, but I had rarely seen such a sorry sight.

We thanked Pam for her time and left quietly.

"Boy," said John. "I almost feel sorry for her."

"I agree." I said. "I can't remember when I've felt such pity for a murderer. We only have two murders left to solve."

Chapter Thirteen

That afternoon, Dr. Meadows was enjoying a sip of brandy on his front porch. How great it was for him to be rid of his troublesome wife and still have his organ transplant ring humming like a fine motor. Nobody was the wiser in this small community. Everybody felt sorry for him, so he could play the despondent husband whose wife imagined everything while on a murderous rampage.

Dr. Meadow's phone rang and he answered after checking the Caller ID. "What do you want?" he asked.

"I want to take over where my sister left off," said Big L. "I know you were having either Samantha or Kate drive the girls and you to Detroit and then taking Amtrak to New York where you were murdering them and harvesting their organs."

"Don't be ridiculous!" Dr. Meadows retorted. "I would never soil my hands in such a degrading business. Now don't call me again."

"I'm not stupid," Big L replied. "My sister, Kate, told me about your operation. If you don't hire me, I'll tell the sheriff everything. Now do I get cut into this deal or not?"

"Since you put it that way," said Dr. Meadows, "I guess I have to include you. I do need a driver to Detroit occasionally when we have a girl lined up. Your sister used to do that, but since her demise, I have to find somebody else. Would you be interested in that?"

"I can do that," said Big L, "but how do you find girls dumb enough to believe you're going to get them to New York and turn them into stars?"

"Don't worry about that. I already have somebody to take care of that end," Dr. Meadow said.

Dr. Meadows disconnected his cell phone and sat back, enjoying his brandy even more. Everything was falling into place.

~~~

On the other side of Cascadia, Mark and Ben returned to The Timbers Bar. Exiting their vehicle, they walked inside and asked the new bartender where Eddy was.

"He quit yesterday and is leaving town with Black Rock's lead singer, Phil McPhail."

"Do you know where we can find him?" asked Ben.

"I think he lives upstairs of one of the antique stores downtown."

Mark and Ben left the bar, not knowing exactly where this excursion was going to take them. Driving through the heart of Cascadia, they saw an old truck that resembled Eddy's from the other night.

Seeing a back stairway to the apartment, they decided to push their luck. They mounted the steps and knocked.

"Who's there?" asked a voice on the other side.

"It's your fairy godmother," said Ben. "Now open this door or we'll kick it in. We just want to ask you some questions. I promise we won't hurt you."

"I told you what you wanted to know; now leave me alone. I have to get out of town or I'm dead," Eddy said.

Inside the room, Phil McPhail looked at Eddy and said, "Don't let them in."

"Don't worry," said Ben. "Nobody saw us come here."

Slowly, the door opened and McPhail and Lavens looked past Mark and Ben to see whether there was anybody else.

"We were wondering if you knew who killed Kate Cather," said Mark.

"Isn't it obvious?" Eddy replied. "She developed a conscience and wanted out of the organ transplant trade. She hooked up with Kent Hendricks and saw him as her new meal ticket. Only Dr. Meadows didn't see it that way."

"How do you know all this?" Ben asked.

"Kate always confided in me," said Eddy. "She didn't trust her roommate, Samantha Perkins, since she was helping to scam the girls also. Her brother was into himself and wouldn't care. I was all she had. I want you to help me get to my truck because I don't trust anybody. Dr. Meadows has a lot of people working for him."

Ben looked at Phil McPhail and said, "What's your role in all of this?"

"Kate and I used to be an item until Kent Hendricks cut in," McPhail replied. "I suspected that Meadows, and maybe his family, was involved in something. I couldn't understand why Kate would leave town unexpectedly with Dr. Meadows and a young girl, and then they'd return days later without the girl. I even followed them once to New York and saw them hand off the girl to some derelict. I wasn't sure what they were doing, but I figured if I followed them long enough, I'd find out. I wanted to win Kate back, but as long as Hendricks was in the picture, I didn't have a chance, and I had to find out what Kate's relationship with Dr. Meadows was."

"Okay, get packed," said Mark. "We'll walk the two of you to your truck."

As they were walking down the steps, a shot rang out. Both Ben and Mark dropped to their knees and unholstered their weapons. They instinctively looked for the shooter, but the assassin was nowhere to be seen. Eddy Lavens was crawling on the ground, badly wounded, as Phil McPhail gasped in horror.

Ben called the shooting into 911. It took longer than expected for the EMTs to arrive, but they finally appeared. Once they exited their vehicles, the EMTs hurried to Lavens and examined him. They took his vitals and stabilized him by inserting an IV into one of his arms. They placed him on a gurney, loaded him into the ambulance, and left with the lights flashing. The sheriff's deputies took Ben and Mark's succinct statements. Both knew who was probably responsible, but it was impossible to prove.

As Ben and Mark drove away from the crime scene, Ben said, "At least we know who killed Kate Cather. Now we just have to find out who took a shot at Eddy, and then we can find the murderer of John Rudolf in New York. I'll call Bill and bring him up to speed."

~~~

After she missed her shot at Eddy Lavens, Samantha Perkins walked to her car and left as soon as possible. Fortunately, the locals and tourists were running toward the scene and didn't pay any attention to a young woman walking away. Samantha had put the pistol in her oversized purse so she would look like all the other tourists. She didn't look forward to telling Dr. Meadows she had missed her chance to silence Eddy Lavens once and for all.

Chapter Fourteen

"Hello," I said as I answered my cell phone.
"Hello, Bill. This is Ben. Guess what? Mark and I just talked to Black Rock's lead singer, Phil McPhail, and he said Dr. Meadows is in this mess up to his neck. He and Kate Cather used to bring young unsuspecting girls to New York, arrange to have them killed, and then sell their organs on the black market. In addition, as we were escorting Lavens and McPhail down to their car some coyote took a shot at us and wounded Eddy Lavens."
"Really? I didn't see that coming," I said. "John and I will have to keep an eye on the wily Dr. Meadows. Thanks for the update. What are you up to now?"
"We'll follow the ambulance to the hospital," said Ben.
"After you follow him to the hospital," I said, "and then check McPhail into a hotel. They're both material witnesses. If they disappear, we might never see them again."
"That sounds like a good idea," said Ben. "I will persuade McPhail to do that."
Unfortunately, that didn't happen.
I called John Baldwin next. After he answered his phone, I said, "There's been a change in plans. Ben just told me Dr. Meadows takes young women to New York under the guise of turning them into Broadway stars, and then he slices and dices them in the organ transplant black market."
"No kidding!" John shouted. "I didn't think even he was that diabolical."
"We'll have to follow his every move," I replied. "I'll meet you outside his house. In addition, someone just shot Eddy Lavens, and Ben and Mark are going to check McPhail into a

hotel and keep an eye on him. Pack an overnight bag just in case we have to travel."

"Sounds good," John said.

John and I rendezvoused at the now sinister physician's house and waited as we consumed several cups of coffee. While John and I were waiting, I stepped out of my vehicle and walked over to Dr. Meadow's vehicle. I knelt down and attached a GPS Tracking Device onto his automobile. Then I returned to our vehicle.

"That was a good idea," said John. "You never know where this bird is going, and we don't want to lose him."

~~~

Late that night, Dr. Meadows emerged from his house and entered his automobile. I turned on the GPS program from Google and allowed our prey to move out while we maintained a safe distance. Our quarry led us to his office where he was met by two women, one of whom appeared to be Samantha Perkins. The two women stepped into Meadows' car and were whisked away into the darkness.

"Well, we'd better follow and see where this leads," I told John.

Before we knew it, the trail led to I-75 and then to Detroit.

"It's a good thing I packed my toothbrush," said John. "I think this is going to be an excursion."

"I agree," I said. Sure enough, the good doctor pulled up to the Amtrak automobile parking lot in Detroit and the three of them exited. They approached the railroad with John and me following from a distance. We watched as they purchased their tickets and proceeded to the terminal bound for New York. John and I swiped our credit cards with the ticket agent and boarded the same train. We stayed several cars back so as not to be noticed.

"We might as well get some sleep," I said. "I think I know where this is heading, but we need proof."

John and I sat back and caught some much-needed sleep.

~~~

The next morning, the Amtrak train pulled into the station. We watched Meadows and his two ladies exit and hail a cab outside the train station. We followed suit, promising our taxi driver a "C" note if he didn't lose the Meadows' taxi in traffic.

After maneuvering through some of the worst traffic in the world, Meadows' taxi came to a halt in front of a seedy apartment complex displaying a sign on the front door that read "Stanley Kramer Talent Agency." We instructed our cab driver to bypass Meadows' vehicle and let us off at the next intersection. After being dropped off, we worked our way back and stood in the shadows of a building across the street. With darkness descending, I said, "Let's have a look inside."

We crossed the street and scaled the dilapidated fire escape. The building was consumed with darkness. John and I wiped the windows to see whether the building was inhabited. John took his knife out, opened the blade, and wiggled it under the sash. Soon the catch popped and John slid the window open. If caught, we were now official burglars looking at five years as guests of the New York penal system. I swallowed hard as I followed John through the window. I pulled out a small flashlight, which I kept for just such a situation. Silently, we moved across the floor, trying not to make a sound that would give us away. We entered the hallway and descended the stairway to the first floor. Like the second floor, it was also pitch black with no hint of recent activity. Old trade papers, empty pizza boxes, and cigarettes in a cobwebbed ashtray made for a disheartening sight. We moved toward the back of the building, looking for a door to the basement.

Slowly, we moved through an office that looked like it had not been occupied for a lengthy period. I shined the flashlight on a doorway, and together we approached it. I turned the handle, but it was locked. John smiled as he took out his locksmith kit. With a few twitches and turns of his tools, the lock released and the door opened. I turned the doorknob and pulled the door toward me. I shined the flashlight down the stairs and could make out the basement floor. We removed our Glocks and crept down the stairs. Upon reaching the basement floor, I shined the light around the room. It appeared to resemble an operating room, complete with a body on the table. We stepped closer to the body and realized it was the young lady Dr. Meadows and Samantha Perkins had transported from Cascadia to New York. The floor was covered in blood, and we dared not get any closer for fear of contaminating a crime scene. We could see from a distance most of her internal organs had been removed.

"Well," said John, "I sure didn't think Meadows would be that bold to continue his organ removal operation with his wife accused of murder."

"I agree," I said, "but obviously he thinks he's too smart for everyone."

"I agree. Now drop your weapons or die where you stand." The male voice shined his flashlight in our faces. I recognized the voice, but I couldn't see his face.

With some hesitation, we dropped our Glocks and turned to meet our adversary. "I am too smart for you two fools. Do you think I didn't notice you following me?"

"Bitch, get their guns before they have second thoughts," Dr. Meadows ordered.

Samantha Perkins emerged from the darkness and stepped toward us. As she was kneeling down to retrieve our pistols, I noticed a surgical instrument on the table next to the deceased young lady's body. I grabbed it and threw it at Dr. Meadows. He fired, but missed. Both John and I dived to the ground and grabbed our Glocks. Before we could fire a shot, both Dr. Meadows and Samantha Perkins disappeared through a secret door in the wall. John and I searched frantically for the door's release button, but to no avail.

"We'll have to call NYPD. Maybe they can catch them before they escape from New York," I said. I took out my cell phone and dialed.

"911. What is your emergency?" the dispatcher asked.

"There's been a murder at Stanley Kramer's Talent Agency. I don't know the street address, but I will stay on the line until the police arrive."

John and I ascended the stairway and waited for the authorities. I knew it wasn't going to be pleasant being at the scene of a young woman who was carved up by a maniac.

Police cruisers arrived while we sat on the front steps. We raised our hands and tried to be conciliatory. The police didn't know us and were on full alert. As a precaution, we were handcuffed and transported to their station. Needless to say, we had a lot of explaining to do upon reaching their station. Fortunately, I had the presence to call my guardian angel, Connie Stevenson. John and I were placed in separate interrogation rooms and we tried to make ourselves comfortable. Before long, the door to my room opened and I smiled as I met Connie's eyes.

"This isn't the Wild West, Bennett," Connie began. "Why didn't you call the police when you saw the doctor entering that dump with that poor girl?"

I tried to think of a good reason, but I had to plead ignorance.

"We weren't sure what the doctor and his accomplice were up to," I said. "We needed proof before we called. What if the police arrived and they were just sitting having a cup of coffee? We'd tip our hand and we'd never catch Meadows or break up his organization."

"So," Connie rebuked, "a young woman gets murdered and what do we tell her family?"

I hung my head and nodded because I knew she was right.

"Can you say emphatically that it was Dr. Meadows in the basement?" Connie asked.

"No, I can't say for certain, but I did recognize Samantha Perkins, who was reaching for our pistols. I saw her face in the light. Should John and I stay in town for a while?"

Connie shook her head in exasperation. "You can return to your beloved Superior Peninsula," she said, "but you'll have to return when you are ordered."

I nodded my head in affirmation. John and I caught the next plane to Michigan.

~~~

After our plane's wings were up, John looked at me and said, "I told you there's nothing good about a big city." I had to agree this time.

After we landed, my cell phone chimed.

"Hello."

"This is Connie Stevenson. I have some bad news. We just found Samantha Perkins' body in a dumpster a few blocks from the talent agency. It looks like we're back to square one with Meadows."

"Maybe, but I think I have a plan to lure the good doctor out of his lair."

I thanked her for the update and disconnected. Now, I had to out-think a maniacal genius who would stop at nothing to continue his organ black market.

Chapter Fifteen

The phone rang and Peter Meadows reluctantly answered. "Hello," he said.

"I have another job for you," said the voice on the other end.

"I'm done with you, Father. Mother is in jail facing murder, and you're still running your organ harvesting ring. Why should I do anything for you?"

Dr. Meadows ignored his son's protest and continued, "I've just been informed by my snitch at Victorious Hospital that Samantha Perkins missed killing Eddy Lavens. He is critically wounded, but not dead. You need money to finish your medical training. I will pay your education bills if you help me."

"I despise you for what you have done to our family," said Peter, "but I guess I don't see any way out." Peter thought for a moment and then said, "I'll help you, but then we're through with each other."

"We'll cross that bridge when we come to it," Dr. Meadows replied. "You're a good son. Maybe, after everything settles down, you can become my partner in the business."

"I will never stoop that low," Peter replied. "Once I get through medical school, I am never coming back to Mesabi County."

They disconnected. Then Dr. Meadows said to himself, "I hope he doesn't become a problem."

~~~

Back in Victorious, we reconvened our weekly meeting at Geno's Pizzeria. After we imbibed our legal limit of alcohol and ate our pizza allotment, Mark started the discussion by saying, "We were escorting Eddy Lavens to his truck when someone shot him. In the excitement, we never saw who fired the shot, but Lavens is still alive."

"With Samantha Perkins dead," said Tyler, "my suspect is out of the picture."

"John and I talked to Pam Meadows," I said. "She admitted to killing Shelia Hendricks, but she didn't have a clue who murdered Kate Cather or John Rudolf."

"Isn't it obvious that Dr. Meadows is pulling the strings? said Carolyn. "He never gets his hands dirty, but he's always behind the action."

"Let's set a trap for the wily good doctor," said John. "What if we inform him that Eddy Lavens is going to tell everything as soon as he is able to? The good doctor will have to come to the hospital to silence him. We can take turns sitting in Eddy's room and wait for Dr. Meadows to make an appearance."

"It's a good plan," I replied, "but there are two problems with that. First, he probably has a snitch in the hospital who would warn him, and second, he does have hospital privileges. He certainly can go anywhere in the hospital without restrictions."

"Good point," said John. "How can we get around those two problems? Are there any suggestions?"

Just then, a light bulb came on for me.

"I have a plan," I said, "but it's very risky. If we fail, we'll get in big trouble."

They all leaned forward to hear my scheme.

~~~

The next day, Peter Meadows called his father. After Peter berated his father for all their troubles, the doctor said, "Are you through? I have more important problems to take care of. My snitch at the hospital has informed me that Eddy Lavens is recovering from surgery. He is still heavily sedated, but by tomorrow, he should be coherent enough to talk to the police. I will visit the hospital tonight and arrange a setback for Lavens. I need you to drive me to the hospital and wait outside by the back door to help facilitate my escape. I don't want to be seen once all the commotion begins with the Code Red."

His son reluctantly agreed to chauffeur him to the hospital and help him escape after the murder.

Part I - The Murders on the Michigamme 77

Later that day, the pseudo-detectives met at Millie's Restaurant to review our plan. We felt the plan was risky, but we had to implement it. I reviewed the plan to make sure everyone was on board.

"Everyone will have to be evacuated," I said. "That will give us time to move Eddy Lavens to another room, and I will replace Eddy Lavens in the hospital bed with myself. We know Dr. Meadows has a snitch in the hospital, but we don't know who it is so we can't trust anyone."

Everyone concurred, realizing the plan had to work or Sheriff Remington would be only too happy to lock us up. We had told Sheriff Remington and his deputies to wait in the back of the hospital, but we didn't dare tell him what we had planned from fear he would naturally shut it down.

Later that night, at precisely nine o'clock I pulled the fire alarm in the hospital hallway. Immediately, the hospital emergency evacuation plan went into action. The hospital personnel were exceptional at evacuating everyone out of the hospital. We allowed Eddy to be moved out to the parking lot along with the rest of the patients. Eventually, the "all clear" was given and the patients were wheeled back inside. After Eddy was moved back into his room, we quickly slipped him two doors down before any hospital personnel had resumed their posts at the nurses' station.

Once in his new room, Eddy was attended by Dr. Carolyn Raft and several private nurses. Meanwhile, I laid down in Eddy's bed and shut the light off. Everything was quiet for an hour. Carolyn Raft had previously hooked up an IV to my arm to complete the ruse. The patients were tucked back into their beds and life returned to normal. We were ready. Ben, Mark, and John were hiding behind the screen separating my bed from the other bed. We didn't allow Mark to lie down on the bed from fear he would fall asleep and start snoring. At ten o'clock, the door slowly opened and a figure crept toward me. With the lights off, it was hard to distinguish who was stalking me. The figure slowly moved closer to me, syringe in hand. As the assailant approached, the would-be assassin said, "Now, Eddy, I am going to give you phenobarbital to help you sleep for a long time. All your worries will be over." The would-be murderer reached toward the IV with the syringe just as I grabbed their arm.

We tumbled onto the floor with the IV stand falling on top of us. Ben, Mark, and John quickly came around the curtain and grabbed the stranger. Mark turned the light on, and to our surprise, it was the head charge nurse, Sharon Conway.

Sheriff Remington and Deputy Roads came in after hearing the commotion. The nursing staff followed right behind them. Dr. Meadows made his entrance and appeared to be shocked. He looked at the charge nurse and said, "Nurse Conway, I can't believe it."

Nurse Conway looked at Sheriff Remington and pointed at Dr. Meadows. "He was the mastermind of the whole ring," she said. "I'll testify against him and give you the names of all the others involved in the organ black market. He made me participate or else he would reveal my dependence on oxycodone."

"That's a lie. I'm chief of staff of this hospital," replied Dr. Meadows.

"Arrest Nurse Conway and charge her with attempted murder," said Sheriff Remington. "As for you, Dr. Meadows, I am personally going to read you your Miranda rights to you to make sure there are no foul-ups."

"Nice job, guys," I said as I shook everyone's hand. "We got our murderer."

Carolyn Raft entered the room. "It sure is hard to get any rest around here," she joked.

The next day, Peter Meadows was arrested for various crimes. During his trial, Peter obtained a reduced sentence in return for testifying against his father. Nurse Conway was found guilty of attempted murder, and in exchange for a reduced sentence, she also testified against Dr. Meadows. With the testimony of Peter Meadows and Nurse Conway, Dr. Meadows was found guilty of first-degree murder for the death of Kate Cather.

During the trial, the poachers, Floyd and Braun Dilfour, admitted seeing Dr. Meadows in the early hours of the day Kate had died as they were returning from poaching in a small motor craft near Kent Hendricks' home. The brothers had seen Dr. Meadows, under cover of darkness, approach Kate Cather unnoticed. He had tied his boat up to shore and then proceeded to engage Kate Cather in a heated conversation. The brothers saw Dr. Meadows finally force Kate Cather into his motor craft, and he departed with her after she resisted, but to no avail.

Upon searching Samantha Perkins' apartment, the police found a single turquoise earring in her jewelry box. The NYPD confirmed Samantha Perkins' fingerprints matched the ones on the turquoise earring found under John Rudolf's body. After checking the Mesabi County airport flight manifesto, the Sheriff's Department ascertained Perkins had flown to New York, which coincided with John Rudolf's murder. Perkins, acting on orders from Dr. Meadows, murdered Rudolf to punish him for having a fling with Dr. Meadows' girlfriend.

Furthermore, the prosecution checked Kate Cather's cell phone call that morning to Kent Hendricks; the closest tower had been a quarter mile from Dr. Meadows. Dr. Meadows' phone records revealed that he had called Samantha Perkins that morning and probably ordered her to pick up Kate Cather's car in Kent Hendricks' driveway. Kate must have managed to call Kent Hendricks in a final plea for help, which Hendricks had ignored. Dr. Meadows murdered Kathe Cather and took her body out to the middle of Lake Michigamme and dumped it, only to have the body caught later that night in the Dilfours' gill net. Based on the circumstantial evidence, the jury sentenced Dr. Meadows to twenty-five years to life.

In return for their testimony, the Dilfours were given probation. Unfortunately, they were sentenced to a life of stupidity. For his testimony, Eddy Lavens, was given probation for withholding information pertaining to a crime.

After the trial concluded, the pseudo-detectives and Sandy Sundell walked down the courthouse steps, enjoying the beautiful fall day. "Thanks for all of your help," Sandy said. "Without you I am pretty sure Kent would have been convicted of murdering his wife. Even so, he's planning to sell his house and move to California."

A nip in the air warned us that colder weather was on the horizon. But for now, we felt good that we had helped solve "The Murders on the Michigamme."

Part II

The Fall of Maderis

Chapter One

There was a chill in the air as the wheels touched down. It was a premonition of what was going to happen. Stella Stevinski, better known as "Maderis" in Hollywood, was returning home. She couldn't wait to see her mother in her hometown of Cascadia. She had left for the bright lights as a budding teenager ten years ago, never having been on a stage larger than the one at Cascadia High School. Now she had starred in several feature films and headlined at several major hotels in Las Vegas. Her public relations assistant, Maggie Grenville, had made sure the media—including *E-News*, *Hollywood Plus*, and *Gossip*—would be waiting at Mesabi International Airport to give her full coverage. It was billed as a starlet coming home to see her hometown, but Stella Stevinski had a darker reason she had not told anyone. Her real reason was so embarrassing that she would be unable to get another movie contract or Las Vegas headliner gig once it was revealed.

My name is Bill Bennett. I am a retired sheriff. I had spent thirty-three years as a law enforcement officer. The last twelve were as sheriff of Mesabi County, which is located in the heart of the Superior Peninsula. Barb, my wife, had just retired, from a counseling career at Victorious High School.

The previous week, my wife Barb and I had been enjoying a cup of coffee on our cottage deck overlooking the Dead River. The clouds were silky white and passing gently overhead, creating a sense of serenity. Boats were casually meandering past our cottage with an occasional wave from their captains and passengers. My pseudo-detective friends and I had just solved a messy series of murders in Cascadia, so I assumed I could enjoy a beautiful autumn day with my wife. I was wrong.

When my cell phone rang, I hesitated to answer it. I didn't want the tranquility to end.

"You should answer that," said Barb. "It might be John Baldwin wanting to go for a bike ride, or one of the kids checking in."

"All right," I said. I picked up the cell phone and said, "Hello."

"Is this Mr. Bennett?"

"Maybe, but it depends; are you selling something, or offering me a free vacation to the Bahamas if I take a survey?"

"No, it's nothing like that. This is Cindy Morgan. I'm Maderis' personal assistant, and we are looking for security next week when we visit Cascadia. I'm sure you may know Maderis is originally from the community and would like to return, but we don't think the police can offer ample protection. Connie Stephenson referred you to us when we were searching the Internet for security people."

"Thanks," I said, "but I'm retired and I don't think my team and I would fit your bill as security guards."

"We will pay your team and you one hundred thousand dollars for the week," Cindy said.

"When do you want us?" I asked.

"We land at Mesabi International Airport next Monday morning at ten o'clock. We think there will be a sizeable crowd. We will need several limousines and protection for our cabins in Cascadia I have booked for the week. We will need round-the-clock protection until we leave the following Sunday. Can you handle that?"

"Yes, I will have my team there when the plane lands," I said.

I hung up and said to Barb, "Now I'm a security guard for Maderis."

"Are you kidding?" Barb asked.

I had four good friends with extensive police background. John Baldwin, Ben Myers and Mark Kestila had served in police agencies for decades before retiring. John's son, Tyler, was a current Needleton Police Sergeant having served in the Army during Desert Storm. To enhance our team, Carolyn Raft, the Mesabi County Medical Examiner, had joined us and had become romantically involved with Tyler.

I called John Baldwin.

"Guess what?" I said. "We're going to be guarding a movie star next week."

"Have you been drinking some moonshine again?" John asked.

"No, I just got off the phone with Maderis' personal assistant. We've been offered a security job to protect her and her entourage for a week."

"I'm not interested in babysitting a spoiled harlot. Count me out."

"They'll pay us one hundred thousand dollars," I said.

There was silence on the other end. Then John said, "For that amount, I will carry her to Cascadia. When do we start?"

"Next Monday morning. You call Tyler, and I'll check with Ben and Mark. I'll call Sheriff Remington also to bring him up to speed. I'll pick you up tomorrow to check out the cabins they rented in Cascadia."

After I hung up with John, I had an epiphany regarding Maderis' security. There would be times when a female would be needed to assure her safety when the pseudo-detectives and I couldn't provide adequate protection. We would need some athletic young women for that. After pondering whom I could call, I remembered Kelly Sanderson and Jenni Durant were home for the summer. They'd had a horrible experience last year, being kidnapped and almost delivered to a prostitution ring in Mexico. Only by luck and sheer determination were we able to rescue them with help from another private detective. The girls had changed their majors to criminal justice since their nightmare experience. They no longer saw the world with rose-colored glasses, but with a degree of cynicism. Maybe the young women would be available to assist us in protecting Maderis, even if she didn't appreciate our help. Unfortunately, like many celebrities, she had a reputation for being rude.

I phoned the Durants and asked for Jenni.

"Who's calling?" her father asked.

"It's Bill Bennett."

"Hello, Bill. Just a minute; she's right here," her father responded.

After a moment of silence, I heard an apprehensive voice say, "Hello."

"Hello, Jenni. This is Bill Bennett. I understand you're home for the summer and not working right now."

"That's right," Jenni said.

"Would you like a paying job for a week?" I asked.

"What do you have in mind?" Jenni asked.

"The pseudo-detectives and I have a protection gig for a famous celebrity, but since she is a woman, we will need additional help. Are you interested?" I asked.

"Definitely. What do I have to do?" Jenni asked.

"Be at Mesabi International Airport next Monday morning at nine. We'll pick up our celebrity and bring her to Cascadia. We have to provide 24/7 protection for her for about a week. I'll pay you the going rate. Are you in?"

"You bet," said Jenni. "Who are we protecting?"

"Maderis."

"Are you kidding? She is the biggest star in Hollywood. I can't believe I'm going to meet Maderis and even be close to her."

"Remember, we have to be professional at all times, no matter how rude she is to us."

"No problem," Jenni responded. "I can sure use the money for college in the fall."

After hanging up, I made the same call to Kelly Sanderson. I knew she would be even more willing since she had martial arts training and liked a physical challenge.

"Hello," said Kelly.

"Hello, Kelly. This is a voice from the past. It's Bill Bennet. I understand you're home for the summer and might be looking for work. My friends and I have been hired to protect a female celebrity for a week, but we need some women to help keep an eye on her. Are you interested?"

Part II - The Fall of Maderis

"Sure, that would be great. What do I have to do?" Kelly asked.

"We're going to guard the Hollywood star, Maderis, for one week. I'll pay you the same I'm paying Jenni Durant. Are you interested?"

"For that kind of money I could even protect Donald Trump," said Kelly.

"Good. Be at Mesabi International Airport Monday morning at nine."

"I'll be there," Kelly said as she hung up.

~~~

The next week was filled with excitement and anticipation. Facebook and Twitter exploded with exciting possibilities that awaited the population of Mesabi County. Imagine a star of Maderis' magnitude coming to Mesabi County. The media was teeming with tantalizing articles of leading Hollywood heartthrobs to whom Maderis was romantically linked. Rumors flew that maybe she was even coming here to make a movie and many of the locals would be cast in the picture. Beauty salons and barbershops were filled to capacity. Clothes flew out of the stores while all the antiquated lawn ornaments mysteriously disappeared. Lawns were manicured and streets were hosed down by overworked city crews. Everybody was under the impression that glamor was just over the horizon. Mesabi County was living the dream.

Chapter Two

The next day, John Baldwin and I pulled up to The Pines cabins. They were accurately named, for the trees hung over them, making them barely visible.

John looked at me and said, "You've got to be kidding. There's no way we can provide security around the clock in this weed patch. Anyone could come from anywhere and break in and we would be unable to protect Maderis and her entourage."

"Let's see what we can do," I replied.

We walked over to the larger building with the "Office" sign hanging by one hinge. I knocked on the door and hoped for the best. When the door opened, we were greeted by an older gentleman who apparently had a grudge against hygiene.

I started the conversation, "Hello, I'm Bill Bennett, and this is John Baldwin. I understand Maderis has reserved all of your cabins next week. We're providing security for her. Can you do anything about the premises?"

"Sure," he said. "The lawn mower is in the back. Help yourself."

"No, that's not exactly what I meant," I said. "We need to trim the tree line back about twenty yards."

As I was trying to explain our dilemma to the gentleman, a car pulled up and a well-dressed, middle-aged man stepped out.

"Can I help you?" he asked.

"I hope so," I said. "We're with the security team protecting Maderis next week while she and her entourage stay here. We were hoping to get your tree line cut back about twenty feet."

"My name is Fred Allen," he said, "and this is my father, Ted. He owns the cabins, but I check in on him from time to time. I can have some loggers come in and cut the tree line back. I've already contracted a local paint company to put a fresh coat of paint on the cabins, and I have ordered new beds and televisions. Is there anything else I can do?"

"As a matter of fact, yes," I replied. "We need one cabin set aside for our surveillance equipment. Is that a problem?"

"No problem," Fred said. "You can have the cabin at the end. Nobody usually stays there anyway."

Feeling a great sense of relief, I said, "That will be great. We'll check back Sunday night."

After we drove away, I said to John, "I think we dodged a bullet there." John smiled and concurred.

∼∼∼

From the woods, a man looked from behind the trees, staring at the cabins, telling himself ole Stella would pay for leaving him, Connor Simpson, high and dry without so much as a Dear John letter.

∼∼∼

Sunday Night

In Las Vegas, Cindy Morgan and Maggie Grenville were consuming their drinks at the MGM bar. In the background, they could hear their employer, Maderis, finishing her last performance before taking a hiatus.

"Here's to us," said Cindy, raising her glass and tipping it toward Maggie.

"What are we going to do in that bug-infested rat hole for a whole week while Maderis cries her heart out to her mother?" Maggie asked.

"Lord, help us," Cindy agreed. "Sometimes, I wonder why I stay with this job. It certainly isn't for the limelight."

They turned around and watched as the audience stood and gave Maderis a standing ovation. Maderis pretended to be overwhelmed and blew kisses at them.

Cindy and Maggie hurried backstage, knowing they had to be waiting when her majesty exited the stage and demanded accolades for her performance.

Maderis walked off stage and threw the flowers handed to her by a stagehand into a wastebasket. "Where can a girl get a drink around this dump?" she shouted.

Cindy and Maggie sprang into action. Cindy poured a stiff drink and handed it to Maderis as she waited patiently for her majesty to be seated in her dressing room. Maggie started reading the latest accolades out loud from *Gossip*, hoping the column would circumvent Maderis' wrath.

"Another wonderful performance was given last night at the MGM by Maderis," Maggie read. "One never tires of watching a true professional dance and sing her way into our hearts. Since she is taking a break from Las Vegas, we will miss her dearly."

"Well," said Cindy, "it looks like you went out with a bang. You should feel great about your time here at the MGM."

"I wish they could hire dancers who could keep up with me and a band that could carry a note," Maderis replied. "It's hard to perform with mediocre talent, but I do my best."

Changing the subject, Cindy said, "We're all packed for Cascadia. I will wake you at seven tomorrow morning. Do you want me to walk with you back to your room?"

"Don't you think I can find my own way back?" Maderis asked.

"No, I didn't mean that," said Cindy. "I just thought you might want company the last night before we leave."

"Don't worry about it," Maderis said. "I have already arranged for one of Ramone's escorts to spend the night. Just make sure everything is ready tomorrow morning. Now get out."

Both Cindy and Maggie left without a word. They walked through the lobby and rode the elevator up to their room, which they shared. After Cindy and Maggie had entered and closed the door, they sat down and discussed their plan.

"How much did you pay that nurse for the medical report?" Cindy asked.

"Two thousand dollars, but it was worth it, if we can embarrass that bitch," Maggie replied.

"You know we will probably have to start looking for new jobs once it leaks out Maderis is HIV positive," said Cindy. "It will ruin her career and she'll become a persona non grata in Hollywood and Las Vegas."

"Yes, but it will be sweet revenge for the way she has treated us. She acts like she's royalty, and she forgets she came from a small town in Michigan. It'll feel great to destroy her career," Maggie stated.

"I even hired a bunch of old codgers to provide security this week," Cindy added. "That should be a hoot. They have a decent reputation, but my sources tell me they'd have trouble guarding a garbage can."

They smiled, undressed, and laid down together in bed. What happens in Vegas stays in Vegas.

~~~

Meanwhile, Maderis had used the celebrity elevator to ride up to the penthouse and enter her room. Overlooking the panorama of the Las Vegas lights, Maderis undressed and waited for one of Ramone's escorts to knock on the door. She contemplated how she was going to tell her mother the heartbreaking news that she was HIV positive. She knew it would eventually become public knowledge, but like most celebrities, she would enjoy the bright lights while she could, the world be damned.

~~~

Back in Cascadia, Stella Stevinski's old boyfriend, Connor Simpson, had waited for the loggers to clear a swath around the back of the cabins. He returned the day after they had finished their work. Behind the cabins, Simpson found a suitable tree, and climbed it halfway up, and attached a tree stand. From the stand, he had a perfect vantage point of the kill zone. Tomorrow, he would make it happen.

Chapter Three

Monday Morning

The team had gathered at the airport well before Maderis' plane would touch down. The press, surprisingly, was out in full force. Not only the local media were present, like Lana Kanton who had been promoted to newscaster for Channel Seven after her predecessor had been murdered in a meth fiasco, but also scores of people with cameras and microphones whom I didn't recognize. I was getting apprehensive.

John Baldwin could tell I was nervous. "Relax, Bill," he said. "It will go fine. Ben is driving the lead SUV. I personally checked out both limousine drivers and they don't have criminal records. You, Kelly, and Jenni will ride with Maderis, and I will follow with her two assistants. We'll go right to the Pines and get them settled in."

"Thanks, John," I said. "I needed the pep talk." I motioned for Jenni, Kelly, Ben, Mark, and Tyler to join us. "I just don't want anything to go wrong on our watch," I told them. "There are a lot of crazies who would like nothing better than to have their fifteen minutes of fame by doing something stupid. Remember, as soon as she deplanes, we usher Maderis to her car, we get the two female assistants into the second car, and we're out of here. Are there any questions?" When there were none, I added, "Everybody get your game face on. Good luck."

The SUV and two limousines were in place as the plane taxied to a stop. Mass screaming erupted as the plane's door opened and the stairway was rolled up to the plane's door. Maderis made her customary exit from the plane, smiling and blowing kisses to the crowd.

We hustled to the end of the stairway and had to push the

media and well-wishers aside as Maderis and her assistants struggled through the crowd. I opened the first limousine's back door and helped Maderis be seated. Then I closed it and entered the front myself. Jenni and Kelly dived into the other rear door.

John, Tyler, and Mark were able to get the two assistants safely into their vehicle, and with that, the motorcade sped off.

In the middle of the crowd, Connor Simpson smirked, telling himself that was the last time Maderis would be enjoying the limelight.

After we were situated in the limos, Jenni held out her hand to Maderis and said, "It's a pleasure to meet you."

Maderis stared right through her and said, "Of course it is." Lighting a cigarette, Maderis turned away and looked out the window.

We sped down M-35, turning onto the county road. I thought it was a good time to introduce myself so I said, "My name is Bill Bennet. My team and I are hired to protect you for the week. I thought you would like to go to your cabins and have a break."

"You thought wrong," said Maderis. "Just do what I tell you. Call that buffoon in the SUV ahead and tell him I want to go to the Cascadia Cemetery."

I bit my tongue and told myself, *we're going to have to earn our money*. I called both Ben and John and told them about the change in plans. John said, tongue-in-cheek, "Can we leave her there?"

As instructed, we drove straight to the Cascadia cemetery, arousing a lot of attention. Seldom does a black SUV and two limousines drive through the heart of Cascadia. The locals smiled and waved. A host of cell phones were pointed in our direction as people hoped to get a picture of their favorite daughter. The motorcade drove into the quaint cemetery and parked. Maderis waited for me to open her door, which I hurriedly did, though I was not used to giving the star treatment.

Maderis stepped out and walked to a marker in the center.

She knelt down and touched the top of the stone. Maderis was motionless for a while before she finally stood and returned to the limousine. She entered, sat down, and she waited for me to close the door. Again, I was remiss at this protocol.

"Now take me to those godforsaken dwellings," Maderis said.

I called Ben and John and updated them on our travel plans. We circled back through town; by now, even more locals had gathered. The Cascadia Township police officer was overwhelmed trying to provide an avenue for our motorcade to inch through.

"Good lord," said Maderis. "I can't believe I used to live here." I knew enough not to say anything.

Upon arriving at the Pines Cabins, Maderis again waited for me to open her car door. She stepped out and let out a sarcastic laugh when she saw the cabins.

All things considered, I thought the owner's son had done a commendable job upgrading. In a week's time, the cabins had been transformed into very habitable structures. The buildings had been painted, the lawn had been mowed, and old signs replaced. Overall, it looked very appealing, but apparently, not to some people.

The owner's son approached smiling with his hand out. Maderis brushed past him and continued walking. The others had joined us and were making our way to the cabins. I saw a glint in the trees behind the cabin. I rushed Maderis, tackling her, causing her to scream a plethora of nasty adjectives. I shouted, "Gun!" Immediately, the others had their Glocks out, aiming at the tree line. I pointed to where I saw the glare. They went into immediate action. John and Tyler ran into the woods, Glocks at the ready. Ben and Mark pushed the two assistants back into their car. I lay on top of Maderis all the while she was screaming at me to get off. I ignored her demands. Not having weapons, Jenni and Kelly, could only lay in the grass, scanning the tree line for a shooter. Hearing shots in the woods, I picked Maderis up, threw her over my shoulder, and carried her into the cabin, dumping her unceremoniously on the floor. I pulled the shades down and pushed her under the bed. Needless to say, she was beside herself with rage, but I didn't care.

In another minute, John and Tyler returned to the cabins. John said, "You were right. There was a tree stand in the woods, and we saw someone carrying a rifle, running away. I shot twice, but I know I missed him."

"I'll call Sheriff Remington and update him," I said. "I know he'll send some deputies."

"Definitely do not call the police," said Maderis. "I don't want any bad publicity while I'm here. Do you understand?"

I nodded reluctantly.

By this time, Cindy Morgan and Maggie Grenville had entered the room, along with Kelly and Jenni. They saw Maderis crawling out from under the bed.

Maderis could not contain herself. She screamed at me, "You stupid idiot!" followed by many other expletives. "You ruined my dress. It was probably some country hayseed trying to get a picture. It happens all the time." Both Cindy and Maggie were fighting to smother laughs, seeming to enjoy seeing Maderis disheveled.

Cindy was the first to speak. "Maderis, I'll run a hot bath for you. That will make you feel better."

"Hurry up about it," said Maderis. "I want to get out of these clothes that this Neanderthal ruined."

I wanted to tell her what I really thought of her, but we had a whole week to put up with her attitude and I didn't want to make it any worse.

"We'll secure the perimeter," I said. "Kelly and Jenni, stay in the cabin and lock the door after us."

"Don't shoot yourself in the foot," Maderis told me. "I would hate to have anything happen to you."

The others heard the entire tirade as I walked out to join them. Mark said, "Why didn't you let the would-be assassin take the shot?" I closed my eyes and pretended I hadn't heard that. We swept through the woods and returned, deciding Ben and Mark would take the pre-arranged first watch. As we left, John looked over his shoulder toward Ben and Mark and said, "Good luck." I'm not sure how he meant that.

Jenni and Kelly would share a bed in Maderis' room, keeping an eye on the prima donna. We had assigned ourselves the remaining cabins. Ben and Mark taking one, John and I another, and Tyler and Carolyn Raft the last one. I walked over later that day with John to relieve Ben and Mark. It was a media circus with every television and radio station within five hundred miles staking out a location. Trailers were parked everywhere, with satellite dishes dotting the skyline. I noticed the owner's son giving interviews, although I wasn't sure what insight into Maderis he possessed. John shook his head and said, "Give me the mountain trails and backwoods anytime to this tinsel world." I concurred as we walked up to Ben and Mark.

"How is everything?" I asked.

"Her highness hasn't been out since we got here," Mark replied. "Maybe she drowned in the bathtub. Let's wait a couple of hours and check."

"We're being paid to do a job, so let's be professional about it," I said. "It's only a week. How long can that be?"

Ben and Mark walked away muttering between themselves.

Chapter Four

Through the open window, I heard Maderis say, "Bennett, get in here."

I didn't appreciate being summoned like a dog. I intended to tell her that as I entered her cabin. Noticing a pile of used tissues next to her on the coffee table, it appeared she had been crying. I again kept my thoughts to myself and said, "What can I do for you?" I motioned for Jenni and Kelly to leave us.

Maderis waited for the two women to close the door. Then she replied through sobs, "Have a seat. I know I'm a bitch and I can't talk to anyone. My life is coming apart, and I have no one to confide in."

I wanted to tell her I was not professionally trained to counsel anyone. I said, "Are you all right?"

"What do you think?" she replied. "My professional life is over, and I didn't want to come back here with my tail between my legs."

"Let me get someone who is professionally trained and very good at counseling," I suggested. "She is very discreet and I know you can confide in her." Maderis nodded, so I picked up my cell phone and dialed a familiar number.

"Hello," said my wife, Barb.

"I need the best counselor available," I began, "and that's you."

"What are you talking about?" Barb asked.

"Maderis is troubled and would like to talk to someone who isn't involved with the glamour and glitter of Hollywood. Can you help her?"

There was a moment of silence. Then Barb said, "I suppose, but she has probably seen the best in Hollywood. I don't know if I can do any better."

"Don't sell yourself short," I said. "Can you come?"

~~~

Barb pulled up within the hour. She exited her vehicle and pushed her way through the mass of humanity. Then she entered Maderis' cabin and sat down.

After introducing them, I left, giving the two of them time to get acquainted.

Several hours passed and night began to settle in before the front door opened and Barb stepped out. She said goodbye and embraced Maderis tenderly.

As Barb approached me, I asked, "Did everything go all right?"

She nodded, and I respected her professionalism for not saying more.

Soon after, Tyler and Carolyn arrived to take the next shift. By now, the media frenzy had settled down to a few independent cameramen trying to take an inappropriate picture and sensationalize it. Not knowing who we were, the cameramen ignored us and kept their equipment trained on Maderis' front door.

As we were driving away, my cell phone rang. I answered it and heard something I thought I would never hear. On the other end, Maderis said, "I got your cell number from Cindy and I just want to thank you for saving my life today and also for having your wife stop by. It was wonderful to confide in someone who wasn't just being nice because of my Hollywood coattails."

"You're very welcome in both cases," I said.

I was about to disconnect when she asked, "Do you think you and your team could help me visit my mother tomorrow? That's the real reason why I came, but I'm afraid to try to get through that media frenzy outside."

"I would be happy to," I replied. I disconnected and thought to myself, *what a metamorphosis*. I looked at Barb and said, "What did you do to help transform her into a human being?"

Barb smiled and said, "She just needed someone to talk to."

Tuesday Morning

After learning where her mother lived in Cascadia, my colleagues and I arranged a hoax. Barb arrived early and put on some of Maderis' clothes. I had Mark drive the SUV up close to Maderis' cabin, and then Barb, disguised as Maderis, stepped outside and into the waiting SUV. Jenni, Kelly, Cindy, and Maggie joined the entourage to complete the ruse. Mark drove off, followed by all the media, who had vehicles at the ready. An hour later, John and Tyler drove up to Maderis' cabin. Maderis and I got into their vehicle unobserved and made our way toward her mother's house.

As we were in route, John said, "I hope the media likes a tour of Mesabi County. Mark is going to take them through every back road and even some dirt ones just to get their goat."

I smiled at the thought of Mark leading a parade of gossip mongers on a scenic tour of Mesabi County.

On the way, my cell phone rang. It was Mark saying, "I just led them on an exciting ride through Victorious and Needleton. Now I think I'll lead them out to the Peshekee Grade. Maybe I can get them lost on the Triple A Road and then circle back to Brown's Road."

"Good luck and thanks," I said.

Once we drove up to Maderis' mother's house, I asked Maderis, "Do you want me to come in with you?"

"No. This is something I have to do by myself," she replied.

Maderis stepped out of the vehicle and transformed herself into Stella Stevinski. She approached the small house and rang the doorbell. The door opened and an elderly lady threw her arms around her daughter. Both cried together. They entered and closed the door. We waited for hours, but we didn't mind. While we were waiting, I told the others what had happened the preceding day. Ben, John, and Tyler seemed to understand. Finally, Stella Stevinski emerged from her mother's house and transformed herself back into Maderis. I opened the car door and she stepped in. I didn't have the heart to ask how it went because it was none of my business. My job was to keep her safe, but it had just become a little more rewarding. We returned to the cabins and saw Mark driving up simultaneously. My wife exited the vehicle and smiled to the media. As they were leaving their vehicles, I heard Mark shout, "Try to photograph my right side because it's more photogenic!" One of the media flipped him off.

Barb and Maderis entered the cabin together and initiated another counseling session. *Maybe everything will work out,* I thought. But I was wrong.

Chapter Five

Tuesday Night

Tyler made his rounds, checking the cabin doors to ensure they were locked. Carolyn Raft was sitting on the front porch of their cabin, reading a gossip magazine under the porchlight. As Tyler approached, he said, "How can you read that trash? You know nothing in those magazines is true."

"I like to keep up with the stars," Carolyn replied. "Who knows? Maybe, we'll be included someday."

Suddenly, a shot rang out. A woman fell down in front of Maderis' front door. Tyler removed his Glock and shouted, "Get down." Carolyn did as she was ordered.

Tyler ran to the fallen woman and saw blood streaming out of her chest. He examined her closer and saw it was Maggie.

Within seconds, the rest of us came out of our rooms, Glocks ready to fire.

"What happened?" I asked.

"One shot!" Tyler shouted. "And it came from the same area where the tree stand had been erected."

Immediately, we ran to the location of the tree stand. Whoever had fired the round was long gone. Jenni, Kelly, and Maderis came out of their cabin. I shouted, "Get back in there. It's not safe." Maderis saw Maggie's body, grimaced, and covered her mouth in horror. She slowly responded to my order to re-enter her cabin.

By now, the media floodlights were turned on and the tabloid photographers had converged like vultures. We had everything we could do to keep them at bay so we could protect the crime scene. Ben phoned it in to the Sheriff's Department, and shortly after, a cruiser was on the scene. EMTs arrived, but they could not revive Maggie Grenville.

Over the next few hours, a band of Sheriff Deputies and employees were on the scene. Carolyn Raft called her assistant to bring the medical examiner's vehicle to the scene. After a cursory examination, Carolyn looked up at us and told us the obvious: a gunshot to the chest appeared to be the fatal cause. Carolyn left with the body in the medical examiner's vehicle. We knew she would be busy for days fulfilling her professional obligation.

Meanwhile, I entered Medaris' cabin and tried to console her. I knew this was a job for a professional, and I knew the best. I called Barb and explained what had transpired.

"I will be there as soon as I can," she said.

I patted Maderis' shoulders and handed her tissues until Barb arrived.

A visibly shaken Cindy Morgan had entered the room and was staring off into the distance. I asked Cindy why Maggie was in front of Maderis' cabin.

Cindy said, "Maggie always liked to smoke a cigarette before she went to bed, but she ran out of smokes and was going to ask Maderis for one."

Maderis' said, "I can't believe Maggie lost her life because someone thought it was me. I feel so terrible. Maggie was with me for years. I can't believe this could happen."

Just then, Sheriff Remington entered the cabin and said, "I'm leaving Deputy Roads here through the night, and along with these guys, you should be okay. I'll come back in the morning. We've gathered all the evidence we can and we have your statements. Try to get some sleep."

Shaking his hand, I said, "Good night, Sheriff."

~~~

Among the crowd, Connor Simpson was trying to be inconspicuous while eavesdropping on the media as they filed their reports. He overheard one of them report the murdered woman was Maggie Grenville and not his former lover, Stella Stevinski. "I'll have to keep trying," he muttered to himself.

Chapter Six

Wednesday Morning

The wheels touched down at Mesabi Airport. Stepping out of his personal jet, movie director Rogue Garrison adjusted his sunglasses. He had come to ask Maderis to star in his next picture. He had the approval of the movie studio executives to offer her top billing in his next enterprise.

After exiting the jet, Garrison walked through the terminal, gathered his luggage, and he walked out to the curb to hail his prearranged Uber driver.

As he entered the vehicle, Garrison asked the driver, "Do you know by any chance where Maderis is staying?"

The Uber driver responded, "Are you kidding? Everybody knows where she is staying especially after the murder last night."

"And what murder would that be?" Garrison asked.

"Maderis' public relations director was shot last night in front of Maderis' cabin," said the driver. "They're pretty sure it was a case of mistaken identity. It was late and someone must have wanted to have revenge on Maderis for some reason."

"Isn't that interesting?" said Garrison, thinking all along how the publicity would do wonders for the picture if Maderis could co-star in his next movie.

The Uber driver drove away with his famous fare in tow, not knowing he was delivering a fly into the ointment.

During the drive to Maderis' cabin, Garrison tapped a phone number into his cell phone. The other end responded, "Hello."

Rogue Garrison asked, "Is this Alfred Snopfs?"

"Yes, it is. What do you want?"

"Did you forget our conversation last week?" Rogue Garrison asked.

"No," said Snopfs. "I haven't forgotten. I get ten thousand if I can persuade my wife, Cora, to get her daughter, Stella, to star in your new picture."

"Has she made contact yet?" Rogue Garrison asked.

"Yes, she has. She came here yesterday morning and talked to my wife. My stepdaughter, Stella, or as you know her, Maderis, is very upset about something. I was unable to overhear the conversation, but it must have been important for my stepdaughter to come all the way here to vent to my wife."

Garrison retorted, "Remember the deal." Then he disconnected. He hoped the old man would come through.

Thursday Morning

The next morning, we were on full alert. The sheriff's forensics people had done their work and given the okay for the owner's son, Fred Allen, to have the crime scene cleansed. After all, a murder scene would be bad for business, and he was only too willing to give interviews to any media personnel who would interview him.

I was posted at Maderis' door, making sure no tabloid muckrakers got past me. I heard Maderis' phone ring. She answered, "Hello, Mom. Yes, I'm okay, but Maggie has been murdered. I don't know what to do." There was silence for a long time, and then I heard Maderis say, "No, don't come over. It will just complicate things. I would worry about your safety. At least I know you're okay where you are. I love you too. Goodbye."

Maderis walked out onto the porch and gazed at the spot Maggie had fallen. "I've all the fame in the world and look where it's got me?" she said. "A good friend died just because some nut thought she was me. I wish I could just go back to being Stella Stevinski from Cascadia."

"You could if you really wanted to," I said.

She looked at me said, "Bill, I wish I could."

~~~

Minutes later, a Uber driver arrived. When Rogue Garrison stepped out of the vehicle, the media converged on him like a lion on wild meat. After motioning for the driver to wait, Garrison faced the media and said, "I am only here to console a dear friend of mine who lost a close companion last night." From the crowd, a rumor mongerer shouted, "Is Maderis going to star in your next picture?"

That was the question Garrison was hoping for. "We'll have to see," he said. "That's up to Maderis."

Having teased the media he turned and walked toward Maderis' cabin. Ben stopped him right away.

"I'm here to see a good friend," said Garrison. "Now step aside, oaf."

With that, Ben had him on the ground in seconds with his arms behind his back and his hands handcuffed in a plastic tie. Maderis stepped out of her cabin and shouted, "He's okay. He is a friend of mine. You can let him go."

Ben released him and Rogue made an uppity sign toward him. When Ben took a step toward him, Rogue Garrison increased his walk to a jog toward Maderis' door.

After walking up the steps to Maderis' cabin, Garrison said, "My dear, how are you? I had to come as soon as I heard. I didn't want you to endure this harrowing experience all by yourself. I simply had to be with you to comfort you in your time of need." Maderis entered her cabin with Garrison's arm around her shoulder.

I looked at John Baldwin and said, "If they were handing out Academy Awards, Garrison could have gotten one right there."

I had to walk away and engage John in a mutual conversation of disgust.

"Where do they get these phonies?" John asked.

"I hear you," I said. "They must grow these plastic fakes under a sunlamp. I hope she doesn't fall for that crap." Once inside the cabin, Rogue Garrison closed the door, took Maderis by the arm, and led her gently to the couch. Watching from the window outside, I could only imagine what Hollywood pretense was going on inside Maderis' cabin.

After several hours, Rogue Garrison exited, giving Maderis a hug first, and closed the door behind him. As Garrison was walking down the path, Cindy Morgan called to him from her porch, "Rogue, would you like some coffee?"

Rogue Garrison, thinking it might help endear him to Maderis, said, "Sure. I like mine with some cream please."

After entering Cindy's cabin, he looked around and said, "Isn't this quaint? I simply have to use a copy of this frontier village in my next picture." He sat down without an invitation and continued, "Well, Cindy, how are you holding up? It's a stroke of luck that it wasn't you who was shot last night."

"Maggie wasn't going over to bum a cigarette from Maderis," Cindy confessed. "Maderis wouldn't give us a glass of water if we were dying from thirst in the Sahara Desert."

"Well, pray tell," asked Rogue, "what was Maggie doing out at such a late hour?"

"She was going to confront Maderis with the truth. We discovered Maderis is HIV positive, and we knew it would destroy her. We were going to blackmail her for a fortune."

"Why are you telling me all this juicy information?" Rogue Garrison asked.

"I think you need her in your next picture. Your last two tanked, and frankly, she's your last hope. With Maggie out of the picture, you can buy my silence. Take it or leave it."

Rogue Garrison pondered for a while before he said, "I think I will leave it. I can get a dozen starlets like Maderis to be in my movie. In Hollywood, they're a dime a dozen. Also, I don't like being blackmailed. I do appreciate you sharing your little secret about Maderis. It will help me persuade Maderis to take my offer to star in my next picture, now at a reduced price, of course."

Cindy had to think quickly, or her opportunity of a lifetime would slip away. "What if I walk out that door and tell the media Maderis is HIV positive?" she asked. "What would it take to buy my silence?"

Rogue Garrison wrinkled his nose. "Well, that is a bird of a different feather. I guess I will have to buy your silence. How about one hundred thousand dollars?"

"Agreed," said Cindy. "I want it deposited into my account within the week. Here's my bank account number."

After slipping the number into his coat pocket, Garrison stood and left, confident he had wrapped up his star for his next picture.

Garrison walked out of Cindy Morgan's cabin and walked over to Maderis' and he knocked on the door. When the door opened, Maderis had a quizzical look on her face.

"Rogue, can I help you?" she asked.

"No, my dear," he replied. "I think it is I who can help you."

Rogue entered and closed the door behind him. After a few minutes, I heard Maderis crying and assumed it was more of Garrison playing on her sympathies after the shooting. Later, Garrison walked out of Maderis' cabin and proceeded down the path. As he neared Ben, he veered off the path, so as not to pass near him.

He hailed his Uber driver and departed with a feeling of confidence that his ship was righted.

Chapter Seven

Thursday Morning

Carolyn Raft had completed her autopsy and released Maggie Grenville's body to a local mortuary where her family planned to have it flown to her hometown in Houston, Texas. Maderis thought it was only fitting that she and Cindy accompany the body to the airplane. I felt her metamorphosis back to Stella Stevinski was continuing. We had arranged for the limousines to pick us up in front of the cabins. Cindy Morgan had walked out of her cabin earlier that day and held an impromptu press conference. Cindy explained, "Miss Maderis and her entourage would like to accompany Maggie Grenville's body to Mesabi International Airport. We hope the press will respect our privacy."

I knew that wasn't going to happen.

When it was time to depart, we opened the cabin door and stepped out. The press came alive with questions that nobody with a sense of decency would have asked.

Some of the questions included:

"Do you feel directly responsible for the death of Maggie Grenville?"

"Have you spoken with Maggie's family?"

"Maderis, are you involved in the shooting?"

We ignored the questions as we walked down the sidewalk and stepped into the waiting limousine, only to have a man charge toward us. Within seconds, Tyler had him restrained and Mark applied the plastic ties to his hands. The man shouted, "Stella, I just want to see you. We loved each other so much once. Can't I just talk you?"

Maderis wound down the car window, removed her sunglasses, and said, "Connor, is that you? Please let him go. He is an old dear friend of mine."

Reluctantly, the boys released the excited man, but they stood next to him in case another episode occurred.

"I can't talk now," Maderis told him, "but when I get back, we have a lot to catch up on. I so want to see you. Gentlemen, please allow him to stay in my cabin while I'm gone."

Ben nodded his head and escorted the young man to Maderis' cabin. Before he opened the door, Ben frisked Connor Simpson thoroughly, emptying Simpson's pockets and even removing Simpson's shoes. Ben escorted Simpson to a chair to sit on and told him not to touch anything. Jenni and Kelly stood ready to restrain Simpson if Maderis' former lover became combative.

~~~

Thursday Afternoon

After seeing Maggie Grenville's body off on the plane, the entourage returned with a weeping Maderis and Cindy Morgan. Everyone entered the small cabin, and Jenni prepared a pot of coffee. Connor Simpson was still sitting on the chair flanked by Ben and Mark. He was the elephant in the room. After a few minutes, Maderis was able to compose herself and say, "Connor, it's good to see you. I wish we could meet under better circumstances. How have you been?"

"What do you care?" Simpson replied. "You ran off to tinsel town and left me for dead. I didn't hear from you, but I still adored you, even though you didn't care."

Maderis was sullen for a minute, and then she said, "I know I let you down, but I just couldn't live here another day. I wanted something better. Can you forgive me?"

Listening to the conversation, I played a hunch.

"Was that you in the tree stand the day we arrived?" I asked Simpson.

"Yes," he said, turning to look at Maderis. "I was so bitter I wanted to kill you."

John asked the next question. "Did you shoot Maggie Grenville?"

"No, I would never do that," Simpson replied.

Ben put his old police hat on and asked, "What caliber rifle do you own?"

"It's a Winchester 30-30 with a 4 power scope."

"That will be easy enough to determine," I said. "Since the autopsy is complete, Carolyn will have the slug. If you're lying, you are in a world of trouble."

"I'm not lying," Simpson replied. "My rifle is in my truck, and you can check it."

"Believe me, we will." said Ben. Looking at Mark, Ben asked, "Would you retrieve the rifle from his truck and bring it to the sheriff's office for them to check the ballistics?"

Mark nodded and stood to retrieve the rifle.

"Would you leave us alone for a few minutes?" Maderis asked. "Connor and I have some catching up to do."

"We'll be right outside the door if you need us," I replied. Mark growled as he stood and stared at Simpson. Then he turned and followed me, reluctantly followed by Jenni and Kelly, who closed the door behind them.

We waited outside, giving the two old flames their privacy and time to reminisce.

"I don't feel good leaving her with that would-be assassin," Mark said.

"I know," I said, "but we have to give them time to patch things up. Right now, Maderis needs all the friends she can get"

"That reminds me," John said. "Where exactly was Cindy Morgan the night Maggie Grenville was murdered?"

We all paused to reflect. I said, "That's right; I didn't see her until well after the shot. She came into Maderis' room after the floodlights were on."

"If you were in your room and heard a loud noise," said Ben, "wouldn't you come out as a natural reaction?"

"I certainly would," said Jenni. Kelly Sanderson agreed.

"Nobody really asked Cindy Morgan where she was," I said. "Let's find out."

We walked over to Cindy Morgan's cabin and knocked on the door.

Ben leaned over and peered through the window. He saw Cindy was placing something high up on her closet shelf.

We knocked on Cindy's cabin door again and then she opened it.

"Is it okay if we come in? I'm not sure about a few things and want to ask you some questions," I said.

"I guess so," said Cindy. "What do you want?"

"We were just rehashing the murder," I said, "and it appears you didn't show up to Maderis' room until a full twenty minutes later. Even if you were sleeping, the sound of the gunshot should have woken you up."

"I sleep with ear plugs, Cindy said, "and I take a sedative before I go to bed."

"Can we look in your closet?" Ben asked.

Cindy looked nervous. "Go ahead," she said. "I don't have anything to hide."

Ben walked over to the closet, opened it, and looked down at her bedroom slippers. They were covered in dirt and dried grass.

"How did your bedroom slippers get so dirty?" Ben asked.

"I liked to sit on the front porch while Maggie smoked her cigarettes," Cindy said.

"But there's no grass on the front porch," said Ben. "Do you want to try again?"

"I think that's enough," Cindy replied. "I want you to leave. You're not the police. I'm packing to leave since I feel it's too dangerous to stay here. I'm quitting my job and returning to Las Vegas. No job is worth getting shot over."

Ben looked up at the closet and asked, "What's in the box?"

"I want you to leave now," Connie said emphatically.

We had no choice but to turn and do as she requested. Even if we did find anything incriminating, it could not be used in court since we had no warrant.

As we left, Cindy slammed the door behind us. She locked it and slid the curtains closed to prevent any further snooping.

"You know as soon as she's on the plane, we'll never see the gun again," said John.

"You're right," I replied. "We have to trick her into using her pistol to implicate herself. But how can we do that? Oh, I think I just thought of something."

The boys gathered around and I explained my plan as they smiled and nodded.

After I explained my plan, we walked over to Maderis' cabin and I knocked on her door. After Maderis opened her cabin door, we entered and I started to explain our last ditch effort to catch Maggie Grenville's murderer.

"Maderis," I began, "I am going to need you to give the performance of your life. We think Cindy Morgan murdered Maggie Grenville, and we need you to persuade her to take her gun and incriminate herself?" I continued explaining my plan in detail.

After I left Maderis alone, she called her mother for some TLC.

"Hello," answered her mother. "Yes, dear. We can talk. Alfred has gone into town. He has been pestering me to convince you to star in Rogue Garrison's next picture. He thinks it would be great for your career. But I want you to do what makes you happy."

"I'm glad to hear that," said Maderis. "I just don't know what to do. It's just nice to talk to you. I have a lot to think about. I'll call you tomorrow. I love you.

"I love you, too, Stella," said her mother.

Chapter Eight

Friday Morning

Cindy Morgan's cell phone rang. Cindy had just stepped out of the shower when she answered it. "Hello, Maderis. Yes, I can come over immediately." She quickly threw on some clothes and hurried over, thinking this would be the last time she would be summoned to appear before her majesty. She knocked on Maderis' door and walked inside. "Please come in," Maderis requested as she motioned for Jenni and Kelly to step outside.

Cindy Morgan was a little surprised by Maderis' contrite behavior. Maybe, it was Maggie's murder that had caused a temporary change.

Maderis started the conversation. "Rogue Garrison called from his hotel in Victorious. As you well know, he has me in a peculiar situation. He knows I am HIV positive, and he's holding it over my head to make me star in his next picture for a pittance. He told me you informed him, but I'm not holding that against you. I've decided against starring in his next picture. He's threatened me that if I don't appear in his next picture, he will tell the world about my illness. I don't want to live like that. Another director, Frank Gorman, called me last night from Hollywood and asked me to be in a picture that will pay me ten times what Garrison is offering. So I'm in a bind and need some time to think it over. I hope you'll continue to be my personal assistant. Now, with Maggie gone, I'll need you more than ever. I thought we could combine your job with Maggie's so you could double your salary."

It was a lot for Cindy to absorb, but she said, "Maderis, that would be awesome. I would like that very much."

"I was hoping you'd agree," said Maderis. "I'll call Frank

Gorman and tell him I'll star in his next picture. I'll also call Rogue Garrison and explain everything to him. I hope he'll agree to keep quiet about my illness."

Cindy Morgan was quick to say, "As your new public relations director let me take care of that. I'll talk to him and persuade him to drop the whole topic. I'll threaten him with an indiscretion I know he's hiding. I know for a fact that Maggie Grenville was raped by Rogue Garrison and she had an abortion that Garrison paid for. Maggie told me confidentially, but with her gone, it doesn't matter. Rogue will do as I tell him, or he'll face the tabloids." Maderis gave her a brief embrace and said, "Thanks for sticking by me. I really need you now." Cindy smiled as she left Maderis' cabin.

Cindy couldn't wait to get back to her room and call Rogue Garrison. There was no way he was going to ruin this sweet deal that had just fallen into her lap. She picked up her cell phone and connected with Garrison.

"Hello, Rogue; how are you?"

After exchanging pleasantries, they discussed how Maggie's murder had to be such a burden on Maderis and how well she was holding up. After discussing some Hollywood rumors, Cindy got down to business. "I would like to talk to you about our conversation yesterday. Can we meet in the Cascadia cemetery?"

"I guess we could," said Rogue, "but I thought we had straightened everything out. Why would I want to meet you in a cemetery?"

"Meet me there in one hour, or I'll walk outside and tell the press about Maggie's rape and abortion."

"All right, but I think this is a dreadful way to conduct business as civilized human beings," Rogue Garrison concluded.

"Shut up and be there," Cindy replied.

~~~

As requested, Rogue Garrison got a ride from a local Uber driver in Victorious to the Cascadia cemetery.

We followed Cindy Morgan from a distance and deployed once we saw her destination, and we waited for the fish to take the bait. It wasn't long before a Victorious Uber driver arrived and Rogue Garrison stepped out. He paid the fare and told the driver to come back in one hour. As the cab drove away, Cindy Morgan walked out from behind an oversized angel headstone. Somehow, there was some irony in that.

They approached each other and Rogue Garrison asked, "Now, darling what was so important that we couldn't talk over a cup of coffee? I thought we agreed you and I will keep quiet regarding Maderis' dreadful illness and Maggie Grenville's abortion, which was a long time ago?"

"There's been a change in plans," said Cindy. She took out her pistol and pointed it at Garrison.

Just then, all of us jumped out from behind the bushes, Glocks at the ready. I shouted, "It's all over Cindy. We know you shot Maggie Grenville. The ballistics on your gun will confirm that. Let's end this peacefully."

Rogue Garrison threw himself behind a headstone and started to whimper. Cindy Morgan turned to fire, but five Glocks rang out simultaneously. She was dead before she hit the ground. We approached the body, and I told Garrison to stand up. "I wasn't involved in anything illegal," he said. "I didn't know she killed Maggie Grenville."

Barb arrived with Maderis. They walked over to Cindy Morgan's body. Maderis looked down and said, "Why do people have to be so greedy? Can't we just live together?"

The metamorphosis is complete, I thought.

Chapter Nine

Both Carolyn Raft and Sheriff Remington arrived with their underlings. The locals were gathering from a distance, wondering what had transpired. Sheriff Remington approached me and said, "Bill, this better be good. I can't wait to hear this one."

I said, "You're going to love my explanation." I proceeded to clarify the events as they occurred. He kept shaking his head, finding the whole story hard to fathom. I left that part out when it came to the part of Maderis' illness. I told the good sheriff that Cindy wanted to continue to blackmail Maderis and Maggie was getting in the way.

"You mean," said Sheriff Remington, "that Cindy Morgan shot and killed her best friend, Maggie Grenville, trying to keep her quiet, and then she was going to murder Rambo here in the cemetery?"

"It looks that way," I replied.

Maderis stepped forward and said, "Bill, you don't have to protect me any longer. Sheriff, the reason Cindy Morgan shot Maggie Grenville and was probably going to kill Rogue Garrison was because I am HIV positive. She and Maggie were planning to blackmail me to keep it a secret, but then she killed Maggie to keep the money for herself, and she was afraid Rogue would let the secret out so she couldn't collect." Then Maderis looked at me and said, "I'm okay with it becoming public knowledge. I've talked to Connor and I'm retiring from show business and moving back to Cascadia. Barb said I can get HIV treatment at Victorius Hospital. After I am tested, the hospital can set me up with the two components of Descovy, which are FTC and TAF. I can take the other antiretroviral medications as needed. Carolyn

Raft tells me I can have a long life, and I hope to share that with Connor."

I gave her a hug. Then we proceeded to return to Victorious to celebrate our success, but before I could drive out of the cemetery, Sheriff Remington flagged me down and said, "Don't go far, Bennett. You have more explaining to do on this one."

I smiled and waved goodbye.

The pseudo-detectives, along with Kelly and Jenni, reconvened at Geno's Pizzeria to toast our success in protecting Maderis.

I looked at Jenni and Kelly and said, "Both of you are fully fledged pseudo-detectives. You did a great job protecting Maderis. I think both of you have a great career ahead of you in criminal justice. If I can help in any way, don't hesitate to call me."

"It was a great experience," Jenni replied, "and I know I speak for Kelly when I say we look forward to working with you again if you need us."

I smiled and shook both their hands. Rick Bonnetelli brought over some pitchers of beer and the usual order of pizzas was submitted.

We all agreed that the re-emergence of Stella Stevinski could only happen with the *Fall of Maderis*.

Part III

The Mayor's Murder

Chapter One

A beautiful autumn day was transpiring in front us as Barb and I drove to Cascadia. This is the time of year when the afternoons are gorgeous, but the temperature drops as soon as the sun sets. The coniferous trees were magnificent with their oranges and yellows exploding from the woods. It was nearly impossible to drive and not smile as one clump of trees was more spectacular than another.

Being from the Superior Peninsula, we have learned to make the most of the weather. In the autumn, outings are planned during the middle of the afternoon knowing full well the night air is not one to fool with. We were looking forward to a wonderful afternoon with our friends, Randy Dunham and his lovely wife, Kate. I had mountain-biked with Randy many times and Barb and Kate had golfed together numerous times. The Dunhams had asked us to come for a meal, and we had agreed to take them up on the offer. With wine in hand, we made our way to their home on Lake Michigamme.

Both Randy and Kate were easy company. After asking polite questions about each other's families, we sat down on their back deck overlooking the majestic Lake Michigamme.

"I never get tired of this vista," Randy said. "Sometimes I just gaze at this panoramic spectacle for hours."

"I agree," I replied. "It is breathtaking what God has created."

"We're lucky to live in such a beautiful location," Randy added. "I only have to look out my window or go for a walk to feel one with nature." I nodded in affirmation.

As the day progressed, cold beverages and a warm homemade meal put everyone in a great mood. Watching the sunset from their deck, Randy expressed his concern about the amount of water that the Michigamme River flows into Lake Michigamme every year. There were rumors that the Environmental Protection Agency and the County Commissioner, who represented Cascadia, were at odds over what the lake's water level should be. The County Commissioner, Pete Runnels, wanted to slow down the river's flow rate into the lake. However, the Environmental Protection Agency disagreed and wanted to allow homeowners and sportsmen to maintain the water at its present level. Both sides had good reasons, but only one side would prevail.

As we sat on the Dunham's deck, in the distance we could see lights from Cascadia glimmering off the lake's surface—a reminder to enjoy the little things in life. Suddenly, Kate stared at the shoreline in disbelief and asked, "What's that floating in the water?"

Standing and straining to see the object in the water with Big Rumsey Island in the background, Randy said, "It looks like a body."

With that, we made our way to the shoreline, except Randy, who walked into his garage and emerged armed with a long pole. Randy walked to the shore and reached for the body. After a few futile attempts, he was able to pull it ashore. He made a cursory examination and said, "I think it's Jack Thompson. He is—I mean he *was* our village mayor for decades." Immediately, I dialed 911 and reported the incident.

It wasn't long before a siren could be heard in the distance. The Dunham's driveway soon became congested with emergency vehicles.

When the sheriff's deputy exited his vehicle and approached us, I recognized him as Andy Roads. He had been seriously hurt last year in a helicopter crash when a jealous lover had sabotaged his chopper. He had miraculously survived and returned to duty, splitting his time between road patrol and emergency helicopter flights.

This was not the time to make polite conversation, so the four of us made it a point to stay away from their investigation. We stepped back, complying with Deputy Roads demand to stay away from the crime scene, knowing this was serious business and no place for curiosity seekers.

The Medical Examiner arrived and proceeded to the body. I motioned to her as she passed me, but Carolyn Raft was all business. She was a true professional whom I respected immensely ever since we had worked closely last year solving some crimes on the Dead River. She had become engaged to my friend's son, Tyler Baldwin, and a wedding was imminent. She bagged the victim's hands and performed a routine examination as her assistant took photographs of the body. I had a bad feeling about this.

"The current is pretty strong," said Randy. "I presume Jack must have fallen in Philomena Bay and was washed down the shoreline with the current."

"You're probably right," I replied. "The question is was it an accident or a homicide."

Randy gave me a quizzical look, not having considered the latter possibility.

After a lengthy examination, Carolyn left the scene with the body. We gave out statements to Deputy Roads, which were pretty cursory. With our evening darkened by the tragedy, Barb and I bid the Dunhams adieu and left for home. I decided to make some phone calls to my pseudo-detective friends to bring them up to speed. I had a feeling we were going to get involved whether we wanted to or not.

Chapter Two

The following day, both *The Mining Ledger* and the local television station, Channel Seven, were unable to provide an insight into how Jack Thompson ended up in Lake Michigamme. This only added to the rumors already flying around Cascadia. According to the locals, Jack Thompson didn't have an enemy in the world, and he had won the last two elections for mayor unopposed. He was an excellent swimmer and even belonged to the local Search and Rescue Unit.

Later that day, I visited the Sheriff's Office and tried to use my inroads, but nobody was talking; even Carolyn wouldn't discuss the events that had transpired.

In the evening, I decided to convene the pseudo-detectives at Geno's Pizzeria. John and Tyler Baldwin, Ben Myers, and Mark Kestila were in attendance. Jenni Durant and Kelly Sanderson had returned to college and were finishing up their Bachelor Degrees in Criminal Justice. As usual, Rick Bonnetelli was serving drinks and taking orders in his bar. Not surprisingly, Carolyn Raft was not present. "She's working on the autopsy and couldn't make it," Tyler explained. I realized she was probably under orders from Sheriff Remington not to divulge any information about the death, and I respected her for that.

"Let's find out what really happened," I said. "John and Tyler, why don't you see if anybody is home and talk to the locals on the Blue Road." Then turning to Ben and Mark, I asked, "Could you investigate the residents on the Brown Road? I'll start asking questions in Cascadia. Let's see if anybody knows anything."

"I have the day off tomorrow," Tyler replied, "so we can start knocking on doors in the morning."

"Sounds good," said Ben. "Mark and I can hit the Brown Road

in the afternoon. Mark probably needs his beauty sleep."

"Why don't you give it a rest?" Mark replied.

As we were adjourning, Rick motioned for me to come over to the bar. "I don't know if this is anything," he said, "but two guys were in here earlier. They said they were from the EPA. They told me the FBI was going to investigate Jack Thompson's death."

"Thanks," I said. "I have a hunch this is going to get complicated before we know what really happened last night."

I walked out the back door of Geno's Pizzeria, but I hadn't taken a step before I was struck from behind. I fell to the ground, unable to comprehend what happened. I heard a voice say, "Let it go, or else you're dead. Do you hear me?"

I struggled to get to my feet, trying to clear my head, but without much luck. When I staggered back into the bar, Rick Bonnettelli ran to me, asking, "What happened?"

"I just got cold cocked and someone threatened to kill me if I didn't drop the investigation."

"You must be on to something," said Rick. "You better stay close to the other guys just to be safe."

"I should, but I can't do that," I replied. "That's not how I roll."

"I'll get some ice for your head," said Rick. "I'll call Baldwin and tell him what just happened."

"Thanks," I said.

Not having the stamina to keep Rick from calling Baldwin, I staggered to the closest bar stool and collapsed. It wasn't long before John Baldwin returned and examined the lump on my head.

"It's a good thing he hit you on the head," he said. "Otherwise, it might have done some damage."

I didn't dignify that with a response.

"There must have been a reason for the attack," John added. "We must be looking in the right direction. Watch yourself tomorrow when you start asking questions in Cascadia. Somebody's hiding something."

"Likewise," I said. "You and your son be careful."

After my head cleared, I limped out to my vehicle and called it a night.

Chapter Three

Bright and early the next day, I was on my way to Cascadia, after leaving a note for my wife regarding my whereabouts and rubbing the lump on my head. I stopped at the only restaurant in Cascadia, The Moose Antlers, which doubled as a social club. If any information existed, I was pretty certain I would get it there. In a small town, nothing happens that doesn't get analyzed over a cup of coffee at the local restaurant.

When I entered, I tried to apply my natural charm.

"How's everything going?" I asked the cashier.

"Fine, can I help you?" she replied.

"I hope so. What's the word on the street about Jack Thompson's drowning?"

Becoming a little defensive, she said, "I haven't heard anything. He was a great guy and everybody liked him. He'll really be missed."

"What projects were going on in the village?" I persisted.

"Nothing much. The only problem is the EPA wants to continue the water flow and our County Commissioner, Pete Runnels, wants to decrease the flow from the dam."

"How do you feel about that?"

"Truth be told," she said, "I don't know why Runnels wants to decrease the river flow. It will upset a lot of landowners. Their shoreline will be a lot farther out."

"That's a good point," I replied. "Thanks for the information."

~~~

Meanwhile, John and Tyler were knocking on doors, trying to find answers from residents living on the Blue Road. Naturally, most people were not home, but finally, they found someone willing to talk to them. The homeowner asked them to come inside, and once they had, John, looking through the back window, noticed a pulp truck parked behind the house.

"This is my son, Tyler, and I'm John Baldwin," said John, introducing them. "We're trying to help the local police find out what happened to Jack Thompson the other night. Can you help us?"

"I'm Lars Larson. What do you want to know?""

"I see you're a logger," said John. "Why is it you're home today?"

Lars Larson replied, "My truck's back axle is broken. I'm waiting for a tow truck."

"Did you see or hear anything the other night?" Tyler asked.

"Yes, as a matter of fact, I did," said Lars. "Now that I think about it, I did see some people on the Indian Bridge in Cascadia that night. I was hauling my load on the Red Road into Cascadia and downshifted as I climbed the hill, and I noticed two men talking on the bridge. I'm pretty sure one was Jack Thompson."

"Why do you think it was Jack Thompson?" Tyler asked.

"He always wore a Stormy Kromer hat and used suspenders to keep his pants up," Lars replied. "I'm pretty sure it was Jack, but I didn't recognize the other man."

"Thanks," said John. "We'll be in touch."

They closed the door on the way out.

~~~

On the other side of the lake, Ben Myers and Mark Kestila were working their way along the Brown Road trying to find homeowners who might have seen something the night of Jack Thompson's drowning. The first few homes met with no luck. Finally, they drove into the local ATV shop where Glenn Magnum was working on a four-wheeler.

Ben and Mark approached Glen and knelt down by the ATV to talk to him.

"Hello, Glenn," said Ben. "We know you're busy, but can you spare a few minutes for us? I'm Ben Myers and this is Mark Kestila. We're trying to find out if there was anything suspicious about Jack Thompson's drowning the other night. Did you see or hear anything that night?"

"No, I can't say as I did," Glenn replied.

A young man had come through the back door in time to hear the conversation.

"This is my mechanic, Sam Waters," Glenn said.

"How about you?" Mark asked. "Did you hear or see anything the other night when Jack Thompson drowned?"

"No, not a thing," Sam replied.

"Well, thanks for your time," Ben said.

Glen Magnum returned to work as Ben and Mark exited the garage. Sam Waters breathed a sigh of relief as he stepped outside and dialed his cell phone.

Chapter Four

Pete Runnels tapped his phone and said, "Hello."

"We're in trouble," Sam Waters said. "Two guys just left here asking if Magnum or I knew anything about Thompson's drowning."

"Were they cops?" Pete asked.

"No, they were just asking questions."

"Relax, Sam," Pete replied. "Nobody saw anything, so we're not in trouble, right?"

"I was on Indian Bridge with Thompson the night he drowned," said Sam. "I just got paroled from prison. You know I won't get a fair trial in Mesabi County. If anybody can put Thompson and me on the bridge, my goose is cooked, and I'll spill the beans about your little shenanigans."

"Listen, stupid," Pete replied. "Keep your mouth shut. Do you hear me?"

~~~

Later that day, I thought enough time had lapsed that I could pay Carolyn a visit at the Sheriff's Office. I entered the building and descended the stairway. I knocked on her door and entered cautiously, not sure how I would be received. She looked up and gave me a look I had seen before. She was very gracious when we were socializing, but she was all business when she was doing her job.

"Look what the cat dragged in," she said. "I thought I'd be seeing you, but I didn't think it would be this soon."

"It's nice to see you too," I replied. "Any results on Jack Thompson's autopsy?"

"The sheriff gave me specific orders not to release any information to the public, especially to you," Carolyn replied.

Remembering a trick I used once before, I asked, "What about a bribe? I have two tickets to the Clint Black—"

"Don't say anymore," Carolyn interrupted. "I'm not falling for any of your tricks. Maybe, I can tell you in a few days when some information is released to the public. Give my regards to Barb."

As I was leaving Carolyn's office, I thought I might stop by Sheriff Remington's office to stay on his good side. I climbed the three flights and knocked on his door.

"Come in," Sheriff Remington said.

As I entered, he said, "I was wondering when you would get around to seeing me. I suppose you already stopped by the M.E.'s office."

"You know me so well," I replied. "Anything up regarding Jack Thompson's drowning?"

"Nothing I can tell you," Sheriff Remington stated.

"Well, for a change I can tell you something," I said. "The other night as I was leaving Geno's Pizzeria, someone knocked me on the head and threatened to kill me if I kept investigating."

Sheriff Remington suddenly looked very interested. "We'll have to wait for Carolyn's autopsy report," he said, "but you definitely got me thinking."

There was a knock on the door and Carolyn entered the sheriff's office. "I have a preliminary report on the Thompson body," she said. She looked at me and then Sheriff Remington. The sheriff said, "Go ahead; he's going to find out anyway."

Looking at her report, she said, "His body contained considerable amounts of phenobarbital. There was bruising on his wrists and neck, meaning there definitely was a struggle. There was no water in his lungs; he was dead before he went into the lake; definitely a homicide."

"I thought there was something wrong with the whole scenario," I said. "He was in good shape, so I doubted he would have drowned from falling from the bridge."

"Bennett, keep this under your hat," said the sheriff. "I don't want to see this in the newspaper before we're ready to release an official news release. Do you understand?"

"Yes," I replied, but I knew I had to tell my pseudo-detective team.

～～～

The five sleuths gathered later that day at Millie's Restaurant for a cup of Joe and to exchange information.

After taking a deep sip of coffee, John Baldwin said, "Tyler and I talked to a logger named Lars Larson. He swears he saw two men on Indian Bridge that night, and one of them was Jack Thompson."

When I looked at Ben and Mark, Ben said, "We haven't uncovered anything in our door-to-door search. Most of the people weren't home, but we will try again tomorrow."

"I got knocked on the head the other night leaving Geno's Pizzeria," I added, "and the assailant threatened to kill me if I didn't quit asking questions. In addition, I was in Sheriff's Remington's office when Carolyn gave her report to him. She said Jack Thompson's body contained phenobarbital and there were bruises on his wrists and neck. Finally, there was no water in his lungs, so he must have been dead before he went into the lake."

I gave the information time to sink in.

"That certainly changes everything," said Tyler. "Only a medical person could have access to phenobarbital. We'll have to find out how the drug got into his body and who could have done it." We all nodded in affirmation.

"We'll have to trace Jack Thompson's movements that night," I added, "and find out how he could have been drugged. Ben, could you and Mark check into the water flow issue? John and Tyler, could you start in Cascadia to see if you can find out where he was that night? I'll check with the EPA to see what light they can shed on this water controversy?" We adjourned with our assignments.

Two well-dressed men stood and followed us out of Millie's Restaurant.

As we were nearing our vehicles, one of them called to us,

"Wait up. Do you have a minute? We'd like to talk to you. We're with the FBI. I'm Special Agent Stone and this is Special Agent Adams. We understand you fellows are looking into the Thompson murder."

"That's right," I said, "but we're not interfering with the federal government or the sheriff's investigations."

"We don't think it's a very good idea for you old timers to be poking your nose into federal business," said Agent Stone. "Stay out of the case, or else we'll have to charge you with obstruction of justice."

Tyler, taking exception to the threat, said, "Who are you calling an old timer? Besides we have the right to ask questions. If you fools can't do your job, we'll do it for you."

"Consider yourself warned," Stone replied, and then the two FBI agents turned and walked to their vehicle.

"They're lucky they walked away when they did," Mark said, "or I'd have let them have it."

Ben rolled his eyes.

Chapter Five

Early the next day, I paid a visit to the federal building in Victoria. I searched the directory on the wall until I found the EPA's office number. I walked down the hall and entered the appropriate office. A young female clerk approached me from behind the counter and asked, "Can I help you?"

"I hope so," I replied. "Is there anyone here who can provide me with information on the EPA's decision to limit the flow of water through the Michigamme River's dam?"

"I think that would be Mr. Wilder's jurisdiction," she said. "Let me see if he's in."

After checking with his schedule, she motioned for me to follow. I entered his office, and after shaking hands and exchanging names, got right to business. "Could you provide me with some information regarding the Michigamme Dam controversy?" I asked. "I understand County Commissioner Runnels wants to draw down the water level, but the EPA is opposed to it."

"It's pretty simple," said Mr. Wilder. "The water level in the lake has to be maintained or it will cause an ecological disaster."

My next question for Mr. Wilder was a little more complicated. "Was Jack Thompson involved in the controversy?"

"As a matter of fact, yes," Mr. Wilder replied. "He was on the committee that made the recommendation to maintain the water at its current level."

"Who else is on the committee?" I asked.

"It's public record, so I can give you a copy," said Mr. Wilder. "I'll print the committee's list." After the printer groaned and spit it out, he handed the list to me. I scanned the list to see if anybody would have easy access to phenobarbital. One name jumped out at me, Dr. Goodney's.

"Was the vote unanimous in recommending maintaining the water table at its present level?" I asked.

"No," said Mr. Wilder. "The vote was 3-2. Jack Thompson's vote was the deciding one."

That made me think his murder had to be tied to his position on the committee. The pseudo-detectives and I would have to find out where each committee member had been the night of the murder.

I asked Mr. Wilder one final question. "Besides Jack Thompson, who else voted to keep the lake at its present level?"

Mr. Wilder thought for a moment before saying, "It's also public record, so I guess I can tell you. Dr. Goodney and Henry Brennen voted to drain the river, and Sara Goodney and Helen Michaels voted along with Jack Thompson to maintain the water level."

"How are Sara and Dr. Goodney related?" I had to ask.

"They're husband and wife."

"Really?" I said. "That must have made for interesting dinner conversation with each voting on the opposite side of the issue."

"I can't comment on that," said Mr. Wilder, shrugging his shoulders. "You'll have to talk to them."

I thanked Mr. Wilder for his time, shook his hand, and left with a boatload of questions that needed answers.

I walked out of the federal building and sat on the top step. I dialed John Baldwin and waited for him to answer.

"Hello," John said.

"Hello, John; change in plans. Forget checking the bars and restaurants in Cascadia. There was a committee that recommended maintaining the water flow from the Michigamme River. Two of the members are married, but they voted differently. Can you check on a Dr. Frank Goodney, who voted against keeping the water level high and his wife, Sara, who voted to maintain the water level?"

"Tyler and I can do that," John replied. "We'll check with you later."

Next, I called Ben Myers and asked, "Could you check with Henry Brennen; he voted to lower the water level. And if possible, Helen Michaels, she voted to maintain the water level?"

"I'll see if I can locate them," Ben replied.

I thanked him and then disconnected.

I thought I'd now return home to enjoy some time with Barb, but that wasn't going to happen.

I had just drove into my driveway when my cell phone sounded. It was John Baldwin.

"I think you better come to Cascadia," John said. "Tyler and I just arrived at the Goodney's residence and there are police cars and other emergency vehicles here."

After obtaining the Goodney address from John, I said, "I'll be there as soon as I can. I'll call Ben and Mark and update them."

"You don't have to call Carolyn," John said. "She's already here along with Sheriff Remington."

I couldn't get to the Goodney's residence fast enough.

Chapter Six

When I pulled up to the Goodney's residence, I was taken aback by the commotion. Sheriff's deputies were taking statements from the neighbors in hopes they might uncover something. Ben and Mark drove up behind me. I stepped out of my car, and nodded to my cohorts who were exiting theirs, and then they followed me up the steps to where John was waiting to give us an update.

"It's Mrs. Goodney," said John. "Apparently, her husband found her dead on the couch from an overdose of drugs."

Meanwhile, Carolyn Raft and her assistant were maneuvering the body and the gurney through the front door. We didn't acknowledge one another because of the perilous circumstances.

I could see a visibly shaken middle-aged man in the doorway watching his wife's body being placed into the coroner's vehicle. Carolyn closed the back doors and stepped into the M.E. wagon, then drove slowly away into the night.

"We'll have to find out tomorrow what transpired here," I said. "I'll wait for Sheriff Remington to see if I can find out any further details."

"Mark and I will check with Helen Michaels as long as we're in Cascadia," said Ben. "Henry Brennen is a pharmaceutical salesman, so he's on the road a lot. I left a voice message for him to call us."

"Let me know what you find out from Helen Michaels," I said. "We can check with Brennen when he gets back into town."

"Likewise," said John, "Tyler and I might as well check the local waterhole to see if anything shakes out."

"Great," I replied. "I'll wait here to talk to the sheriff. Then we can all talk tomorrow. See all of you later."

They entered their vehicles and drove to their appointed meetings.

Eventually, Sheriff Remington exited the Goodneys' residence and walked down the path toward me. He greeted me with, "What do you want, Bennett? You know I can't tell you anything."

"But maybe I can tell you something," I said. "For starters, both the good doctor and his wife were on the water level committee, but voted against each other."

"Really?" said Sheriff Remington. "I'll have to tell Carolyn to be extra suspicious in her autopsy on Mrs. Goodney. Thanks for the tip." I nodded to him as I left.

Driving through Cascadia, Ben checked his Google Search for Helen Michaels' address and discovered her residence was only a few blocks away. When Ben and Mark drove to the front of Helen Michaels' dwelling, they noticed the lights were on. They figured she must still be up, so they left their vehicle and approached her front door. After they rang the doorbell, the door opened. An attractive young woman stood there who had obviously been crying.

Ben was starting to make his introductions, but he interrupted himself to ask, "Are you okay? My name is Ben Myers," pointing toward Mark, "and this is Mark Kestila."

"I'm sorry," said Helen Michaels. "I just heard some horrible news. My good friend, Sara Goodney, was found dead on her couch. I'm still in shock."

"That's perfectly understandable," said Mark. "Are you up to answering a few questions?"

"I guess I can try," Helen replied.

"We just want to ask you a few questions about the water level committee," said Ben. "We understand you voted for it along with Jack Thompson and Sara Goodney. You understand you're the only one still alive who voted to maintain the water level."

"I guess I hadn't given it any thought," Helen replied. "I was under the impression Jack Thompson drowned and Sara overdosed on drugs."

"They're calling Jack Thompson's death a homicide," said

Part III - The Mayor's Murder   147

Mark, "and, of course, we don't know the circumstances of how Sara Goodney passed."

"Did anybody threaten you while you were on the committee?" Ben asked.

"Pete Runnels told me I was on the wrong side," said Helen, "and that I would regret not voting against the recommendation to the EPA."

"I think that's enough for one night," said Mark. "I can see how upset you are. We can come back in the morning."

"For your safety," said Ben, "I think you should check into a motel for a few nights. We can follow you to the motel if you like."

"No thanks. I think I'm okay here," Helen answered.

"Would you mind if we stuck around for a little while, just to ensure your safety?"

"Okay. I would appreciate that," said Helen.

After Helen had closed the door behind them, they walked toward their car. Ben dialed my cell phone number, and after I answered, he said, "Ms. Michaels is really upset over Sara Goodney passing, and she doesn't realize she may be in danger. She told us that Pete Runnels made a mild threat regarding voting in favor of lowering the water level. I'll feel better if Mark and I camp out here for a few hours."

"Good idea," I said. "You can follow up with her when she has had time to absorb everything."

~~~

Driving toward Cascadia and leaving U.S. 41, John and Tyler had driven into an empty parking space in front of The Timbers Bar and stepped out. As they approached the bar, they could hear a ruckus, which described the activity in many bars in the country that time of night.

John and Tyler entered the Timbers Bar and they ordered two beers.

As soon as they sat down, a young man stood and walked out the door. "In all my life I have rarely seen a man leave a full beer on the bar," said John. "Let's check this guy out."

Following the young man out the door, Tyler called to him, "Wait up. We want to ask you some questions."

The young man stopped in his tracks, turned, and he glared at them. "Get away from me and stay away," he said. Then he continued walking toward his truck.

Tyler caught up and spun him around, saying, "I'm only going to ask you one time. What's your name and do you know anything about Jack Thompson's death?"

Appraising Tyler's strength and size, the young man thought better of trying to test his metal and said, "My name is Sam Waters. I was on Indian Bridge with Jack Thompson the night he died. He was trying to help me by sponsoring me with AA and I just got out of prison. Jack followed me to the bridge and talked me out of committing suicide. He was a great guy, but I don't know anything about his death."

"If someone spots you in the Timbers Bar," said John, "that's a parole violation and you could be back in the slammer."

"I might as well be because I've got nothing to live for," said Sam. "Now leave me alone." He stepped into his truck and drove away.

John looked at Tyler and said, "I think we have what might be called a genuine suspect. I'll let Bill know in the morning. Let's go back and finish our drink."

~~~

As Waters drove away from The Timbers Bar, he phoned his accomplice.

"Hello," Pete Runnels answered.

Waters said, "Two more guys just stopped me outside of The Timbers and asked me what I knew about Jack Thompson's death. I don't know if I can keep this charade up."

After hanging up from talking with Sam Waters, Pete Runnels felt he had to come up with a solution to this problem. He phoned his other conspirator.

"Hello," said the voice.

"Yeah, this is Runnels. We have a problem with Waters. Some men have been around to ask questions about Jack Thompson's death. Should I take care of it?"

"No," said the voice. "Let me do that. Everybody knows he has a drinking problem. We'll have to arrange an accident for the poor man. If he can't be quiet, he'll have to be dealt with." Both disconnected simultaneously.

Sam Waters' cell phone rang and he answered.

"Hello."

"Sam, there's been a change in plans. Just sit tight for a while until I can figure this out," said Pete Runnels. He tapped off his phone before Sam could reply.

Chapter Seven

I should have known better than to try to visit Carolyn Raft early the next morning to see whether I could gain an insight into Mrs. Goodney's untimely death. But then I left common sense at the M.E.'s entrance door and took my chances by entering Carolyn's lair. I was ready for the worst, but I had to find out as much as I could.

"I can tell you," said Carolyn when she saw me, "that Mrs. Goodney had several anti-depressants in her body. They included tricyclic antidepressants. Mrs. Goodney's blood level had .10 mg/L alprazolam, which is Xanax. There was .43 mg/L of cocaine and .25 mg/L of morphine. Her urine showed .2 mg/L of morphine. Being a doctor's wife, she would have known how horrible and slow the death would have been, including three to six hours for the drugs to work, convulsions, uncontrollable seizures, heart failure, and respiratory problems. If a person is looking for a quick painless death, drugs are not the way. Only 2.5 percent of depressed people who use drugs and try to commit suicide are successful. Many are left with a combination of pain, vomiting, fever, convulsions, respiratory depression, organ failure, heart palpitations, and other unpleasant effects."

"Are you insinuating," I asked, "that she might not have taken the antidepressant drugs on purpose because she knew what they would cause, or that someone ingested her with tricyclic anti-depressants?"

"I guess I'm saying that," Carolyn replied. "I was leaning toward the latter, and I'm glad I don't have to prove this murder. That's Sheriff Remington's and your problem."

"Thanks for the information," I said, "and let me know when you have a final autopsy."

With so many leads, I didn't know where to start.

~~~

In Cascadia, Dr. Goodney's cell phone rang.

When he answered, Helen Michaels said, "I have to see you. I feel so guilty about your wife taking her life. Do you think it was an accident or a suicide?"

"We'll have to take it easy for a while and cool it," said Dr. Goodney. "Of course it was an accidental overdose. I don't believe she would take her life. I have to plan Sara's funeral, so I won't be available for a few days. Take care and I love you."

Helen could barely say goodbye as she hung up because she was so worried about her future.

~~~

Henry Brennen drove through Mesabi County listening to the local news. He couldn't believe the Sheriff's Department had released a statement that Jack Thompson's death was not a suicide, but a homicide. Further, he heard from his office that one of his clients, Dr. Goodney's wife, had passed away from an apparent drug overdose. He started sweating profusely, thinking he had to get out of Cascadia as soon as possible. He had provided both Jack Thompson and Sara Goodney with barbiturates to help them deal with emotional problems. Not only could he lose his job, but he could also be sent to prison for the rest of his life.

Henry pulled into his driveway, only to see two figures sitting in a vehicle. John and Tyler Baldwin were waiting. Henry Brennen decided he would try to blow them off and pack his bags and disappear.

As Henry Brennen stepped out of his vehicle, John and Tyler Baldwin did likewise. They approached Brennen and introduced themselves.

"Hello," said John. "I'm John Baldwin and this is my son, Tyler. We're trying to help the police solve the murder of Jack Thompson. Can you help us?"

"Not really. I'm in a hurry. Can you come back later when I have more time?" Henry Brennen asked.

"This will only take a minute," Tyler said.

Part III - The Mayor's Murder

Henry Brennen made a disgusting sound and said, "Hurry up. I'm late for an appointment already."

John started by saying, "We understand you were on the water level committee and voted in favor of reducing the flow. Is that correct?"

"Yes. So what? I had the right to vote as I wanted."

"It's sure a coincidence," said Tyler, "that two of the three members who voted to maintain the water level are dead."

"I don't know anything about that," Henry Brennen replied. I've been out of town. Now if you will excuse me, I have to be someplace." Brennen was thinking to himself he wanted to get as far away from Cascadia as possible.

John and Tyler Baldwin returned to their vehicle and drove away, wondering how they could make him divulge pertinent information.

Henry Brennen entered his house and started to pack his clothes into his suitcases. At first, he didn't see the figure enter his bedroom. When he turned around, he said to the figure, "You scared the shit right out of me. Why didn't you call first, and how the hell did you get in here?"

"You shouldn't leave your key under the front doormat. It's much too easy," the figure said. "Besides, I wanted to be sure you'd be here when I paid you a visit. What did those two guys want?" asked the figure.

"To see if I knew anything about the two deaths," said Henry Brennen.

"I hope you didn't tell them anything," said the figure.

"No, I promise I didn't say a word. I just want to get as far away from Cascadia as possible," Henry Brennen said. "You will have to excuse me. I need to use the bathroom." After a few minutes, he returned. The figure was still waiting.

"I want you to leave now," said Henry Brennen. "If you don't mind, I have some packing to do for my trip."

"Maybe, I can help you." The figure pulled out a syringe and stabbed Brennen in the neck with five grams of sodium phenobarbital. The figure said, "Don't worry; you're going on a long trip and you're not coming back."

Brennan slumped to the floor, seemingly unconscious, as the figure took another syringe loaded with Midazolam. He tied a rubber band around Brennen's left arm above the elbow and slammed it into Brennen's vein. The figure then threw *The Mining Ledger*'s clipping of Sara Goodney's obituary on the body, picked up Brennen's pharmaceutical bag, and left.

Chapter Eight

The pseudo-detectives met that evening at Geno's Pizzeria with Rick Bonnetelli front and center serving up cold beer and great pizza. I was glad to see Carolyn there along with the other pseudo-detectives.

We had a lot to discuss, and I wanted to get right to it. At this point, we were not aware of Henry Brennen's demise, but we had a lot to hash out nevertheless.

Carolyn began the discussion. "As you probably know by now, Sara Goodney died from a drug overdose, and there was sodium phenobarbital in Jack Thompson's body. It's anybody's guess whether Sara Goodney died from an accidental overdose or committed suicide."

"We talked to Sam Waters the other night," said John Baldwin, "and we don't know if we can trust what he said. He admitted being on Indian Bridge with Jack Thompson, and he said Thompson talked him out of committing suicide. We're going to keep an eye on Waters to see where it leads. In addition, Tyler and I talked to Henry Brennen, but he said he has been out of town and didn't know much."

"Mark and I are going to tail Helen Michaels," said Ben. "She was sure upset the other night over the news of Sara Goodney. Maybe there's more to the story."

"I'll locate Pete Runnels and shake his tree a little," I said. "I think he's up to his neck in this scandal. We don't have to worry about Dr. Goodney for a while. He's busy tending to his wife's funeral." We adjourned and agreed to meet the following Monday night.

~~~

Sara Goodney's funeral was the next morning, so Ben and

Mark waited at Helen Michaels' residence for her to return from the church. Helen pulled into her driveway, exited her car, and she was walking into her house when Ben Meyers and Mark Kestila left their car and tried to catch her before she could get inside. When they approached, they noticed her eyes were red from crying.

"Is this a bad time?" Ben asked. "We can come back tomorrow."

"No, let's get this over with," Helen replied. "Please come in and I'll put some coffee on."

They followed her into her house and seated themselves on the couch. Then they waited for her to return from the kitchen. When she entered with their coffee, Mark said, "We understand you and Sara were close. Is there anything you can tell us about why she might take too many barbiturates?"

"I guess it doesn't matter anymore," Helen replied. "Frank and I were seeing each other. Sara found out and she was devastated. Both Frank and I agreed to break off our relationship, but Sara was emotionally destroyed."

"So you're pretty sure it wasn't an accident," Ben continued. "Is it reasonable to assume she got the barbiturates from her husband?"

"I suppose that's reasonable," Helen replied. "I know Frank wouldn't knowingly give her any drugs. She must have stolen them somehow from his office. She would visit him every Tuesday and they would have lunch at The Moose Antlers."

"Have you received any threatening phone calls since we last talked?" Mark asked.

"No," said Helen. "I don't think my life is in jeopardy."

Even as she spoke a shadowy figure was watching her from a distance.

Ben and Mark finished their coffee and left, offering their apologies for the loss of Sara.

Ben and Mark walked to their car, and Ben dialed my number. When I answered, Ben said, "We just talked to Helen Michaels and she admitted she and the good doctor were having an affair, which is why Goodney's wife may have taken her life."

"That helps start to put the puzzle together," I said. "I'll talk to you later."

Ben disconnected and Mark said, "Did you see something move in the woods across the street?"

Ben scanned the woodlands until he saw something move. "Let's act normal and proceed to our vehicle," he said to Mark. "We'll leave and come back on foot."

"Good idea," Mark agreed.

They entered their car and parked their vehicle around the corner.

"Here's where it gets dicey," said Ben. "Let's double back and see if we can sneak up on the stalker."

They slowly worked their way through the woods until they could see the culprit peering at Helen Michaels' residence.

"Don't move!" Mark shouted.

In a flash, the chase was on. The perpetrator ran through the woods toward a waiting car. Both Ben and Mark pursuing, with Ben tackling the goon from behind. The suspect brandished a knife and slashed at Ben. Mark arrived and kicked the knife out of his hand. Mark and Ben wrestled him to the ground and turned him onto his stomach.

"Okay, it's all over," said Ben. "We can sit on you all night, or you can act right, and we'll let you up."

"Fine, let me up," said the assailant.

Mark and Ben turned the perp over and saw his face. It was Sam Waters.

"Do you know how this makes you look? There are two people dead who voted to maintain the water level, and you're hiding in the woods watching the third person."

"Come on. Out with it," said Mark. "Why are you here?"

"I was scared," Sam replied. "I was on the Indian Bridge the night Jack Thompson died, but I never pushed him."

"Why didn't you tell the police that?" Ben asked.

"I have a criminal record and I just got paroled from state prison for vehicular manslaughter," said Sam. "I served my time, and Glen Magnum was nice enough to hire me. If the police can put me on the bridge with Jack Thompson, I don't have a prayer."

"You should really be looking at Pete Runnels, Sam continued. "He's the one behind all the criminal activity. When I first got out of prison, he hired me to be a cruiser for his logging company. I was marking trees at the watershed near the Michigamme River when I found some gold nuggets. After Jack Thompson's death, Runnels made me promise to keep quiet, or he would turn me into the police for murder. I had no choice. Runnels had the nuggets assayed and they're real. He wants to drain the river as much as possible and buy the mineral rights along both sides. In order to do that, of course, the river would have to be lowered. That's why he wanted the water level committee to vote in favor of lowering the river. I whacked Bennett on the head the other night trying to discourage him from continuing digging up any evidence that could incriminate me."

"Why were you peering at Helen Michaels' house?" asked Mark.

"I was hoping to see her and ask her if she could help me," said Sam. "The night of Jack's death, we had an AA meeting at the church and Jack followed me through town. I was contemplating suicide by jumping off Indian Bridge. He was able to persuade me not to do it, but instead to continue coming to AA meetings. As I was leaving Indian Bridge, I looked behind me and saw two people talking to Jack. They seemed to be arguing. It was getting dark and I couldn't see well, but I think one was Helen Michaels."

"Isn't that a nice little story," said Mark. "Why should we believe you?"

"Because it's the truth," said Sam, whimpering.

"Get out of here and don't get in anymore trouble," said Sam. "Your story had better check out."

Sam Waters entered his car and left the scene.

"We'd better call John and Tyler and save them some time looking for Waters," said Ben. He dialed John and said, "Hello, John. Mark and I just talked to Sam Waters and he has quite a story to tell. Don't bother looking for him. You might be better off seeing if Henry Brennen is back from his trip."

After John got off the phone with Mark, he related to Tyler what Mark had said and then suggested, "Let's see what Henry Brennen has to say. Maybe, he's finally home."

After locating Brennen's residence on Google Search, they drove there. Once they arrived, they exited their car and walked up to the front door. They knocked, and then as they waited for someone to answer, Tyler said, "Do you smell that?"

"Unfortunately, I do," John replied. He called 911, and then together, they broke down the door. Both John and Tyler put handkerchiefs over their mouths and noses. Together, they entered Brennen's bedroom and opened the windows. The odor was starting to get pungent. Examining the body, there were no signs of a struggle, but Brennen had moved on to the hereafter.

"We're not getting any information from him unless we bring in a psychic," said John.

Within minutes, the sheriff deputies arrived along with Carolyn Raft. She walked into the room, acknowledged John and Tyler, and she knelt over the body.

"Rigor mortis has set in," said Carolyn, "so this man was killed between twelve and twenty-four hours ago." The body was fully discolored. She noticed the needle marks on his neck and left elbow. "I suspect this man was killed last night about eight o'clock. It appears to be an overdose, but I won't know for sure until we run toxicology reports."

Sheriff Remington had arrived by now. He was watching over Carolyn's shoulder. "Just what we need," he said, "another dead junkie."

John and Tyler needed some fresh air. Both exited the house and then John said, "I don't know how Carolyn can do that because I never get used to that odor."

Tyler agreed, saying, "Carolyn's one tough cookie."

"I'll call Bill and bring him up to speed," said John. He dialed my number and said, "You can cross Henry Brennen off your list. We just found him dead. Carolyn said he died about eight o'clock last night." I had just hung up from talking with Ben, so I informed John what Ben and Mark had uncovered regarding Sam Waters.

"It looks like Dr. Goodney and Pete Runnels are our prime suspects," I said. "How about you and Tyler check out the good doctor, and I will pay a visit to Pete Runnels."

"That sounds good," said John. "I'll talk to you later." We disconnected and pursued our query.

Checking my Google Search on my cell phone, I arrived at Pete Runnels' logging office. It was just a rundown trailer. I could hear someone bellowing, followed by several meaty loggers exiting and cursing under their breaths. I took that as a bad omen. I knocked on the office door and sheepishly entered. An older secretary looked up from her desk and asked, "What do you want?"

"Could I speak with Mr. Runnels?" I asked.

"Who are you and why do you want to see Mr. Runnels?" she replied.

"I'm Bill Bennett," I said, "and it's about the unsolved deaths that have been occurring."

"This is not a good day to see him," she stated.

"That's okay," I said. "I don't have many good days."

"You're on your own," she replied. "Go back and follow the shouting."

"Thanks."

I walked down the narrow trailer aisle toward the sound of a man screaming into a phone. I waited for his phone conversation to end and then knocked on his office door.

When he didn't respond, I knocked again and heard, "Yeah, what is it?"

I opened his office door and said, "I'm Bill Bennett. I want to ask you some questions regarding the recent murders?"

Pete Runnels thought for a moment and then said, "What do you mean murders? I thought only Jack Thompson was murdered. Who else bit the dust?"

"There is some question as to how Sara Goodney passed," I replied, "and they just found Henry Brennen's body."

"It appears it was bad luck to be on the water level committee," said Pete.

"Especially if they wanted to keep the water level up," I said, watching for a reaction, but there was none. "I heard you stood to make a lot of money if they lowered the water level."

This time Pete Runnels raised his eyebrows and said, "That useless Waters must be talking. Listen, buster; I didn't kill anyone. Now get out of here."

"The tough guy act doesn't intimidate me at all," I said. "I used to arrest punks like you all the time when I was sheriff. My friends and I are going to keep digging until we find out the truth. Have a nice day." As I left, I slammed his office door for effect.

After I left, Pete Runnels dialed a number and said, "Let's meet tonight." Disconnecting and staring out the window, Runnels tried to figure out how he was going to solve this dilemma.

Chapter Nine

John and Tyler arrived at Dr. Goodney's residence. The drapes were drawn closed and it looked like nobody was home.

"We came this far," said John, "So we might as well see if anybody is there."

As John and Tyler approached the house, the curtain moved ever so slightly.

"Well," said Tyler, "I suppose we should ring the doorbell even though someone knows we're here."

After ringing the bell and waiting an appropriate time, Tyler was about to ring it again when a woman opened the door. John said, "I'm John Baldwin and this is my son, Tyler. We're trying to help the police solve the mystery of what happened to three people: Jack Thompson, Henry Brennen, and, of course, Dr. Goodney's wife."

"I'm Helen Michaels," she replied. "I'm a friend of Dr. Goodney. Won't you please come in?"

They entered and she led them to the rec room, then she said, "I'll see if the doctor is up to seeing company. His wife's death has been hard on him."

Helen left the room. While they waited, John and Tyler looked at Dr. Goodney's animal hunting trophies on the walls. Just about every big game species in North America had a head mounted with an inscription under it. Tyler and John passed the time examining each mount until they finally heard, "Aren't they something?" Dr. Goodell entered the room and said, "Please be seated."

John introduced himself and Tyler and then said, "I'm very sorry for the loss of your wife. It must be very hard, but we would like to ask you some questions if you're up to it."

"Fire away," said Dr. Goodney. "My memory is a little fuzzy at the moment, but I'll do my best."

Helen Michaels came in, seated herself next to Dr. Goodney, and joined in the conversation. "Dr. Goodney has been through a lot," she said. "The police have already been here, so you can always check with the sheriff's department for details."

"Thanks," said Tyler, "but we would prefer to hear firsthand what he has to say."

"Did you see Jack Thompson the night he died?" John asked.

"Yes, I did," said Dr. Goodney. "We were discussing the Michigamme water level vote. As you know, I voted to lower the river level, but Jack thought we should maintain it. Even though we disagreed, I had a lot of respect for Jack. When I left him on the bridge, he was alive."

Tyler looked at Helen Michaels and asked, "What about you? Someone saw two people with Jack Thompson on Indian Bridge. Do you know anything about that?"

Helen Michaels was taken aback. "No, of course not," she said. Dr. Goodney looked at her with a puzzled look.

"Doctor," John asked, "were you with your wife earlier in the evening before she passed?"

"Of course," said Dr. Goodney. "We ate our evening meal and then I went for a walk. When I came home, I thought she was sleeping on the couch. Just before I went to bed, I went to wake her and realized she had passed. There was nothing I could do but call 911."

"What about you?" Tyler asked Helen. "Are you able to account for your whereabouts?"

"I was home watching television and retired early," said Helen.

Although he already knew the answer, John asked Dr. Goodney, "How well did you know Henry Brennen?"

"I saw him about once a month in the office when he had new pharmaceuticals to show me," said Dr. Goodney. "Other than that, I didn't see him socially."

Pushing the envelope, Tyler now looked at Helen and asked, "How about you? Did you know Henry Brennen?"

Pausing for a moment to reflect; she said, "I saw him around town, but I never had any dealings with him."

John stood and motioned for Tyler to follow, saying, "We've taken up enough of your time. Thank you. If we have any questions, we'll get back to you. Goodnight."

John and Tyler showed themselves out. After they left, Dr. Goodney turned to Helen and said, "You were with me on Indian Bridge when we talked to Jack Thompson the night of his death. We should have told them the truth."

"I don't want to get involved," Helen replied. "We have enough problems without being accused of murder."

"I wanted to tell them that you and I confronted Sara the night of her death with the truth," said Dr. Goodney, "but I couldn't bring myself to say it."

"That's right," said Helen, "and if you ever tell anybody, they're going to become suspicious. Let's go to bed."

~~~

The next morning, I worked up the courage to drive over to the Sheriff's Office. After entering the building, I descended the stairway to the M.E.'s office. Wanting to find out if Carolyn knew any more about Henry Brennen's passing, I tried to act nonchalant as I came through the doors, but as usual, Carolyn saw right through me.

"Are you here again?" Carolyn asked.

I smiled and tried to be congenial. "How's the Brennen autopsy going?" I asked.

"He did have a massive cardiac arrest," Carolyn replied, "but that's not what killed him. Someone poked a needle loaded with Sodium Thiopental into his carotid artery, causing the cardiac arrest."

"We now have two murders," I said, "and maybe a third if Sara Goodney was filled with barbiturates against her will."

I thanked Carolyn and left the lab with a lot on my mind.

Chapter Ten

Later that day, I called John and Ben with the information regarding Henry Brennen's murder. Both said they would pass it on to our compatriots. I opened a cold one and sat back on my deck, watching the boat traffic meander by. It was therapeutic for the soul, but it didn't last long. Before I could finish my beverage, my cell phone rang. I didn't recognize the number on my Caller ID, but I took the call anyway. It was Dr. Goodney.

"I have to see you," he said. "It's urgent that I talk to you. Can you come right away?"

"Certainly," I said. As I drove to Cascadia, I called the other pseudo-detectives and asked them to come immediately to Dr. Goodney's residence. Each said he would be there ASAP. I arrived first, and when I did, the door was open. Without waiting, I entered and took my chances. Seated at the chair under a mounted grizzly bear head was Dr. Goodney. He had a shotgun pointed at his face. The other pseudo-detectives rushed in and saw the potential tragic sight. We all screamed in unison, "Don't do it!" But it was too late. A large blast made a deafening sound as the good doctor shot into his face. It was one of the most horrific scenes I have ever witnessed.

After regaining my composure, I noticed there was a blood-splattered envelope on the end table. Instinctively, John called 911 to report the tragedy. Meanwhile, I picked up the envelope, not being able to restrain myself. I opened it and read the letter out loud.

To Whom It May Concern:

I have lived with guilt for what I have done. For my infidelity, I have broken my loving wife's heart. She took her life and I must do the same. It was Helen Michaels and me on the Indian Bridge with Jack Thompson. We had a clandestine meeting whereby Jack Thompson told the two of us he saw us in a compromising situation at the state park. We begged him not to tell anyone. He gave us the choice to tell Sara or he would. I left Helen alone with Jack Thompson that night and returned home. I believe she may have killed Jack Thompson.

Unbeknownst to me, Helen came to our home when I was out and confided everything to Sara. My wife was broken-hearted and left me a note forgiving me. But I cannot forgive myself. Through my business relations with Henry Brennen, Helen was able to blackmail Brennen into supplying her with the lethal drugs. She threatened Brennen that if he didn't supply her with the drugs, she would persuade my partners and me to switch to another pharmaceutical distributorship. Please forgive me.

As I was finishing the letter, sirens could be heard in the distance. We left the crime scene, moved to the living room, and we prepared for a real grilling from the sheriff's deputies.

Helen Michaels was arrested that evening, and after reading Dr. Goodney's suicide note, she confessed to both Jack Thompson and Sara Goodney's murders.

When she was pressed by Sheriff Remington regarding the murder of Henry Brennen, she claimed she didn't know anything about his murder.

I happened to stop at Sheriff Remington's office later that day. When he told me Helen Michaels confessed to two of the murders, but not the third, I had to wonder who could have done it. Surely, she would have admitted to the third murder if she had been involved.

I called another meeting that night at Geno's Pizzeria with everyone present, including Carolyn Raft.

I started the meeting by asking, "Do any of you have any suggestions for who could have been responsible for Brennen's murder?"

John Baldwin was the first to respond. "Maybe the doctor killed him," he said. "After all, he certainly had the medical knowledge and the drugs available."

"That's certainly a possibility," I said, "but I don't think he had it in him to kill an innocent man."

"Maybe, it was Pete Runnels," Ben remarked. "He was worried about making a fortune with the gold discovery, and he wanted the vote to go his way. Brennen may have been an accomplice."

"Possibly," I said.

"Maybe," Mark added, "Helen Michaels is holding out for some reason. After all, she admitted to killing two people. She probably isn't thinking right."

"That's a possibility, but I doubt it," I replied.

"Let's work the murder backward," Carolyn suggested. "Who would stand to gain by Henry Brennen's death?"

"I have an idea to smoke the murderer out," I added. "Let's get the word out that the governor is going to appoint new replacements to the committee, and it's going to include Randy Dunham, who is an avowed critic of lowering the river's water level."

We agreed that I would obtain the Dunhams' permission and we'd stake out their house to see if the villain made an appearance. Then we adjourned for the evening.

~~~

The next morning, I called Sheriff Remington with the suggested plan. He agreed to call the governor and get him to sign off on it. The governor not only agreed, but even agreed to release the names of the replacements.

That evening, I picked up our local newspaper, *The Mining Ledger*, and read the headline that mentioned the governor was appointing replacements to the committee. The article included Randy Dunham's name. The game was on.

When I called John Baldwin, he agreed to take first watch, with me relieving him after midnight. I retired for the evening only to hear the alarm clock sound all too soon. I rolled out of bed, dressed, and taking my Glock, I drove toward Cascadia. Along the way, I called Ben and arranged for him and Mark to relieve me at dawn. I didn't know it would all be over by then.

I drove into the cottage next to Randy and Kate's home and parked next to John's vehicle. I knew the residents' cottage was abandoned until next spring, so it would not be a problem. Walking the shoreline over to the Dunham's house, I could see light in the kitchen. John was sitting in an easy chair, reading the most recent issue of *Guns and Ammo.* When I knocked on the door, he gave me a look of acknowledgment. Unlocking the door from the inside, Ben motioned for me to enter. Ben holstered his pistol and prepared to leave when we heard a noise outside. The Dunhams were fast asleep, so we knew they could not be responsible for the commotion. I shut off the light and we both crept toward the front window. We could see someone hiding behind a tree, slowly making his way toward the front door.

"Let's allow him to enter," said John, "and we'll take him alive."

"Sounds good," I said.

The intruder broke the glass on the front door and proceeded to reach in and unlock the latch. We had our Glocks aimed at the door if he wouldn't surrender. Slowly, the door opened and the invader stepped inside.

"Hold it right there or you're a dead man! Make up your mind!" I shouted.

The intruder turned and attempted to run outside and down the steps. John was on him like a cat. He dove on top of him before he reached the last step. They rolled over and over, finally coming to a halt with John on top. I jumped the last two steps and hurried to help. Shoving my Glock in the thug's face, I shouted, "Freeze!"

John slowly rolled off the desperado and I shined a flashlight into the would-be murderer's face. To our surprise, it was the EPA administrator, Fred Wilder. We disarmed him and pulled him to his feet.

"What do you have to say for yourself?" I asked Wilder.

Trying, but unable to compose a plausible excuse for why he might have been trying to break into the Dunhams' residence, he finally confessed.

"I was hoping to make a lot of money along with Runnels," Wilder said, "by buying up as much property along the tributary that empties into the Michigamme River. Runnels told me about the gold he found after having it assayed, and he assured me we could both make a fortune. Brennen approached Runnels and I to cut him in on the water level deal, and Brennen agreed to increase the dosage for Dr. Goodney's wife, hoping she would overdose. With her out of the way, Runnels hoped to have me appointed to the committee, and then we would be home-free. After Sara Goodney committed suicide, Brennen became expendable as well as a loose cannon. Runnels knew I was a former pharmacist and told me to take Brennen out. I found some Sodium Thiopental and opium in Brennen's suitcase and loaded a syringe with the Sodium Thiopental and I stabbed him in the neck. I finished him off with the opium to make it look like an overdose."

"Well, you can tell that to the sheriff when he arrives," I said.

The Dunhams emerged after hearing the commotion and approached us with caution.

"Here's Henry Brennen's murderer," I told them. "He and Runnels were going to clean up after they made sure they could re-vote to lower the water level on the Michigamme River."

"I can't believe so many lives were lost over greed," Randy said.

John called 911 and reported the attempted murder. It wasn't long before we heard sirens in the distance. Wilder broke down and cried, thinking about his greed and the ramifications of his actions.

After Deputy Roads pulled up and stepped out of his vehicle, I explained the whole sordid affair to him. He radioed it into his office and an arrest warrant was sworn out to pick up Pete Runnels for complicity in Henry Brennen's murder.

Pete Runnels never made his fortune in gold along the Michigamme River, but he had a long time to think about it in prison. Later, we discovered that it's not uncommon to find sprinklings of gold in riverbeds that have been undisturbed for centuries, but there was no likelihood of finding any significant amount of gold in the riverbed. So many lives were lost over love and greed. It was tragic, but we wouldn't forget *The Mayor's Murder.*

Part IV

The Moose Shed Murders

Chapter One

The Superior Peninsula is famous for its natural beauty and wildlife. One such form of wildlife is our prized possession: the moose. Originally native to the Superior Peninsula, they had slowly died out in the area. Then in the 1980s, the moose were transplanted back here from Canada. My family and I were fortunate enough to observe one such release in the 1980s. The locals wishing to observe the moose-release were bused into the Peshekee Grade where we were met by Department of Natural Resource personnel, state dignitaries, and politicians who, it appeared, were quite proud of this endeavor. I think the dignitaries were there to ensure much sought-after publicity in the state media. Once we arrived at our destination, we were ushered into a fenced-in enclosure where we could see the moose crates prepared, and on cue, one-by-one, the crate doors were slid open as the confused moose sauntered out and ambled up a trail into the wilderness. It was a huge success and probably helped some of the dignitaries win their next re-election. Nobody asked the moose what they thought of this relocation project.

Fast forward a generation and the moose appear to have established a thriving foothold in the Superior Peninsula. They not only provide a chance for lucky nature lovers to catch an occasional glimpse of the four-legged beasts, but they also started a new pastime—searching for moose sheds.

Many people spend countless days in search of the dropped moose antlers better known as moose sheds. Typically, the peak of the rutting season for moose is the first two weeks of October in the Superior Peninsula.

Over the years, John Baldwin and I have enjoyed many excursions as we searched for moose sheds after the rut was over. One of the best woodsmen I know, John, has been able to call a bull moose within earshot. A bull moose that hears the yearning calls of a cow moose in estrous will investigate, and may even vocalize his approach. John will even walk into the swamp to call the moose, trying to gain a peek at the monstrosity. Erring on the side of discretion, I usually wait by our ATV in case a hasty retreat is in order. Countless times, John has walked right up to a bull moose, which is extremely territorial during this time. John has had many face-offs with a bull moose. The creature will defend its territory to the death, so John has had to retreat carefully while facing the moose down. To run would entice a bull moose to charge.

Before a bull moose goes into rut, it will usually be found in the higher elevation areas. A bull moose will seek out cooler and thicker areas of the forest, which are higher in elevation, trying to escape insects and predators. However, once the rut begins, cow moose and their calves will stay in the lowlands near water. The cows seek out water for two main reasons: food and safety. Calves are vulnerable, so if predators should attack, especially wolves and bears, a cow with calf will use the water as an escape. Even though the insects are a bother in the lowlands, the safety of water will outweigh this.

When the moose rut begins, and likely for a few weeks before the beginning of the rut, a bull moose will move down into the lowlands to seek out the cows in hopes of getting the breeding done. As the rut winds down, the Bull Moose will once again move back to the higher elevations, dropping its no longer needed antlers.

With this idea in mind, John and I will forage into the woods in early spring in search of our prize, a pair of large moose antlers.

This spring day was still cool and the snow was melting slowly. This made for a perfect morning as John and I decided to venture into the woods to obtain our trophy. We were armed with a thermos of coffee, binoculars, and a GPS tracking device on our cell phones, not to mention our Glocks in case we encountered any danger. The tracking device would allow us to set waypoints to enable us to retrace our steps back to where we had started. We were looking for a fun-filled day of adventure, but that was not going to happen.

On the Peshekee Grade, we had put several miles behind us as we traversed higher and higher in elevation. Our escapade led us to a set of large tracks that we believed belonged to a bull moose, so we thought we might be getting close. Maneuvering through some of the toughest brush in the North, we managed to stay on the track as we climbed almost straight up. We reached the top of a peak and stopped for a break. I turned to gaze at Mother Nature's beauty. We could see for miles in every direction as the trees looked microscopic and the landscape was a soft silky residual of white. We truly were a very small part of God's plan. As he unscrewed the thermos, John said, "It doesn't get any better than this."

"For once, John, you're right," I replied.

We sat in silence as we breathed in God's splendor. No words were necessary between us. Some folks would never appreciate the surreal beauty of our peninsula.

As we transcended the peak, the elevation leveled off, enabling us to pursue our quarry at a faster pace. John had to wait as yours truly tried to keep up, but I was no match for this man who had spent most of his life in the woods.

Finally, we came upon our treasure. Our quest led us to one antler rack lying among a patch of thickets. We could barely see the tip of the antlers protruding through the hardened snow. Cleaning the ice off our prize, we knew the other one couldn't be too far away. I tied the huge antler rack to my pack and proceeded to follow John, who by now was moving at an accelerated pace. I tried to keep up with my tall lean comrade, but I was no match. I motioned for him to continue; I would catch up by following his tracks. It wasn't long before I heard a jubilant shout over the next rise. I knew he had found the other half of the moose shed. Catching up to him and gasping for breath, I said, "Great job.

These will look great lacquered and varnished." John attached the second half of antlers to his back and we proceeded to retrace our steps using the GPS app on my cell phone.

Chapter Two

Approaching our vehicle as dusk was settling in, I noticed something on the side of the road.

"What's that?" I asked John.

"Let's check it out," he replied.

We stored the moose antlers in the back of my truck and stepped toward the object. As we neared the entity, we realized it was a conservation officer's vehicle. Opening the driver's side door, we could see the officer was unconscious, with a huge loss of blood running down his right side. Using our Red Cross training, I leaned over and carefully felt the carotid artery for a pulse, but I was unable to locate one. "We'd better phone this in to the Sheriff's Department," I said.

Our euphoria over, finding the moose sheds was immediately curtailed as we now had to secure the scene until a deputy arrived. We were back in the real world and had to deal with its ugliness.

It took a long time before we spotted the flashing blue and red lights in the distance. We shined our flashlights toward the advancing cruiser and it slowed to a halt. Deputy Roads stepped out of his vehicle and said, "What do you have?"

"A deceased CO," I said. "We didn't want to contaminate the evidence. I felt for a pulse, but I was unable to obtain one. We searched the area, but we didn't find anyone else."

Deputy Roads proceeded to tape off the area and wait for the other authorized vehicles to arrive. Soon, Sheriff Remington, other deputies, and the M.E., Carolyn Raft, arrived on the scene.

Carolyn removed her equipment, and along with her assistant, she proceeded to the body. She knelt over it and performed a cursory examination. She removed the officer identification from his wallet and said, "His name is Charley Rollins." She held up a picture of the CO with presumably his wife and child. We both grimaced as we absorbed the thought of a wife and child now having their loved one deceased. Sheriff Remington called the Department of Natural Resources, which sent one of its personnel to confirm the CO's identification. John and I retreated to my truck for this tragedy to play out and also to stay out of the way.

After carefully examining the body, wrapping the hands, and checking the interior of the truck, Carolyn and her assistant removed the body and placed it in a transport bag. Then she judiciously zipped it closed.

She approached Sheriff Remington and said, "After the other personnel arrive to confirm the CO's identification, I will remove the body to my lab and examine it."

"Was it a suicide or a homicide?" Sheriff Remington asked. "Let's get this right. We owe it to his wife and child to be accurate."

"I always get it right," said Carolyn. "Right now I can't tell for sure. The shot was to his right temple and his pistol is still in his holster."

"I want this investigation kept in-house with no leaks to the media or would-be detectives," said the sheriff. "There will be a lot of pressure to solve this death."

"Okay," said Carolyn. "We'll keep it in-house with no leaks to the outside."

The Department of Natural Resources Officer arrived and stepped out of her vehicle. The CO approached Carolyn, saying, "I'm CO Lindsey Haynes. I worked with CO Rollins and knew him well." Carolyn slowly unzipped the top half of the body bag for her to identify the body. CO Haynes gasped and said, "That's Charley all right. I can't believe it's him."

"I'm sorry for your loss," said Carolyn. "I think the sheriff has some questions for you."

Carolyn re-zipped the body bag and closed the tailgate on her vehicle. Carolyn and her assistant stepped into their vehicle and drove away, leaving us with a swirl of flashing lights and a plethora of unanswered questions.

Chapter Three

Sheriff Remington walked over to CO Haynes and said, "I'm sorry for your loss, but was CO Rollins supposed to be in this area?"

"Yes, he was looking for cougar poachers," said Haynes. "Officer Rollins was assigned to this quadrant, and I was taking the next section. We found a tracking collar a few days ago in this area that belonged to a mountain lion that migrated here from North Dakota. Apparently, a poacher killed the cougar and discarded the device."

As soon as I heard the term poacher, a light came on. The pseudo-detectives and I had had a run-in with two of Cascadia's most infamous poachers last year, Floyd and Brawn Dilfour. If anybody knew anything about cougar poaching, those two desperadoes would.

"Tomorrow at daylight," I said to John, "we'll have to check out the Dilfours. There's no point checking with Carolyn Raft before she's had time to finish the CO's autopsy. Let's get reacquainted with the Dilfour brothers."

"If there's any lawbreaking going on in Cascadia you can bet the Dilfour brothers are involved," John agreed.

We returned to Victorious, planning to set out on our mission early the next morning.

The next day as we were driving to Cascadia, I asked John, "Where would be a good place to look for the brothers-in-crime?"

John pondered the question before replying, "Probably where we found them last time—at The Timbers Bar."

"Do you think they'll be there this early in the morning?" I asked.

"I'd bet on it," John replied.

"I won't take that bet," I said, and it was a good thing I didn't. Sure enough, as we parked our vehicle and walked into the bar, we saw the two sorry-looking malefactors slamming down some rotgut. John and I went up to the bar, and I said, "Well, boys. It's good to see you're still taking good care of yourselves."

"What do you want?" Floyd Dilfour asked.

"Boys, we just want to ask you a few questions," said John.

"We heard there's one less CO to bother us," Floyd replied. "We don't know anything about his demise. Now leave us alone to enjoy our breakfast."

"What do you two coyotes know about the cougar poaching on the Peshekee Grade?" I asked.

Brawn turned to take a swing at me, but before he could, John thumped his head against the bar. Floyd stood and also tried to swing at me, but I karate-chopped him in the throat. As the Dilfours were getting their air back, I said, "Boys, we want some answers."

Floyd whispered, "We don't know anything about cougar poaching. Leave us alone."

"With your reputations, why don't I believe you?" John asked. "Maybe, we'll have to continue this conversation at the buck pole."

"I heard how you operate outside of the law," said Floyd. "We did take that cougar, but we didn't harm the CO. We had nothing to do with the CO's death."

"Wasn't that easy," I said. "I thank you kindly, boys. You have a nice day."

John and I turned and walked out the door. We entered our vehicle and returned to Victorious.

"We found out what we wanted," said John, "but I guess I can cross them off my Christmas card list."

<center>~~~</center>

Later that day, I felt it was time to check in with Carolyn without the sheriff's knowledge. John and I picked up Tyler

Baldwin, and together, we drove to the Sheriff's Department. We entered the front door and used the back stairs to reduce any chance of being seen by the sheriff's personnel.

Upon entering the M.E.'s office, I heard the familiar "Oh, no, not you guys. I have strict orders not to say anything to you, Bennett, and your pseudo-detectives."

"Don't worry, Carolyn," I replied. "We're just here to pay you a social call. Tyler was wondering if you would like to eat tonight at the new restaurant that just opened."

Tyler gave me a quizzical look and said, "Yes, that's right. Would you like to dine out tonight? It'll be my treat."

"Sure," Carolyn replied, "but I'm still not going to tell you anything about CO Rollins' autopsy. Pick me up at 7:30."

Tyler, John, and I, knowing we had been outmaneuvered by a smarter person, turned and walked out the door.

"That went really well," said Tyler.

"As a matter of fact, it did," I replied. I pulled out the autopsy report Carolyn had left on the table. I opened it and proceeded to read it to them: 'The entrance was on the right occipital region. A CT scan shows the skull fracture and a large underlying cerebral contusion. The victim suffered major ballistic trauma to the cerebellum with the projectile finally resting in a cavity near the cortex."

"That must have been a powerful shell to penetrate that far through the brain," said Tyler.

"That's good information," I said. "Now all we have to do is return the report without Carolyn finding out. Let's go back in; you work your magic, and I'll replace the report."

"Are you nuts?" Tyler asked. "If she finds out you took the report, she'll kill all three of us."

"Come on, Tyler," John said. "Here's your chance to be a man. Now get in there and distract her while Bill returns the report."

We returned to Carolyn's den, hoping we wouldn't see her, but as luck would have it, she was having a sip of coffee at her desk. I motioned for Tyler to approach her and butter her up.

Tyler walked over to Carolyn and said, "I was just wondering what wine you would like to have tonight with your meal."

Carolyn looked up and said, "The same wine I have every date we go on. Don't you remember?"

Tyler walked over to the window, causing Carolyn to turn her back to me, which gave me crucial seconds to slide the Rollins' autopsy under some papers.

Tyler continued to make small talk until he noticed I had returned the autopsy back to the desk. Tyler then said, "I'll pick you up tonight, and maybe we can catch a movie after dinner."

"That sounds fine," said Carolyn, "but you'll have to leave now because I have a lot of work to do."

As we turned to walk out the door, Carolyn said, "Bill, I hope you put the autopsy report back in the right stack." I couldn't catch a break.

Chapter Four

The three of us decided to pay a visit to Sheriff Remington while we were in the building. We mounted the mandatory flights of stairs, and then I knocked on Sheriff Remington's door.

"Come in," I heard.

"Good morning, Sheriff," I said, opening the door. "I just left Carolyn's lab, and you'll be happy to know she didn't tell me a thing."

"Good. I want to keep a tight lid on this," said Sheriff Remington. "There's something fishy about the CO's death."

"What do you mean?" I asked.

"As you know," he said, "the gunshot entrance was on the right side, but his widow, Cindy Rollins, told us he was left handed. Forensics proved his gun was holstered, and our ballistic people say the gun hadn't been fired. It has to be a homicide, but I want you to promise me you won't let this information get out to the media."

"Scout's honor," I said.

John, Tyler and I left Sheriff Remington's office eager to start our unofficial investigation.

"It's too early to ask Rollins' widow any questions," I said. "That can wait. However, we can pay a visit to Rollins' office to see if anybody knows anything."

John, Tyler, and I drove to the Department of Natural Resources Office and entered. The mood was somber and restrained. When I saw a black bunting on a desk in the corner, I assumed it belonged to CO Rollins. I approached the counter and said, "My friends and I are looking into the unusual circumstances surrounding CO Rollins' death. Can anybody help us?"

Nobody looked eager to say anything. Finally, an older officer stepped forward and said, "I'm Commander Sternwall. This is neither the time nor the place to conduct any questioning. Are you with law enforcement?"

"No," I said, "but we're trying to help find out what happened. It appears it wasn't a suicide."

Everyone's ears perked up when I said that.

"What do you mean it wasn't a suicide?" Commander Sternwall asked.

"For starters," I said, "he was shot on the right side of his temple, and he was left handed. Secondly, his Glock was still holstered and unfired. Someone else must have fired the shot very close to him in the vehicle. Who do you think would have been able to get that close to him and fire the fatal shot?"

All eyes turned on one of the other COs. It was the officer who had responded last night—Lindsey Haynes. She stood and left the room without looking back. I motioned for John and Tyler to wait. Then I followed her into the back rooms and found her crying at a table in the lunchroom.

I decided to pursue the case. I approached CO Haynes and asked, "May I sit down?" She nodded, wiping away tears from her eyes.

"You'll probably find out, so I might as well tell you," she said. "Charley and I were lovers, even though he was married. We knew the romance wouldn't last, but it just happened. We were on a lot of assignments together, so we just became close. It became romantic a few months ago, but Charley ended it when he realized he couldn't leave his wife and child."

"Where exactly were you last night?" I asked.

"I told you we were checking different quadrants looking for poachers. We had met briefly for coffee at The Moose Antlers, but it was just professional. We both had our assignments, and I never saw him again until the M.E. unzipped the bag. I can't believe he's gone."

"The sheriff is probably going to ask for your Glock to check ballistics against the fatal shot that killed Rollins," I said.

She nodded. Then I stood and left the grieving CO to her

sorrow.

As we exited the state building, Tyler asked, "What did she say?"

"She told me CO Rollins and she were intimate," I said, "but he broke it off a month ago."

"That certainly gives Lyndsey Haynes a motive if she felt rejected," said John.

"Do you think she could have shot her former lover?" Tyler asked.

"Everyone's a suspect until they're cleared," I replied.

As Tyler and I were leaving the state building, a burly man walked past and brushed us, causing Tyler to turn and say, "Hey, watch it buddy."

The man ignored us and continued into the building.

"Let it go," I said. "I think everyone is on edge here with last night's murder."

"I guess you're right," said Tyler. "I'll give him that one."

We entered our vehicle and drove toward Cascadia. Along the way, I called Ben on my cell phone.

"Ben," I asked, "could you get ahold of Mark and meet us at The Moose Antlers. Maybe we can come up with a plan to solve CO Rollins' murder."

"How do you know it was a murder?" asked Ben. "From what I heard, it sounds pretty cut and dried to me."

"The circumstances aren't good," I replied. "The gunshot wound was on the right side and he was left handed. Besides, his Glock was holstered and it hadn't been fired. In addition, he had been seeing his fellow CO, Lindsey Haynes, romantically. She said Rollins had recently ended it, but who knows?"

"I'll call Mark," said Ben. "We'll see you there in an hour."

I disconnected and deliberated on a plan to solve the murder.

Soon after, Tyler, John, and I arrived to a congested full parking lot at The Moose Antlers. We made our way inside and found a table in the middle of the room. I thought that would be perfect because then we could eavesdrop on any loud conversation if it pertained to CO Rollins' untimely death. I was soon joined by my cohorts. We had to talk loudly to be heard since the dull roar was getting louder by the minute.

Mark started by saying, "I understand there were a lot of mysterious circumstances relating to CO Rollins' death." I explained to everyone what Sheriff Remington had told me. We had to come up with a plan, continuing our conversation over some hot Joe with customers coming and going.

Just then, a loud male voice was heard over the dull roar of the restaurant. "I don't care what anybody says; it had to be his girlfriend, Lyndsey Haynes. My brother-in-law dumped her a month ago and she couldn't take it."

At the other end of the restaurant, another bruiser stood and shouted, "That's my sister you're talking about, and I'll be damned if I'm going to sit here and allow you to accuse her of murder." I recognized the first heavyweight as the man who had brushed past us as Tyler, John, and I were leaving the Department of Natural Resources. Both men stormed toward each other, but they were restrained by the crowd.

As they were pulled apart, each threatened to kill the other the next time they laid eyes on one another. I hoped I wasn't present when that event occurred.

After the ruckus settled down and both ruffians had left, I asked the man in a booth near me, "Do you know those two?"

"Yes," he answered. "The first one is the deceased's brother-in-law, Tom Renfrow, and the second one is Lyndsey Haynes' brother, Jack Carver."

"I can see they're a couple of scrappers and both their nerves are on edge," I said.

"You got that right," the man replied.

I looked at my comrades and said, "I think we have two suspects to follow up. Are there any takers?'

"Tyler and I can check into Lyndsey Haynes' brother, Jack Carver," John said.

"Mark and I can follow up on Renfrow," Ben replied.

After finishing our coffee, I said, "Let's give the investigation some time. I want to attend CO Rollins' funeral tomorrow to see if anything happens there. Let's meet here tomorrow after the funeral."

"I think we should all attend," John replied, "just to see what the funeral might uncover."

The others concurred. We agreed to meet the next day at the Cascadia church before the funeral began.

Chapter Five

The next day, people were filing into the church in a somber mood. Scores of law enforcement were present from all over the county who had come to pay their respects. As we maneuvered into our seats, I contemplated whether the murderer was present. The pseudo-detectives and I perused the pews, trying to glean an insight into anyone who looked out of place, but we were unsuccessful. It was hard to watch CO Rollins' widow with her arm around her young son absorb the sadness as everyone passed by and paid their respects. Her brother, Tom Renfrow, stood ramrod straight as he consoled his sister and nephew.

Finally, the minister asked everyone to take their seats and the pews quietly filled to capacity. The eulogy was beautiful as many officers provided testimonials and humorous antidotes of CO Rollins' humor and wit. At the conclusion of the service, the choir sang "Amazing Grace," as the attendees slowly filed out.

I looked over my shoulder and noticed Lyndsey Haynes slowly walk up to the casket. Lyndsey Hayes placed a single rose on top. Rollins' widow jumped up, grabbed the rose, and she threw it back in Haynes' face, saying, "Haven't you done enough?" Haynes broke into tears, but consoled by her brother, Jack Carver, she shuffled away through the side door. It was pretty obvious that there was no love lost between the two women.

With the funeral concluded, we adjourned to Millie's Restaurant to reflect on the events.

Mark started by saying, "That's the kind of funeral I want, with lots of people crying and everyone saying nice things about me."

"The only way that will happen is if you pay them," said Ben.

Mark and Ben started exchanging insults. I could see the

discussion would only deteriorate from there. "Let's concentrate on solving the murder," I said. "I have to think there must be a clue with the widow Rollins hating Lyndsey Haynes so much. I can follow up with Lyndsey Haynes to see if she'll divulge more information regarding her love affair with the late CO Rollins."

"As I said yesterday," John said, "Tyler and I can check with the brother, Jack Carver."

"Mark and I can find Rollins' brother-in-law, Tom Renfrow, and see how involved he is."

"That leaves me with Lyndsey Haynes," I said, "and we can wait to talk to the widow Rollins." We finished our coffee and left the restaurant to complete our assigned tasks.

~~~

Later that day, after checking the search app on Google Earth, John and Tyler maneuvered to Jack Carver's house. They exited their automobile, walked up to his house, and rang his doorbell. Shortly after, a sound could be heard inside and a disheveled Jack Carver opened the door.

"We'd like to ask you some questions about Charles Rollin's death. May we come in?" John asked him.

Carver stammered, "What do you want? I want to be left alone."

"We just need a few minutes," John persisted. "We're trying to help the police solve a murder and your assistance could be valuable. I'm John Baldwin and this is my son, Tyler."

Carver responded, "All I know is that everybody thinks my sister, Lindsey, killed Charley Rollins."

"What do you think?" asked John Baldwin.

"My sister couldn't hurt anyone," Carver shot back. "She's just not that kind of person. She was upset when Charley and she broke up, but she understood Charley wanted to keep his family together. If you want a suspect, try looking at Charley's brother-in-law, Tom Renfrow. Now leave me alone."

After having the door slammed in their faces, John and Tyler returned to their vehicle. After entering their vehicle, John looked at Tyler and said, "Maybe Carver has a point, but we will have to see what Ben and Mark uncover about Tom Renfrow."

On the other side of Cascadia, I arrived at Lyndsey Haynes' apartment parking lot, prepared to ask some tough questions. I exited from my vehicle and approached her apartment. After I knocked on her door, I could hear the television being turned down. When Lyndsey Haynes opened the door, I could see she had been crying. Wiping tears from her eyes, she said, "Mr. Bennett, how can I help you?"

I decided to soften my questions, feeling compassion for the love forlorn CO. I started by asking, "How are you holding up?"

"Okay," she replied.

"Do you know if CO Rollins had any enemies?" I asked.

"He was a CO and did a commendable job," Lyndsey replied. "He cited violators and poachers as they deserved and didn't play favorites."

"Would there be a list of his arrests and citations at the DNR command post?" I asked.

"Yes, the command post keeps everything for five years and then it is logged onto a permanent CD."

"I'll try to stop there and check that out," I replied. "Thanks. I won't keep you any longer." I bid her adieu and returned to my vehicle.

Meanwhile, Ben and Mark were scouring Cascadia for Chris Rollins' brother, Tom Renfrow, who had disappeared after the funeral. They checked his house and even drove by his sister's home, but both reconnaissances were futile.

The next morning, I drove to the Department of Natural Resources' command post. After I exited my vehicle, I was approaching the front door when a shot rang out. I felt a stinging sensation in my shoulder and I collapsed to the ground. DNR officers scrambled out the front door and scoured the area. The sniper had disappeared into the woods, leaving only a spent shell casing which one of the officers retrieved. An ambulance was summoned, and before long, I was hustled to the Victorious Hospital. My family and the pseudo-detectives were waiting there for me.

I felt I was entering the Pearly Gates, but the good Lord wasn't ready for me. I was sent back to harass my family and friends. The sad part about the whole event was that I couldn't let them know I was going to make it. For days, my life was touch and go and my family took turns sitting with me. Finally after four days of unconsciousness, my eyes opened and there were my family and friends. The doctor said, "The bullet missed all of your vital organs so you're destined to live to a ripe old age."

I thought I heard a groan from John Baldwin.

~~~

The next day, my head was clear enough to hold a bedside pseudo-detective meeting. Ben and Mark were still hunting fruitlessly for Tom Renfrow, who had vanished into thin air. John and Tyler had been persuaded into thinking Jack Carver couldn't be the shooter or Charley Rollins' murderer because it was too convenient and easy. Carver didn't have an alibi and he sure had a reason to dislike Charley Rollins. I explained to them that my interview with Lyndsey Haynes was interesting to say the least. I said, "Lyndsey was so emotional when I interviewed her that I could have been fooled. Lindsey Haynes was the only person who knew I was going to the DNR office the next day. Was it possible she could have had a sniper waiting for me?"

One final thought did enter my mind. Why wasn't I killed? Did the shooter purposely graze me and allow me to live in order to put the appearance of guilt on someone else. My head was filled with these questions, so I couldn't wait to get out of the hospital.

My wife drove me home from the hospital, and she only had one stipulation: that was I was not to work on the case for at least one week. Reluctantly, I complied, but the wait seemed endless.

Finally, after serving my penance, I was allowed to call a meeting at Geno's Pizzeria. Still weak and recovering I had to help solve this mystery. The pseudo-detectives and I now took this case personally. The presumed murderer had tried to circumvent the investigation by killing the lead investigator: me. As I entered the pizzeria, I got a cell phone call from one of the suspects, Tom Renfrow.

"I believed I'm under suspicion for shooting you. I want talk to you," he said.

"Where do you want to meet?" I asked.

"Behind The Timbers Bar because I don't think you will try anything there," he replied.

"When do you want this soul cleansing to happen?"

"How's an hour from now?" he replied.

"I'll be there," I confirmed.

Disconnecting the cell phone, I looked at my partners and said, "You'll never guess who just called me. Tom Renfrow wants to meet me. Let's discuss who our suspects are."

"Could one person shoot both Rollins and you?" asked John. "Or maybe we have two suspects working together."

"What about the Dilfour brothers?" asked Ben. "Wouldn't they be at the top of our suspect list? If they were poaching, maybe Rollins caught them red-handed, so the Dilfours felt they had to eliminate him or face a fine and prison."

"Being a CO, Lindsey Haynes would have the ability and the motive to shoot her former lover," said Mark.

"Possibly," I said. "Even his widow would have a reason to shoot her husband for being a philanderer."

"I think the rest of us should come with you in case you run into trouble," said John.

I didn't like the idea of them accompanying me, but I had dodged fate a week ago, so I decided I better not venture there alone.

"I don't like it," I said, "but you're probably right."

We finished our drinks and then we proceeded to our vehicles as we bade Rick Bonnetelli a hearty farewell.

Later that evening, we arrived at the Timbers Bar in time to see the last patron drive away. The bar's lights were shut off, and we noticed only two vehicles were left in the parking lot. Soon, the bartender exited the bar, locked the door, and proceeded to his vehicle. He entered his vehicle and drove away, leaving us in a darkened parking lot. We stepped out of our vehicle and approached the last vehicle. Looking in the windows, we could see it was unoccupied. Shining the flashlights around the property's perimeter, our eyes fell on a ghastly sight. In the back of the bar's parking lot, hanging from the buck pole, was a man I thought I recognized. When we approached the body, our fears were confirmed. Tom Renfrow was dangling from a rope like a trophy buck. John took out his knife and cut the rope as the rest of us lowered Renfrow to the ground.

"You know this makes us look like prime suspects for what we have done in the past using this buck pole to interrogate suspects," said John. "Remember, we used the buck pole to question that bartender last year."

"We'd still better do the right thing and phone it into 911," I said.

After calling it in, Ben said, "I just remembered we also threatened to use it on the Dilfour brothers. You don't suppose...."

"That's a great observation," I said. "They'd definitely have motive, plus the ruthlessness and capability to commit both homicides and attempt to murder me."

Before long, several sheriff deputies' vehicles drove into the parking lot. Deputy Roads stepped out and said, "My God, I can't believe there's another murder. What's going on around here?"

"We cut him down hoping we could save him," I said, "but he was already dead. His name is Tom Renfrow; he called us about an hour ago to meet here while we were at Geno's Pizzeria. Rick Bonnetelli can vouch for us."

"That's good," said Deputy Roads, "because all of you are going to need an alibi."

Carolyn pulled into the parking lot with her M.E. vehicle. She exited her van and approached the body.

"Good God," she said. "Don't you guys ever take a day off?"

"Believe it or not, we had nothing to do with this murder," I said. "Renfrow called us an hour ago to talk to us, and when we got here, this is how we found him."

"Remind me not to arrange a meeting with you guys," Carolyn said.

The next several hours were spent giving out depositions and thinking how we could move on from this predicament.

Chapter Six

The next morning, we convened at Millie's Restaurant over some hot Joe.

I started the discussion by stating, "We have three suspects, Lyndsey Haynes, her brother, Jack Carver, and the Dilfour brothers."

"Don't forget Rollins' sister, Chris," added Ben. "Never underestimate a woman's scorn."

"I supposed you're right, but why would she, with the help of an accomplice, want to hang her brother? It just doesn't make sense," I said.

Mark added, "It would take at least two people to subdue Tom Renfrow and hang him."

"The Dilfour brothers," Ben replied, "would have no trouble subduing Renfrow and doing the deed, but what would be their motive?"

"That's a good point," I said. "Why would the Dilfour brothers want to hang Tom Renfrow?"

"Maybe, Renfrow saw them doing something illegal and he was going to report it to his brother-in-law Charley Rollins," said John.

"If that was the case," I asked, "why wouldn't the Dilfour brothers murder Renfrow first and then Rollins later?"

Everyone nodded in agreement.

"Don't forget Lindsey Haynes," Mark said. "I think she was involved in the murder up to her eyeballs."

"I could see why she might want her boyfriend dead," I said, "but why would she want Renfrow out of the way? Besides, she'd need help overpowering Renfrow. Let's each take a subject and check them out."

"Mark and I can check on the widow Rollins to see if she is ready to talk about her husband's death," said Ben.

"Tyler and I can check back with Jack Carver," said John. "Maybe, he'll be more sociable now that Renfrow is dead. After all, Carter told us to check on Renfrow."

"I can check with Lyndsey Haynes," I said. "I hope she can think of someone who might remember something. If nothing works out, we can meet later tonight to see if the Dilfour brothers are at The Timbers."

We dispersed with our assignments, eager to uncover evidence that would point to a suspect.

~~~

Later that afternoon, I drove to the Department of Natural Resources Office. As I entered, I asked the administrative assistant at the counter, "Do you know where I might find CO Haynes?"

"One minute, please," she replied. "I'll get Commander Sternwall." She left and returned with Commander Sternwall following her.

"I understand you're looking for CO Haynes," said Sternwall. "Right now she is on the Peshekee Grade near seventh bridge where CO Rollins was found. She thinks some cougar poachers are still active in the area, so she wants to find them."

"Thanks," I said and turned to walk outside to my vehicle. Just as I reached my truck, my cell phone chimed.

"Hello, Bill," John said.

"What's up?" I asked.

"Any luck with CO Haynes?"

"She's on the Peshekee Grade looking for poachers," I said. "I think I'll drive there and see if I can find her."

"Tyler and I drove to Jack Carver's residence and knocked on his door, but nobody was home," said John. "We'll wait a few hours to see if he comes back."

"Sound good, John. I'll talk to you later," I said. I disconnected and continued driving toward Cascadia.

I called Ben Myers to see whether he'd had any luck

questioning Chris Rollins.

"Hello," Ben said.

"Right back at you, Ben. How are things going at the Rollins' residence?"

"A teenage girl just entered the Rollins' residence and Mrs. Rollins just came out. I'm guessing the teenager is a babysitter."

"Follow Mrs. Rollins to see where she goes," I said.

I disconnected and continued driving, but I didn't know I was heading straight into trouble.

My cell phone chimed again.

"Hello," I answered.

"Hello, Bill, It's John. Jack Carver just came home and unloaded some groceries. It looks like he's in for the evening."

"As I told you," I replied, "Lyndsey Haynes is supposedly looking for poachers on the Peshekee Grade near seventh bridge. Why don't you meet me there?"

"Okay. Tyler and I will see you soon."

I had just disconnected the phone and was about to turn off U.S. 41 when a car maneuvered past me and continued at a high rate of speed. As the vehicle passed me at warp speed, I recognized the driver as the widow, Chris Rollins. I wondered why she would be driving so fast. When she turned onto the Peshekee Grade ahead of me, I slowed down so I wouldn't appear to be following her. I continued driving, following her dust track and staying just far enough back not to be seen.

I called John and said, "Guess what? Chris Rollins just passed me on the highway and is heading toward seventh bridge."

"We'll be there ASAP," he replied. "Don't do anything until we get there."

My cell phone chimed again. This time it was Ben Myers. "I have some bad news," he said. "We lost Mrs. Rollins going through Cascadia. We stayed so far back we couldn't see where she went."

"Don't worry," I said. "I just picked her up on the Peshekee Road. I think she's driving toward seventh bridge. John and Tyler are on their way also."

"Don't do anything stupid until we get there," said Ben.

I guess they had little confidence in my ability to take care of myself. Eventually, the partners caught up with me, and together, we caravanned behind Chris Rollins, being sure to stay out of sight so she wouldn't see us. We continued to climb in elevation and the foliage got thicker. The sun was setting over the tree line, and the shadows were getting longer. Twilight was settling in, and soon we would have to use our headlights, making it impossible to keep up without Mrs. Rollins seeing us. I decided to take a gamble and called John Baldwin.

"Hello, John," I said. "I'm going to try following Mrs. Rollins without my headlights. There is a full moon tonight so that will help. Naturally, I'm going to have to slow down considerably. Don't ram me from behind. Call Ben and tell him what I'm going to do."

"We'll have to do the same thing. We have no choice." Almost simultaneously, we turned our headlights off and relied on our instincts to guide us.

Our pursuit continued sans headlights, but I had a good idea of where she was going. We continued driving into the darkness, using the moonlight as our guide. We crossed many of the bridges that traverse the Peshekee River, hoping our tires would stay on the bridge. The rumble of the vehicles across the bridge made it even more nerve-racking. I could see lights ahead so I we knew we had to be close. I slowed down, and John and Ben did likewise, swerving to the side of my vehicle, narrowly missing the back of my truck as they came to an abrupt halt.

We exited our vehicles and slowly inched our way forward. I knew something was afoot. Nobody drives out to seventh bridge this time of night. Peering into the darkness, I recognized a conservation officer vehicle, which I assumed had to belong to Lindsey Haynes.

The pseudo-detectives and I knelt down and strained to hear their conversation. The five of us edged forward as deliberately as possible, being careful not to make any noise. We could now see Chris Rollins talking to Lindsey Haynes, but they were not

Part IV - The Moose Shed Murders

alone. There were at least two people in the shadows holding CO Haynes. I had to hear what they were saying, so I crept ever closer, trying to hear their conversation. Finally, as I moved almost on top of them, I could hear their exchange.

"You think you're so smart," Chris Rollins was saying. "I played you like a fool, and now you're the main suspect in both my husband's and brother-in-law's murders. Now we just have to make it look like a suicide and leave your inconsolable suicide note, and by the time the law finds your body, the animals will have picked your carcass clean."

Lindsey Haynes tried to struggle, but it was no use. The two men now stepped into the light so that I could see they were Floyd and Braun Dilfour. I motioned for my comrades to spread out so we could encircle them and leave them no way to escape.

Once we had them surrounded, I stood and shouted, "It's over Dilfours and Rollins! Drop your guns! We have you surrounded!"

Both Dilfours fired and started to run into the bushes. That was enough for the pseudo-detectives to jump into action. All four of my comrades leaped into the bushes, tackling the two would-be murderers. I grabbed Mrs. Rollins, forced her to the ground, and bound her hands.

Braun Dilfour finally got the fight he wanted with John, but it didn't go well for the poacher. In a matter of minutes, John had the bloodied poacher begging for mercy. I had to pull John off Braun and separate him from the burly thief. Floyd Dilfour tried to escape Tyler by running into the darkness, only to run right off a cliff and fall to his demise. There wasn't a tear shed by any of the pseudo-detectives.

"Well, that saves us a trial," said Mark.

I untied Lyndsey Haynes and freed her from her ropes.

"Thanks a lot," she said. "I had a hunch the Dilfours were responsible for the cougar poaching, so I followed them. I had just arrested the Dilfours when Chris Rollins struck me from behind. When I regained consciousness, I was tied up, and then you and your friends intervened. I have a lot to tell you.

"Chris Rollins just finished explaining everything to me,"

Lindsey continued. "She said she was insulted that her husband and I had an affair. The night of Charley's murder, she followed Charley out here, snuck up on him, and shot him in his truck while he was waiting to catch the two Dilfours."

"But why would Chris Rollins get caught up with the two Dilfours?" I asked.

"She made a deal with them to cover up the murder," Lindsey replied. "She even contracted them to shoot you and murder her own brother. Apparently, Renfrow had unraveled the murder. Chris borrowed one of her brother's handguns without her brother's knowledge, and when he discovered it had been recently fired, he was going to have it tested. Chris couldn't stand the idea of going to prison so she paid the Dilfour brothers to murder her own brother."

"Why did they shoot me?" I asked.

"You were starting to ask questions that might lead directly to Chris," said Lindsey, "and if the widow turned evidence, the Dilfours would be indicted."

"How did Chris Rollins know to come out here and help the Dilfours after you had arrested them?" I asked.

"It was the night of the big payoff," said Lindsey. "Chris was going to square up with the Dilfours, and I happened to get in the middle of it."

"I'm sorry I ever thought you might be a suspect and I apologize," I said.

"That's okay," said Lindsey. "I understand why I would be a suspect given the circumstances. I just feel sorry for the Rollins' boy; he's lost a father and a mother in a week."

In the distance, we could hear sirens approaching. I could only imagine what Sheriff Remington and Carolyn Raft were going to say when they saw this carnage.

~~~

Months later, with the conclusion of the trials, Braun Dilfour was given life without parole for his part in my attempted murder and for the premeditated murder of Tom Renfrow. He was still sentenced to a life of stupidity. Chris Rollins was also given life in prison without parole for murdering her husband, the attempted murder of yours truly, and for conspiring to murder her own brother.

The Rollins' son was adopted by his paternal grandparents. He would have the unenviable task of growing up knowing his mother had murdered his father.

After giving us all a thorough tongue lashing for being responsible for so many deaths, Carolyn had to agree that the pseudo-detectives had brought justice to *The Moose Shed Murders*.

Part V

The Revenge of ISIL

Part V - The Revenge of ISIL

Chapter One

My grandson Clay had just finished his tour in Afghanistan, and after a brief visit home to Cascadia, where his wife Donna lived, he received his next assignment. He was soon whisked off to Egypt and from there to Andahar, finally landing in Baghdad and being trucked twenty miles north to Camp Taji, Iraq. Battery, A 1st Battalion, would be his new unit. Upon reporting for duty, his CO, Captain Kormel, greeted Clay with a firm handshake and "Welcome to Hell." Clay was then briefed on their assignment, which was to train Iraqi soldiers to fight ISIL.

After the captain had finished the briefing, Clay asked, "When do we go on patrol?"

"We don't," said Kormel. "Our mission is to train the Iraqis so they can protect their own country."

Clay knew better than to press the issue. He had gained experience leading troops in Afghanistan, and with time, he knew he could do the same in Iraq, but his job was to follow orders no matter how restrictive they might be.

Clay returned to his barracks, unpacked, and prepared for a long disappointing tour in Iraq. The first chance he had, Clay skyped Donna, trying to reassure her that he was all right and was only doing routine training.

Within weeks, Clay was settled in and training a handful of Iraqi volunteers, teaching them how to be proactive in addressing threats and the proper way to search house-to-house, and giving them courses in weaponry, obstacle courses, and, for the officers, planning missions.

Most of his trainees had joined after the ISIL invasion and had chosen the Iraqi military because of its pay and pension. The American personnel knew the Iraqi trainees couldn't be completely trusted so the Americans and Iraqis were separated at night to prevent unprovoked attacks by an occasional disgruntled trainee against his American allies.

Clay made up his mind to learn the culture and religion of his new assignment. He learned that ISIL while establishing an ISIL caliphate and had established Sharia law throughout its domain. He learned that Sharia law regulated public behavior, private behavior, and even private beliefs. Its strict laws included amputation of the right hand for theft, and death was the punishment for criticizing the Quran, criticizing Muhammed, denying Allah as the only god, becoming a non-Muslim, leading an army away from Islam, or marrying a non-Muslim. Clay was surprised to learn other Sharia laws included allowing a man to marry up to four wives, and the need for four men to testify in her favor if a woman was raped since a woman could not testify in court.

Over time, Clay became close to some of his trainees, and through an interpreter, he was sickened to learn of how horrific many of their lives had been, but while he learned to empathize with them, but Clay still never completely trusted them. Most of the trainees' families had been terrorized by ISIL, so the young recruits wanted to avenge their relatives' fates.

Clay befriended one Iraqi who showed a distinct desire to become a good soldier and avenge his parents' deaths. His name was Mohid Malek. Every day, Mohid was the first to arrive, and he couldn't learn enough regarding armaments and military strategy. It was hard for the new recruits to learn to fire in short bursts rather than spray the area, which resulted in running out of ammunition. The American soldiers taught the trainees that their enemy would try to bait them into making that mortal mistake. It was up to Clay and his fellow trainers to break them of the habit.

Ignoring warnings from his fellow officers, Clay took Mohid under his wing and started spending time with him. Mohid opened up about his personal life, and Clay did the same. They even shared an occasional coffee, but Clay could never get used to how strong Iraqis liked their coffee. Clay knew he had little in common with Mohid, but it seemed Mohid loved to hear about life in America. People in Clay's country could come and go and not be afraid to walk in the open streets. Likewise, Clay found it hard to comprehend that walking a short distance in Iraq could be a mortal mistake.

ISIL would love to get an Iraqi trainee, better yet, an American Army officer in its sights and kill him. Fortunately, ISIL was kept at bay, but there was always the chance one suicidal bomber would drive into the American compound, willing to sacrifice himself to gain entrance to Paradise.

Mohid's parents had been captured by ISIL during its advance in 2014, leaving Mohid and his younger sister, Amreen, to persevere. Mohid and Amreen's grandparents were murdered in the Al-Anfal genocide conducted between 1987 and 1989. Al Hassan al-Majd, acting on orders from Saddam Hussein, oversaw the murder of 100,000 Kurds near Halabaja. Mohid and Amreen's parents were relocated to the south by the new government. In 2014, ISIL established its caliphate, and anyone who did not follow Sharia law was killed, including Mohid and Amreen's parents.

Mohid and Amreen were forced to take refuge in Al Taji. Mohid and Amreen's baiti (house) had been burned out, but they had repaired it enough to make it livable. Holes in the ceilings made the first floor a mud hole when the rains came, but Mohid and Amreen saw it as their home and were staying.

On one of his days on leave, Clay ventured with Mohid to his house in the center of town. Upon meeting Amreen, Clay tried to impress Amreen with his knowledge of Kurdish by saying in Kurdish, "Peace be unto you and so may the mercy of God and His blessings." Amreen nodded and smiled. Clay tried to continue to show off his knowledge of the Kurdish language, but it only ended with Amreen giggling and chuckling. Clay finally relented and used Mohid as his translator, which was only a little better. Kurdish was a unique language, so it took Clay time to understand the phonetics.

Mohid and Clay sat down at the family dinner table. Amreen was proud to bring out a display of vegetables, which, back home, Clay would have assumed was a side dish. He was getting acclimated to their cultural meals such as dolma, Masgouf, biryani, and kababs. Clay never mentioned that most of the food they consumed was provided courtesy of the United States Army with a little assistance from himself. Clay learned it was acceptable for everyone to eat from the same bowl.

Time seemed to pass faster when Clay could come to Mohid's house, and his command of the Kurdish language improved. The three of them exchanged stories about their countries, and Clay liked it when Amreen became involved in the conversation. "I'll never get used to watching an animal get its throat slit," Clay said, but he was impressed by how fast the meat was prepared. Within an hour, the meat was ready to be consumed.

"We can eat it as long as it is blessed first," said Mohid, "and of course we can never eat pork."

"Would you like some vegetables and eggs?" Clay asked. "We always have a lot of extra. Most soldiers don't care for veggies, so they get thrown out and the kids pick through them. In addition to what I have brought, I can bring some okra, potatoes, eggplants, and tomatoes; we have plenty of them in the mess hall."

"That would be very gracious of you," Mohid said. "We don't have enough usually, and that will certainly help Amreen."

That was all Clay needed to hear. Clay said he could bring them some food from the commissary that he knew they would appreciate. Fresh eggs and bananas made Amreen's eyes light up, so Clay would load up his rucksack before he visited Mohid and Amreen's *baiti* again.

Clay skyped with Donna less as he became enamored with Amreen. He knew it was wrong, but he blamed it on his need for companionship. He and Amreen would occasionally go for walks when he was able to steal away some time from his post. Clay was careful to keep his CO and fellow comrades in the dark, knowing that consorting with foreign women would result in retribution by his fellow soldiers and perhaps a transfer by his CO. He was always careful to be gone only a short while so as not to arouse suspicion.

Chapter Two

The next day, Captain Kormel gave Lieutenant Clay Bennett new orders.

"Your troop is to be part of a major sweep west of Baghdad," said Kormel. "Intel reported ISIL is building up a major supply depot in Fallujah and they plan to springboard to other places in Iraq. One of ISIL's leaders, Ali al-Badri, is believed to be leading them. Your troops are to search and destroy any contraband discovered in nearby villages and deny ISIL access to the city. Bennett, keep your head down. ISIL has infiltrated the villages and terrorized the locals. We're hoping this sweep will result in building up the Iraqi morale and show the locals their soldiers can protect them. You are to provide support, but the National Police (NP) must enter the villages and conduct the house-to-house searches. Is that clear?"

"Yes, sir," Clay replied.

"We deploy at 06:00 tomorrow morning," said Kormel, and he gave Clay the coordinates to follow.

"Clay could hardly contain his enthusiasm as he returned to his barracks and packed his equipment.

The next day, after putting on the fifty pounds of equipment, including a flak vest, gas mask, and Kevlar helmet, Clay and his Iraqi troops were ready to conduct searches for ISIL.

This would be Clay's first actual encounter with ISIL, and he hoped he was up to the task. The next morning, the 1st Battalion rode for several miles in Armored Personnel Carriers (APC). Approaching the first village, Clay's troop was ordered to dismount and begin searching for ISIL combatants. As instructed, the NP entered the village first and encountered heavy fire, including RPGs. The NP fought valiantly, but was losing ground. Clay radioed in for orders, and after explaining the dire straits of the NP, Kormel gave him the green light for him and the supporting American troops to invade. The NP had to be supported or risk losing face with the villagers if it was forced to pull back.

First Battalion charged into the village and started house-to-house search-and-destroy procedures.

ISIL was being driven back through the tenacity of the American grunts who knew how to comb the homes and get results. After several hours, ISIL was down to its last fortification. It would now fight to the death. First Battalion was up to the task. With heavy fire and casualties, it cleaned out the last bastion of ISIL in the village. After the fighting subsided, Clay ordered his men to gather Intel from the bodies.

"Will you look here?" one of the soldiers shouted.

He held up an ID with Ali al-Badri's name on it.

Everyone gathered around, unable to believe their good fortune. Ali al-Badri was the brother of Zawhi al-Badr, the ISIL leader in Anwar province.

"This will certainly be a blow to the command structure of ISIL in our AO (area of operation)," said Clay.

Everyone slapped each other on the back. They didn't realize what the repercussions would be.

"Okay," Clay ordered, "let's gather up our wounded and head back to Camp Taji."

After waiting what seemed an eternity, APCs rumbled into the village and scooped up the tired men of the 1st Battalion.

Upon returning to Camp Taji, Clay couldn't help noticing how demoralized his Iraqi troops were.

He approached Mohid and, in broken Kurdish, asked him, "Why are you and your fellow soldiers so down?"

In Kurdish, Mohid responded, "We did not fight well today. You and your troops had to take the initiative and drive the ISIL dogs out."

"Don't worry," Clay replied. "ISIL are experienced fighters

and had all the advantages. We had to invade every house and drive them out. You and your men are going to get better every time we do this."

Mohid seemed to perk up at these words, and he relayed the vote of confidence to the other Iraqi soldiers. They seemed to appreciate Clay's belief in them. No one knew what was coming.

Camp Taji became relatively quiet with only a few sporadic attacks, lulling Clay into a false sense of security. When Mohid finished his training, he was immediately sent west to fight ISIL. It was a tearful goodbye, with Clay vowing to look after Amreen while Mohid was away fighting. With Mohid now gone, Clay visited Amreen's home even more, rationalizing that he had to look after Amreen and bring her fresh food since she was unable to provide for herself.

~~~

With ISIL defeated in the west, conditions improved at Camp Taji. Villagers were even seen walking openly in the streets during the daylight. As it often happens, fate intervened. Clay and Amreen were walking down an alley when gunfire erupted. Before Clay could react, he felt a burning sensation in his chest. He tried to move, but he could only watch as ISIL fighters climbed the wall and approached them. Amreen was grabbed and carried off, but not before one of his black-shrouded enemies kicked Clay in the head, causing him to black out. When he regained consciousness, he was in an Army triage tent, IV hanging above him, and medical personnel swirling around him. He fell asleep under the influence of anesthesia, not regaining consciousness for over a day.

When Clay finally became clear-headed, Captain Kormel was standing at his bedside.

"How are you feeling, son?" asked the captain.

"It's hurts, but I know I will get better," replied Clay.

"Don't worry, Lieutenant; you're getting the best care Uncle Sam has. You're going to be on your feet in no time and on a plane home," Captain Kormel said.

Clay had not even thought about being sent home. He said, "I was walking with a young woman who was grabbed by the men who shot me. Were we able to get her back?"

"No," the captain replied. "I'm sorry; they took her, and I think you know what is going to happen to her."

Reality set in for Clay. How could he get her back? What would he tell his friend Mohid?

"You take care," said Kormel. "I'll draw up the papers to have you flown to Germany and from there back to Michigan. You will probably receive a purple heart and even get an early leave from us."

Clay didn't want the damn medal. He had done nothing to deserve it except get Amreen kidnapped.

He fell into a deep depression, unable to tell anyone about Amreen being kidnapped and being forced into a life of hell. He didn't even get a chance to contact Mohid and tell him what had happened.

~~~

A few days later, Clay was flown to Ramstein Air Force Base in Germany and from there stateside. He was admitted to Walter Reed Hospital and treated like a war hero. He felt he was anything but that.

Chapter Three

In Andahar province, the news of ISIL's defeat and the death of Ali al-Badri incensed the leaders, including Ali-al-Badri's brother, Zawahi. Zawahi al-Badri wanted to know all the details of his brother's death. He sent spies into Camp Taji to find out who was the commander who had killed his brother. Weeks later, one of the spies reported back that a Lieutenant Bennett was responsible for the attack, but he was wounded days later when some of their freedom fighters scaled a wall in the city, shooting Bennett, and capturing a young woman who died in an American Tomahawk attack days later.

Zawahi al-Badri swore revenge on the young lieutenant. He accessed ISIL's website and called for a jihad to avenge his brother's death. Zawahi al-Badri's sources informed him Lieutenant Bennett lived in a place called Michigan. In Detroit, one particular extremist decided this would be a good way to gain martyrdom.

Back in Mesabi County, Clay's homecoming was sweet for the family—at least for most of us. We couldn't wait for the wheels to touch down at Mesabi International Airport. It seemed like the whole county turned out. The military brass was there, making sure it got its picture taken with a true war hero. For the rest of us, it wasn't everyday a local got to have his or her picture taken with someone who was wounded in combat.

When Clay stepped off the plane, Donna ran to him, shouting, "Honey, I've missed you so much. I'm so glad you're home." That's all she could say before she broke down and cried.

Clay gave her a forced smile and said, "It's good to be home." Clay's mother and father had a hard time getting the words out.

We all understood and felt relieved that he was home at last. I shook his hand and Barb gave him a hug that I thought would last forever. There wasn't a dry eye on the tarmac.

"What do you want to do first?" I asked him.

"I haven't thought about it. I have some time off before I have to start my therapy," Clay said.

"Let's go home, honey," said Donna. "I just want you to rest. Everything is just as you left it."

Clay gave her another forced smile and nodded. Returning to Cascadia wasn't the magic solution for him that everyone had hoped. Days turned into weeks and Clay seemed to be recovering physically, but I could tell something was bothering him. I thought he would talk when he was ready. Taking him fishing seemed to be a good idea. A lot of problems were solved over a fishing pole and a cold beverage.

A few days later I drove to Cascadia with all the fishing equipment my truck could hold. As I approached the house, I saw Clay sitting on the front porch.

"How about giving the fish a run for their money?" I said. "It's a beautiful day and we could catch our limit by sun down."

"I don't know, Gramps," Clay replied. "I don't feel like it."

"I might need some help if I latch onto a big one," I said. "Come on; it'll do you good to get on the water."

We drove to the boat launch in Cascadia and backed our boat into the water. The boat floated off the trailer with Clay in it and I parked my truck before crawling into the boat beside him.

"Remember when you caught your first walleye here when you were a youngster?" I asked. He barely acknowledged me.

I was hoping he would open up when we were in the middle of the lake, but he didn't have that spark he used to.

"Can I tell you something?" Clay finally said.

"You can tell me anything and it stops right here," I said.

"In Iraq, I made some friends."

"That's great. What's the problem?" I asked.

"Near Camp Taji, I was walking with a girl I met when we were attacked by ISIL. That's where I was wounded and they kidnapped her. They're probably going to give her to some ISIL fighter as a prize. Even worse, her brother became a good friend of mine. After he was trained, he was sent west to fight ISIL. I never had a chance to tell him the bad news, or even help try to get his sister back."

"That's pretty heavy stuff, Clay," I replied, "but you can't hold yourself responsible for the girl being kidnapped."

"It was my fault," Clay stated. "We used to go for walks around town. The ISIL fighters were probably waiting."

All I could think to say was, "Sometimes in war, people can't control what happens. Iraq is a very dangerous place. You risked your life trying to help those people. Nobody holds you responsible."

"But I do," he replied.

"Talk to Donna and let her in," I suggested. "In addition, we both know a pretty good counselor who could help you." Clay smiled as he cast his line.

We fished in silence for the rest of the day. At least I knew what was eating him. I had sworn myself to secrecy, so I couldn't tell my wife, even though I knew she could help him. I had to hope time would help heal both his physical and mental wounds. PTSD is a bitch.

Chapter Four

In western Iraq, Mohid Malek was counting the days until he could return to his hometown, Al Taji. He had not spoken or received any mail from Amreen in weeks. Nobody knew what was happening. He had to return and speak with his good friend, Clay Bennett. The lieutenant had promised to take care of his sister, and Mohid knew he could count on him. Days later, there was a lull in the fighting, so Mohid was granted permission to return home to Al Taji for a week if he promised to return.

Mohid couldn't wait until the antiquated bus dropped him off near his home. He ran into the decaying structure, hoping to see his beloved sister, Amreen, but she was nowhere to be found. He searched the neighborhood for blocks, but nobody knew where she was. One villager told him ISIL attacked their village and some women were carried away weeks ago. Mohid ran to Camp Taji to find his friend, Clay. Surely, he would know and have a good explanation. Arriving at the gate, Mohid begged to be admitted, but he was denied.

"Could I see Lieutenant Bennett?" Mohid asked. "He trained me and we are good friends."

"Lieutenant Bennett was wounded several weeks ago and was air lifted back to the States," the MP replied. "You'll have to move along."

Mohid Malek felt alone. He needed time to think.

Over the next few days, Mohid continued to search for his beloved sister, Amreen, but without any luck. He found a coffee shop and accessed an ISIL website. His worst fears were confirmed. There he saw dozens of captured Iraqi soldiers being forced to kneel down and then beheaded. He saw on the ISIL website that many young women from Al Taji were being given to ISIL fighters as rewards for fighting bravely to protect their beliefs against the infidels.

For weeks, Mohid tried to gain access to intelligence regarding Amreen's whereabouts. It was anyone's guess where she would have been moved within the caliphate. He talked to every driver who made it to safety from the ISIL-controlled territory, but no information surfaced that could lead to his attempt to rescue his beloved sister.

He finally learned what had happened from one family who had made their escape across hundreds of desert miles from the Al-Raqqa province. They swore they had seen Amreen under the control of an ISIL fighter. As the family was fleeing, an American drone flew high over their village. Within minutes, American tomahawk missiles rained down on them, killing hundreds of ISIL fighters, but also innocent civilians. The family was certain nobody could have survived that ultimate decimation.

Mohid's heart became full of hate for ISIL; his sister's death left a hole in his heart. He had to contact his good friend Bennett and find out what had really happened. Bennett surely would have fought to the death to defend his sister. His sister had lived in purgatory until she was vaporized by American tomahawk missiles. Mohid wanted to find Lieutenant Bennett and hear from him in his own words what really happened that horrible day of his sister's kidnapping.

Mohid had to get to that place called Michigan and find Bennett. If Amreen died a horrible death, at least Mohid could find out the truth from Bennett. He hitchhiked and walked northward. He would have to find passage to Europe and from there gain access to a ship leaving for the United States.

~~~

Mohid joined the nine million refugees flooding north. Once in Turkey, he was able to fight his way onto a boat and dared to cross the Mediterranean Sea. Landing in southern Greece, he made his way through Albania and the rest of the Balkan Peninsula. Arriving in Vienna, Austria word on the street was that there was a plane of Syrian refugees was flying out soon to

Toronto, Canada. He had to be on that plane.

Early in the morning of the plane's departure, he went to the Syrian embassy in Vienna and tried to gain a voucher for the refugee plane; being turned down, he was not deterred. While leaving, he noticed a well-dressed man exiting the embassy.

"Do you know anything about the plane of Syrian refugees leaving today for Toronto?" Mohid asked in Arabic.

"As a matter of fact, I do. I just paid for the last seat. It cost me almost everything I own, but it will be worth it," the man replied.

"I see," said Mohid. He walked the man to his car, making casual conversation. Upon reaching his car, Mohid pushed the man out of the car, grabbed his plane voucher, and sped away. He asked Allah to forgive him for what he was doing, but Mohid had to find Bennett to hear from his lips how Amreen was kidnapped. He drove the vehicle down an alley and proceeded to change into some clothes the man had in his luggage. Having only a short time to make the flight, Mohid turned on the GPS as he drove toward the airport. The stewardesses were closing the refugee plane's door as Mohid ran up the stairway. He entered just before the door was closed. Sitting down in the plane, he was not proud of what he had done, but the truth had to be explained.

Chapter Five

In Detroit, Abu al-Krik disconnected his web browser and placed his hand on his Kalashnikov AK-12. He had recently purchased the weapon from a gun store in Detroit. The AK-12 had a 30-round magazine with a range of 2,000 feet.

On the ISIL website, al Krik announced his jihad by stating, "To reach martyrdom and paradise, I will kill this Lieutenant Bennett and his whole family. Only then will I gain entrance into heaven." After searching a few hours on the Internet, he found Bennett's address in Cascadia. He gathered up his belongings and his AK-12 and headed north on I-75 to complete his martyrdom.

In Cascadia, Clay was starting to accept what had transpired. He had survived an ISIL attack, Amreen had not, and Clay's friend, Mohid, had lost everything he held dear that day. Clay was visiting a psychologist who specialized in PTSD. He was actually starting to smile and enjoy life again. He became ecstatic when he learned his wife, Donna, was pregnant, and the news soon spread throughout Cascadia.

Meanwhile, Mohid Malek disembarked from the refugee plane in Toronto. The refugees were herded into a waiting area and told to wait for the proper paperwork to be processed. He waited overnight, but still there was no sign of being released. He saw an airport cleaning employee placing a "wet floor" sign at the entrance to a restroom. He followed the man inside and attacked him from behind; placing him in a chokehold that Lieutenant Bennett had showed him. Within minutes, the cleaning employee was unconscious. Mohid quickly undressed the employee and switched clothes. He exited the restroom and pushed the cleaning cart slowly through the throng of restless refugees. With a wave, the security guard motioned for him to leave the area after checking his ID and the cart for any contraband. Satisfied, the guard motioned for Mohid to move along.

Meanwhile, Abu al-Krik arrived in Cascadia. He was taken aback by the lush green foliage that surrounded him. He had lived in an urban environment that never provided so much beauty. Putting that out of his mind, he checked Google Search on his cell phone and located his victim's residence. He would scope it out before he completed his jihad. He repeated "Death to the infidels" as he drove to Bennett's house.

Donna and Clay were preparing the baby's room, and we all knew the nest had to be ready. Not wanting to know the sex of the baby, they had opted to paint the walls yellow and light green. Naturally, all hands were on board in preparation for the new Bennett arrival. It was great finally to see Clay happy again. The baby crib had been assembled with minimum obscene words being used. A mobile was hung at just the right height on the crib. After all, it was important for everything to be just right when Baby Bennett made his/her arrival. Bedding was washed and prepared. Ample *How to Take Care of Baby* books were purchased and examined in case something had changed over the last two thousand years. Everything was ready. All we needed was that darn baby.

Abu al-Krik drove slowly through Cascadia, having identified young Bennett's house. He would have to determine when he should conduct his jihad for maximum effect. He would kill not only Bennett and his immediate family, but as many family members as possible. Justice would prevail.

At the airport, Mohid walked through the terminal, pushing the cleaning cart. He saw a group of youngsters who appeared to be on a school trip. The chaperone was trying to contain them and wasn't paying attention to her purse. In one quick swoop, Mohid picked up the purse and deposited it into his cleaning cart. Entering the closest restroom, he left the cart behind and examined the purse. There was a large stash of Canadian currency, credit cards, and a cell phone. Praise to Allah.

He exited the restroom and ignored the commotion where the chaperone had "misplaced" her purse. Mohid continued to the escalator, leading to the main exit. He flagged a cab and said, "Take me to the first restaurant off the airport property." The cabbie set his meter and drove out of the airport. Within minutes, the cabbie pulled into a restaurant parking lot and Mohid held out all of the chaperone's money to the driver, after taking more than enough money the driver left Mohid in the parking lot with the dilemma of how to get through United States' customs.

Walking into the restaurant, he noticed a truck driver sitting at the lunch counter. The driver was wearing a baseball cap with a petroleum logo on the front. Mohid scanned the parking lot and saw a logo on a corresponding tanker. It was a gamble, but it had to be taken. He walked out to the tanker and climbed up on top of it. Then he unscrewed one of the covers. He lowered himself down inside and was almost overcome by the gasoline fumes, but he left the cover off so he could at least breathe fresh air.

Chapter Six

Barb and I were enjoying our morning coffee on our deck as boats navigated past our view. My cell phone rang with an unfamiliar ringtone.

"Hello," I said.

"Hey, stupid," the voice on the other end answered.

It took me a minute, but eventually the light came on. "John Crane, how are you?" I asked. I was partly afraid of his answer. He was a crack private detective who had saved our lives last year. He had served in the military as a Green Beret, distinguishing himself in combat.

"Guess what, Bennett? My sources at Quantico tell me you have trouble coming your way. A jihadist named Abu al-Krik is trying to gain entrance into Paradise by killing your grandson. Not only that, the State Department has it on good authority that a Kurdish fighter who served under your grandson has snuck into the United States via Canada. You better be on your toes or you'll be burying loved ones."

The line went dead before I even had time to thank him for the warning. If someone else had sent that ominous warning, I wouldn't have taken it seriously. Coming from John Crane, it meant trouble was coming our way. I called John Baldwin.

"Hello, John," I said. "We got trouble. John Crane called with a double-edged sword coming at my grandson. A jihadist is on his way, and apparently, a Kurdish freedom fighter has an axe to grind with Clay."

"We'd better be ready," John said. "I'll alert the others. We can put a 24/7 guard on Clay whether he wants it or not."

"I agree," I said. "We can't take a chance with either one of these men. They have nothing to lose and are willing to die trying."

~~~

Mohid Malek was crossing the International Bridge into Sault Sainte Marie, Michigan, by hanging onto the ladder inside of an oil tanker. He knew he was getting closer; soon he would have his questions answered by Clay Bennett regarding his sister's kidnaping and death.

~~~

Abu al-Krik had pulled up in front of Clay Bennett's house and was watching the family conduct normal activities. Suddenly, a SUV arrived. The pseudo-detectives in camouflage jumped out and fanned out in all four directions. Abu al-Krik accelerated his vehicle driving away from the Bennetts' residence to rethink his jihad.

~~~

Ben, Mark, John, and Tyler deployed to the edges of the Bennett property and knelt down scanning the perimeter of their kill zone. There was no lighthearted joking or teasing of one another. This was serious business, and someone was probably going to get killed. They were professionals, so I felt better as I entered the house to confront an uncooperative grandson.

After hearing of the imminent attack, Clay shook his head and said, "I don't want any protection. I can protect my family without your assistance." After hours of cajoling and pleading, I could see it was no use.

"I agree to pull the pseudo-detectives off and let you provide your own protection," I finally said. Clay removed his service weapon and checked to see whether it was loaded. I shook my head, saying, "That won't be enough." I knew arguing with him was past the point of reason. I called for my friends to load up and leave Clay to defend his home alone.

As we drove away, we knew what we had to do: ignore his demand.

"I'll take the church steeple that overlooks Clay's backyard," said John.

"There's an empty house down the street that will serve nicely for an eastern vantage point," said Mark.

"The garage next door has an attic I can climb up and enter after dark," I said.

"I'll take the lumberyard," Tyler added. "It's a quarter mile away, but I will prep my Chey Tac M200, which allows me to hit a target up to 2,000 meters away."

Without Clay knowing it, we had created a 360-degree killing zone.

"I don't have to tell you we'll have to shoot to kill and ask no questions," I said. "If you don't want to do this, I understand."

All four of them looked at me with determined looks. I knew that would be their answer, but I had to ask in case things went bad.

We deployed that night and communicated with our cell phones only as needed.

~~~

The oil tanker stopped at a corresponding gas station in Victorious to top off the station's tanks. Mohid Malek slid down the side of the tanker and slithered into the grass. He examined his stolen cell phone and checked Google Earth. He realized he was in close proximity to Cascadia. There was a fast food restaurant next door, so he casually strolled through the parking lot, looking for a trusting driver who had left his keys in the ignition. It wasn't long before he found one. He slid in, turned the ignition key, and soon was on his way to Cascadia to have his questions answered.

I was half asleep when my cell phone rang. John said, "Do you see that? There's movement at 6:00." All of our attention was immediately trained on the potential target. Our safeties were off ready to kill the bogey without batting an eye. Someone was crawling through the bushes that dotted the back line of the property. I trained my scope on the assassin. I was preparing to squeeze one quick shot so the perp would be motionless. But nobody moved.

At that moment, Clay emerged and saw the protective

perimeter we had established around his house. He noticed I was trained onto a target. At the last minute, he shouted, "Gramps don't shoot! It might be my friend, Mohid Malek. Do not shoot under any circumstances."

I relieved the presser from the trigger and complied with his request. There could be others, and we could ascertain later who the assassin was. This was no drill and the pseudo-detectives had to be at the top of their game. All of us slid down from our positions and approached the potential assassin. We were in no mood for sarcasm. We wanted the truth, and we were willing to beat it out of him if need be.

As I approached the man Clay identified himself as Mohid Malek, the man seemed to relax. He looked at me and said, "You must be Lieutenant Bennett's grandfather. The family resemble is striking."

Clay approached Mohid Malek with apprehension.

How could one of his trainees come so far from his homeland?

What was his goal in coming?

What could he tell him about his murdered sister?

They approached each other and let emotions take over. They ran to each other and embraced for an extended time. Neither said a word. We stood around the newly-bonded friends, believing some answers would be forthcoming when this reunion calmed down. We let it run its course before I said, "Clay, it's not safe outside. Let's move this happy reunion inside, away from possible enemy sniper fire?"

Both Clay and Mohid concurred. Neither took their arms from one another's shoulder as they entered Clay's house.

"There is so much I want to tell you," said Clay.

Clay said, "Whew, Mohid, you sure smell like gasoline."

Mohid responded, "It's a long story and I'll start at the beginning."

Once inside, Clay asked, "How did you get here?"

"I'm not proud of how I got here," said Mohid, "but I had to see you. My heart was broken when I learned Amreen was killed and you had left the country. I had to find out what happened."

"I can't tell you how sorry I feel," said Clay. "I felt I let you and Amreen down. Some assassins shot me and then jumped the wall and kidnapped Amreen. I couldn't do anything to stop them. I woke up the next day after they removed the bullet and Captain Kormel told me what had happened. Mohid, can you forgive me?"

Mohid looked Clay in the eyes and said, "I forgive you. I just had to hear what really happened from you. I know you would have protected her if you could." They embraced and cried in each other's arms.

Meanwhile, outside, we waited in our positions until dawn when several sheriff deputies' vehicles arrived and relieved us.

"I can bring Mohid to my house where I have an extra bedroom," John offered. We didn't like it, but dangerous times called for dangerous measures.

"Let's go home and come back at sundown," I said. "Make sure you get plenty of sleep." They nodded as they left. As they were walking away, a dark sedan slowly circled the block, trying to see where the deputies were going to be posted. I said, "Do you see that?" The pseudo-detectives grunted in unison.

"I think we've got some more work to do," said Mark. "This would-be assassin is going to be a whole lot more dangerous. I believe this jihadist may be more concerned about dying for his cause than carrying out the death order."

Ben identified the vehicle the jihadist had been driving, including the vehicle's license plate. That would make it really easy to neutralize him if he tried something. We tipped the deputies about the lone vehicle circling and I said, "We'll be back at sundown to relieve you."

~~~

That night, we again posted ourselves in our assigned protective hiding places, making sure the entire perimeter was covered. Suddenly, there was lots of commotion in Clay's house. Both Clay and Donna stepped out of the house with Donna shouting to him to "Bring the car around, get the baby bag, and call the hospital, your family, and my mother!" Clay made the mistake of asking which of those orders he should do first. I felt sorry for the boy when she was done with him. A new term was introduced to my grandson that night better known as "multi-tasking."

It's amazing what the human body can do when properly motivated. Within seconds, the vehicle was loaded, calls had been made, and they were on their way to the hospital.

From my vantage point, I noticed the dark sedan followed at a safe distance. We all climbed down and made it to the rendezvous point, agreeing we had better hurry to head off the potential assassination. Without due care for the speed limit, we high-tailed it as fast as possible to the Victorious Hospital. We noticed the dark sedan was also parked across the parking lot and staying in the shadows.

"That's enough!" Mark shouted. He jumped out of the SUV and sprinted as fast as he could toward the sedan. The vehicle accelerated toward U.S. 41 and was gone in minutes.

"That should discourage him from coming back," said Ben.

"You might be right," I replied, "but next time, he will pick his place and time more carefully."

I called Barb and all the other relatives who would like to be updated. It wasn't long before the delivery waiting room was filled to capacity. After several hours, Clay emerged, beaming from ear to ear, proclaiming he and Donna were the proud parents of a baby boy.

Clay looked at me and asked, "Gramps is it okay if we name him after you?"

I was almost too choked up to respond, but I was able to say, "That would be great."

Everyone shook Clay's hand and professed how happy they were for him and Donna. Lots of good-natured teasing abounded about which grandparent the baby resembled. It was truly a moment that comes only once in a lifetime when you put all your cares away and live in the minute. Barb and I were enjoying that moment. We didn't know what was coming.

Chapter Seven

Everything was quiet in Cascadia for the next few weeks. Clay and Donna were consumed with caring for little baby Bennett as we continued our surveillance. John Crane's tip had been invaluable, but could we continue to safeguard my grandson, Clay, and his family?

The next order of business was young Bill's baptism. It was scheduled for the following Sunday. As we drove to the church, a thunderstorm approached. It rained so hard the windshield wipers couldn't keep up with the deluge. Somehow, we made it to the church, and running with our coats over our heads, we made it inside. We were determined not to let Mother Nature spoil this special day. A packed house was guaranteed with Mohid Malek seated in the front row next to Clay and Donna.

As un-Christian as it seemed, I felt we had to be armed in case of an attack. As usual, Father Don gave a spiritual homily. Finally, the big moment came. Father Don held baby Bill up for the congregation to see. All of a sudden, gunfire erupted from the back of the church. Some thought it was the thunder overhead, but the pseudo-detectives and I knew better. Many parishioners dived under their seats. The gunman was shouting in Arabic, but he never got a chance to finish his threat. The pseudo-detectives and I opened fire. Everything happened so fast it was hard to tell which of us hit his mark first. The gunman fell to the ground and we continued firing until the body was motionless.

Mass chaos followed with everyone making for safety. The pseudo-detectives approached the body with pistols ready. The body was covered with Kevlar body armor. Ben pulled the assailant's mask off and revealed a bloody mess with five bullet wounds to the head.

Everyone was stunned as Father Don approached the body

and prayed over it. It wasn't long before sirens could be heard in the distance. By now, the church was empty except for the body and the pseudo-detectives. Sheriff Remington entered and stared in disbelief.

"What the hell happened?" he asked.

"It's a long story," I said. "You better have a seat." We both sat in a pew and Remington listened intently as I explained the cause-and-effect of this would-be jihadist.

Clay came inside and walked up to me. "Thanks, Gramps," he said. "I didn't know how serious this was. I thought I could protect my family myself, but I sure needed help." He shook all of our hands and embraced me as tightly as he could. Tears welled up in my eyes. Neither of us could speak, but words weren't necessary.

"You and Mohid are good friends," I said. "I will see what I can do to help arrange for Mohid to obtain a visa and, maybe, even citizenship. You couldn't have prevented what happened to Mohid's sister. War is hell. You were just a small part of it, and now you owe it to your family to put the war behind you and go on."

He seemed to agree as he hugged me and I returned his embrace as tightly as I could.

"Gramps," said Clay, "I'm happy we named our son after you."

"That's great," I said. "I am truly honored."

The thunder and lightning subsided and the sky opened up, revealing a beautiful rainbow. Wiping tears from our eyes, we beheld one of God's beautiful gifts to his children.

∼∼∼

Upon hearing of the failed jihad in America, Zawihi al-Badr again turned to the Internet and wanted to encourage a full-fledged jihad to avenge his brother's death. Zawihi al-Badr went into his communication tent, logged into one of ISIL's websites, and as he was calling for another jihad he heard the sound of an American tomahawk missile finding its mark, thus bringing an end to the *Revenge of ISIL*.

Part VI

The Lion of Michigamme

Chapter One

Monday

Excitement wasn't the word. Every child in Mesabi County was ecstatic with the news that the circus was coming to Cascadia. It would be here for a full week, and every exotic animal would be on display before and after each performance. Every child badgered his or her parents until they purchased a ticket for the magical show.

To enhance the euphoria, summer vacation had just commenced for the children. Although it is quite different today with video games and cell phones taking precedence over outside activities, I felt it was paramount that children be exposed to as much outside stimulation as possible.

When our grandchildren begged us to take them to "the greatest show on earth," we relented. The big day arrived, and we began our escapade with a stop at a fast food restaurant and soon we were on our way to Cascadia. Upon arriving at the ballfield, which was doubling as the circus parking lot, there was no stopping the children in their excitement as they raced euphorically to the big tent. I felt sorry for the exotic animals as I viewed them in their cages, pacing back and forth. Exotic animals were created to live in the wild, but these animals were destined to live out their lives doing tricks with the threat of cattle prods and bull hooks. I contemplated in my mind why these wild animals had to perform these meaningless tricks to avoid punishment. I now understood why organizations like Last Chance for Animals (LCA) and PETA were trying to eliminate animals in circuses. Maybe, the time has come for a change.

Upon entering the circus tent, we were overwhelmed by the noise and excitement. The children scurried to find their seats with Barb and me trailing behind. Naturally, an order of beverages and popcorn was required. After sufficiently filling our grandchildren's stomachs and emptying our wallets, Barb and I were relieved when the house lights dimmed and the ringmaster made his entrance. His booming voice resonated throughout the arena. All eyes were on center stage as he introduced the acts individually.

The three rings were filled with exciting acts, but again, I couldn't help feeling sorry for the animals. The tigers and lions performed wonderful acts of submission by jumping through hoops of fire. Later, two brothers kept us spellbound as they drove their motorbikes inside the "Sphere of Death." Their death-defying coordination was impressive.

Finally, the climax to the circus performances arrived. The stars of the show were the two high-wire aerialists, Gabriela and Villarreal. They made their entrance with great pageantry, doffing their capes before they climbed their respective poles.

The ringmaster, Jeb Stalworth, enhanced the atmosphere by ordering the net to be cut down. While this was occurring, Gabriela and Villarreal warmed up by performing simple catches that were amazing by themselves. Finally, the net was laid on the ground and the ringmaster announced Gabriela would do a triple somersault in the air before being caught by her partner, Villarreal. Everyone held their breath as Villarreal proceeded to swing back and forth higher and higher. With a drum roll, Gabriela leaped from her perch and somersaulted three times in the air before being caught by Villarreal. The arena erupted with applause and Gabriela and Villarreal smiled and waved to the enthralled onlookers below. With the conclusion of the aerial act, the circus performers paraded one last time around the interior of the tent to the applause of the crowd.

Exiting the circus tent, the grandchildren begged for one last look at the circus animals. As we approached the cages, I could see the children were impressed with the massive size of these beasts. The handlers were using bull hooks to herd the animals into their respective cages where the animals would remain until their next performance. It was hard for me to watch the animals being shepherded into their cages as one of the lions unleashed one last ferocious growl of defiance. One of the handlers said, "That's Chico. He likes to show off his rebelliousness."

As we entered our vehicle, the grandchildren were abuzz with the excitement of the performances. Driving back to Victorious, I tried not to think of the animal cruelty, but instead, to enjoy the children's happiness.

Chapter Two

Tuesday

The next day, Barb was running her four-mile morning constitutional and I was pacing myself so as not to over-exert myself by grabbing some much deserved shut-eye. When my cell phone chimed, I reached over and picked it up. "Hello," I said.

It was John Baldwin, my right-hand man among the pseudo-detectives. "You'll never guess what happened," he said.

"Good," I replied. "That saves me time. Goodbye."

"Wait," he said. "It's important. They found a body on the Cascadia public beach this morning. They think it might be one of the circus performers."

"No kidding," I said. "I'll meet you at Millie's in one hour. Call the others and let's see what's up."

"Sounds good," he replied.

~~~

The five of us pseudo-detectives arrived almost simultaneously. Besides myself and John, also present was John's son, Tyler Baldwin, our current Needleton police officer; my neighbor, Mark Kestila, a retired military officer who had participated in drug enforcement while stationed in Germany; and Ben Myers, a retired Victorious police officer who had helped reduce drug crime in our city.

Carolyn Raft, our newest member of the pseudo-detectives and the county M.E., was working, so she naturally wouldn't be available. I would pay her a visit later to see what she could reveal to me without getting in trouble with her boss, Sheriff Remington, who often loathed our law enforcement procedures for sometimes skirting the letter of the law.

We entered, sat in the first available booth, and we ordered before getting down to business.

After taking a sip of coffee, Ben said, "My sources in the sheriff's department tell me the deceased was the star of the show, Gabriela. Her real name is Maria Garcia from Galena, Mexico. Her aerial partner, Villarreal, is her brother, and his first name is Javier. The circus is owned by Henry Bartle and the ringmaster is Jeb Stalworth."

"That's a good start," I said. "Let's see what Sheriff Remington comes up with before we start digging. I'll visit Carolyn after I leave here to see if she's discovered anything about the young lady's death."

"If you don't mind," said Tyler, "I'd like to tag along. I want to see if she really earns her money."

"Is that why you really want to come?" I asked.

Tyler just smiled and accompanied me out the door.

It was a short drive to the sheriff's department, and we knew where we would find Carolyn. Entering her laboratory, we saw her bending over the body of a young lady on the table. We knew we could not approach, so we took a seat and waited for her to finish her autopsy. After a few minutes, she shut the overhead light off and approached us. She said, "I can only imagine what you two want to know."

"We're not going to start that again are we?" I asked.

"I can give you some information," she replied, "but you have to keep it to yourself."

"Promise," I said.

"She died of an overdose of methylenedioxymethamphetamine or MDMA," said Carolyn. "It's street name, as you know, is ecstasy. The MDMA affected the brain by altering the activity of chemical messengers. MDMA raised her body temperature and released norepinephrines, which likely caused the increase in heart rate and blood pressure, which led to her death."

Carolyn waited for that to sink in for us before continuing.

"Miss Garcia's stomach content had over two hundred milligrams of MDMA, which was more than enough to kill her.

Her blood alcohol level was 1.5, which meant she was probably intoxicated when the attack occurred. She was not sexually attacked, but her body was moved from where she was killed. Her body had lividity, which did not match the pictures of the crime scene. That's why I can say she was definitely moved. The time of death was approximately eleven o'clock last night."

We thanked Carolyn for the information, and then Tyler and I swore we would only tell our fellow pseudo-detectives as we stepped through the double exit doors.

"I guess we have a murder on our hands," said Tyler

"No doubt," I replied. "The circus is leaving in six days and the murderer may be among them. I suggest we meet tonight at Geno's Pizzeria and assign the group different persons of interest to question."

Tyler concurred, so I called the others and arranged for us to meet at our favorite waterhole at eight o'clock.

We gathered later that evening at Geno's Pizzeria, entering with a wave to our favorite bar owner, Rick Bonnetelli.

Rick delivered a few pitchers and he didn't even have to ask what pizzas to bring.

"Here's what we know," I said. "Maria Garcia was filled with ecstasy, intoxicated, murdered, and dumped at the Cascadia public beach. We have six days to find out who murdered her because once the circus leaves town, it will be next to impossible to solve the case. Ben, could you check out the ringmaster and see where he was last night after the performance? John and Tyler, could you interrogate some of the circus stars like the Gomez brothers and see where they were last night? Mark, could you check with the brother, Javier, and see if he can provide an alibi? I'll check with the owner, Henry Bartle. I don't have to tell you time is of the essence. Let's meet here tomorrow morning at eight o'clock and drive to Cascadia together."

As we adjourned, I could tell they didn't appreciate working under a deadline, but we had no choice.

Chapter Three

Wednesday

The pseudo-detectives drove into the designated parking lot for the circus. The village had removed its baseball fence to accommodate the circus.

Exiting our car, John and Tyler could see the Gomez brothers practicing inside their "Sphere of Death." John said, "We'll see what these two birds have to say. We'll meet back here in an hour." Ben, Mark and I nodded as we stepped out of the vehicle and dispersed to find our respective query.

Tyler and John watched spellbound as the two brothers, Carlos and Tomas Gomez, drove their laps inside the sphere, barely missing each other by inches. Finally, they slowed down and an assistant opened the door, allowing the two motor bikers to emerge unscathed. John motioned for them to drive toward them. To John and Tyler's chagrin, the two daredevils increased their speed to warp drive and headed right for the two amateur detectives. John and Tyler dove at the last minute and barely avoided being run over.

The cyclists turned and drove toward them, slowing down and in Spanish asking, "*Que quieres?*"

Both Tyler and John stood and dusted themselves off. John had to restrain Tyler as he stepped toward the Gomez brothers with his fists clenched. John said, "Tyler, wait a minute. We need some information from them." They asked the assistant if he could interpret for them.

"Si," the assistant replied.

Needless to say, strong words were used before the interrogation started. Through the interpreter, Carlos Gomez said, "We thought you were with the USDA and were coming to close us down."

John settled down, looked at the assistant, and he said, "Tell them we're not with the government. We're trying to help solve the murder. We just want to find some answers regarding last night. Ask these two clowns where they were the night of the murder?"

Through the interpreter, Tomas Gomez said, "We heard about Maria's death, but we didn't know she was murdered. We went to The Timbers Bar and had a few drinks. Most of the circus performers were there, including Maria and Javier Garcia."

"Did Maria leave with anyone?" Tyler asked.

Through the interpreter, Tomas said, "We're not sure because it was so packed we didn't notice whether she left with anyone."

John asked the interpreter, "What time did they leave the bar last night?"

After interpreting the Gomez response, the interpreter said, "They don't remember because they were so drunk. They woke up in their trailer and heard the tragic news about Maria."

Tyler stepped toward them, preparing to use physical force to encourage the Gomez brothers to be more forthcoming.

John held him back, saying, "They're definitely lying, but we'll see them again when it's more conducive for our questions."

The Gomez brothers and John and Tyler stared each other down as John and Tyler walked away, entered their car, and drove to the circus trailers to wait for the rest of us.

"I don't believe for one minute that they attacked us because they mistook us for USDA agents," Tyler told his dad. "What do they care if the show gets shut down? They can just hook up with another circus."

"I agree," said John. "I want to keep an eye on those two coyotes."

Ben walked through the parking lot, looking over his shoulder in time to watch the Gomez brothers miss John and Tyler by inches with their motorbikes. Ben said to himself those two bikers don't know who they're dealing with.

Ben walked through the quiet avenue of trailers until he came to one with a star on the door. He gambled that the trailer belonged to the ringmaster, Jeb Stalworth. Ben knocked on the door and heard, "Go away." Ben opened the door and stepped into a one-man shrine. Everywhere there were glossy pictures of all sizes of the ringmaster introducing acts over the years. Focusing his eyes on a moving heap of sheets on the bed, he heard from underneath, "If you're selling something, I'm not interested. If you're looking for work, I'm not hiring. It's been nice talking to you. Don't let the door hit you on the way out."

Ben walked over to the bed and gave it a good kick. He heard a woman scream in pain. Ben stepped back and said, "I'm sorry. I thought you were alone."

"As you can probably tell," Jeb replied, "I'm not alone. Now get out."

Ben cleared his throat and said, "I'm here to ask you some questions about Monday night. We can talk now, or I can drag you outside. Make up your mind."

"Are you with the police?" Jeb asked.

"No, my friends and I are helping the police find out who murdered Maria Garcia Monday night. The M.E. said she was full of ecstasy and booze. Someone wanted to knock her unconscious and have his way with her."

The ringmaster threw off the bedding and sized up Ben, realizing he didn't want any part of this fellow who looked like he could handle himself. Jeb slapped his bedmate on the behind and said, "Later."

His bed-partner wrapped a sheet around herself, stood, and made her way to the back of the trailer. She gathered her clothes, entered the bathroom, and she closed the door behind her. Ben recognized her from the circus poster, but he decided her interrogation would have to wait until later.

"Now that we're alone," said Ben, "maybe you can tell me what the hell happened last night."

"It's a tragedy that Maria died," Jeb replied, "but I don't know anything. We all congregated at The Timbers Bar, and then I remember waking up with that bimbo," he said, nodding toward the bathroom.

"Was Maria there?" Ben asked.

"Yes," Jeb replied. "We had a drink together, but she had eyes on someone else. I couldn't see who it was, but he must have money because Maria didn't waste her time with barflies."

"Here's my cell number," said Ben, handing Jeb his card. "Call me if you remember anything."

"Sure, but next time wait outside."

~~~

My quest took me past the animal cages. I guess I just couldn't get away from them. The animals looked so pathetic pacing in their cages when they belonged in the wild, not in a freak show. Asking directions as I made my way through the circus village of trailers, I came upon the largest trailer with a sign marked "Office." I walked up to the door, and as I was preparing to knock, I heard, "Get the hell out of here! I'll pay you when I get the money."

"I'm not looking for money," I said. "I just want information regarding the murder of Maria Garcia Monday night."

The owner opened his door and said, "Sorry; I thought you were with the USDA. They're hounding me every day to pay my fines."

"I'm with some friends who are helping the police find out who murdered Maria Garcia last night," I replied.

"I knew she died," Henry Bartle said, "but I didn't know she was murdered. How did it happen?"

"She was full of ecstasy and alcohol," I said. "Do you know who might have done it?"

"Look around," said Henry. "This is a circus. We hit a new town every week. My employees come and go. I don't even know half of them. I'm just trying to keep this extravaganza afloat. I feel terrible about what happened to Maria, but I have to find a replacement by tonight."

"Did you see Maria Monday night after the performance?" I asked.

"No. I was exhausted. I turn in early every night. I'm seventy years old and I have all I can do to keep this business going."

"Well, thanks for your time," I said. "If you think of anything, let me know. I'll be in touch."

I walked away to find my cohorts and assess our situation. As I was looking for my pseudo-detective partners, a great commotion was heard near the cages. Some employees were running away from the area while the handlers were running with stun guns and billhooks toward the commotion. I had to follow the excitement. Large animal roars could be heard the closer I got to the cages. The animal trainer, Emil, was cracking his whip, trying to get some of the big cats to retreat into their cages.

Apparently, a cage door had been left open for only a moment while a handler was reaching for more food. One lion, Chico, in one leap, bounded past the handler, terrorizing him into running for his life, thus leaving the gate wide open. Numerous cats, including the other lions, tigers, and cheetahs, made the best of the situation. They not only walked out of the cage, but also took the liberty to stroll casually among the other cages. It appeared they were enjoying their newfound freedom. Nevertheless, Emil cracked his whip and forced most of the large cats to retreat. Only Chico seemed ready to challenge him. Emil gave Chico many stern commands to back into the cage, but the big cat just roared.

Henry Bartle appeared with his rifle in hand, ready to put Chico down.

"No, don't do it!" Emil shouted. "Without the elephants the only exotic animals we have to showcase are my cats. I'll get Chico back into his cage. He's just showing his defiance in front of the other cats." After several nail-biting minutes, Emil was able to persuade Chico to give up his newfound freedom for the security of his cage. Once back inside, Chico continued to snarl at his handlers and Emil.

"Next time," warned Henry, "I'll put a bullet in his fat head and be done with him. That's the last time he causes trouble in my circus. I can't wait to get to the end of the season and be rid of him."

Emil was forced to acquiesce.

Not hearing the commotion, Mark Kestila had worked his way through the maze of trailers. Finally, he saw one with a black bunting on the front door. He approached and knocked softly. He heard in English with a heavy Spanish accent, "What do you want? Can't you see I'm in mourning?"

Mark hesitated, but then he remembered the time restraint we were working under. Mark called out, "I know you are grieving, but I would like to ask you some questions if you feel up to it."

Javier opened the door and said, "Can't you leave me alone. I have to take my sister from this godforsaken land and return with her to Mexico."

"I'm very sorry for your loss," Mark said. "Are you able to tell me anything that might help find her murderer?"

Javier gasped and said, "What do you mean 'murderer'?"

Mark realized he had said too much, but he continued carefully, "The M.E. said she had a high content of ecstasy and alcohol in her system. Can you think of anyone who might want to hurt her?"

Javier wanted to say something, but he thought better of it. He finally said, "No, I can't think of anyone who would want to hurt my sister."

"Javier," Mark continued, "do you remember where you went after the performance Monday night?"

Javier glared at Mark and said, "Maria and I went for a drink at The Timbers Bar, but I lost sight of her in the confusion. There were a lot of people there. I left about twelve and came home."

Mark could tell Javier wasn't being truthful, but to continue this line of questioning would be pointless.

"Thanks for your time," Mark said. "I'm sorry for your loss." Mark closed the trailer door on his way out.

After questioning John Stalworth, Ben had waited outside for

Stalworth's elusive mistress to make her exit. He followed her a few feet, and then, when he was sure they were out of earshot of Jeb Stalworth's trailer, he said, "Excuse me. Do you have a minute? I'm Ben Myers, and my friends and I are helping the police try to solve Maria's death. Can I ask you some questions regarding Maria Garcia? I recognize you from the circus poster."

"I'm Consuela Garcia," the young lady replied. "Maria and I were cousins, but I'm not getting mixed up in her death."

"The M.E. thinks it was a homicide," said Ben. "By the way, I can see Jeb Stalworth was consoling you. You hide your sorrow pretty well."

"A girl has to eat. You don't know how tough it is to make it in the circus world," Consuela replied.

"What's your role in this spectacle?"

"If you must know, I was Maria's understudy. If she was sick, I took her place. Otherwise, I assist Emil with the cats in the cage."

"With Maria's death, I guess you become the star of the circus," Ben replied.

Consuela reeled and said, "That's nonsense. Maria and I were like sisters. I will miss her very much, but I have to keep that pig, Stalworth, happy, or else I'm out on my butt."

"Well, it's been nice talking to you," Ben said. "I'll see you around."

Consuelo Garcia walked away, wiping tears from her eyes.

~~~

As Ben, Mark, and I drove back to Victorious, we started to exchange reports. After we were brought up to speed, Ben had a quizzical look on his face. "The entire group of circus people, except the ringmaster," he said, "acted surprised to find out Maria was murdered. When I told him about the death being a murder, he didn't bat an eye. How would he have known that unless he knew something?"

"You're right, Ben," I replied. "I think we have our prime suspect. We continued to exchange information as we waited for John and Tyler.

~~~

Before leaving the circus grounds, John and Tyler took it upon themselves to examine the Gomez's trailer. It wasn't a good idea to try to run both Baldwins over, and if you do try to run them over, you better succeed. Payback's a bitch.

They meandered around until they discovered a pile of motorcycle parts lying in a heap next to a rundown trailer. Both Tyler and John looked at each other and knew this had to be the Gomez's trailer. Prying open a window was child's play for these two battle-tested detectives. Not getting caught was another story. They slid the window open and hoisted themselves inside. Once inside, they held their noses because the stench of marijuana was overwhelming.

"I think they have their own scam going," said John. "Let's say we shut it down."

Both Tyler and John pulled out dresser drawers and examined them for false bottoms. No luck. Next, they pulled the LP stove out and examined it for illegal activity. No luck. They slid the stove back into place with a feeling of futility. Finally, John had an idea. He stepped outside and paced off the length of the trailer. Then he reentered and paced off the inside.

"The trailer is four feet longer on the outside than on the inside," he said. With that, the Baldwins approached the back of the trailer to the Gomez's sleeping quarters. A large picture was hanging on the back wall between the single beds. John and Tyler lifted the picture from its hook and smiled as they gazed on dozens of marijuana bags packed into the back of the trailer.

"I think we got our payback," said Tyler.

"You're right," said John, "but we found it through an illegal search. Now we have to trick them into showing their hand."

John and Tyler replaced the large picture and exited the trailer, making sure everything was just as it was before they entered.

Driving back to Victorious, John brought us up to speed regarding the Gomez brothers' illegal marijuana operation.

"We'll have to put that sting on the back burner," I said. "I'd like to solve Maria Garcia's murder first. What do you think?"

"The Gomez brothers can wait," John agreed. "We'll get them before they leave town. I'll have to think of something that won't be jeopardized by our illegal search."

Chapter Four

After we returned to Victorious, I decided to pay a visit to our Mesabi County Sheriff, Strom Remington. I entered the department headquarters and assailed the three flights of stairs to his office. Knocking on his door and hearing the familiar, "Come in," I entered with hopes of obtaining additional information on the murder.

Much to my chagrin, Sheriff Remington was in no mood for small talk.

"What's up in the world of law enforcement?" I began.

"I just got off the phone with the DEA," he said. "It seems there's a trail of illegal drug sales that follows the circus wherever it goes. They were just in Cincinnati, Ohio and Des Moines, Iowa, and there is currently an epidemic of heroin overdoses laced with Carfentanil."

"What's Carfentanil?" I asked.

Sheriff Remington was only too happy to show off his knowledge of the illegal drug world. "It's a sedative used on elephants. Two milligrams can knock out a 2,000-pound African elephant. Drug suppliers are using the illegal drug to cut their heroin so their supply lasts longer. Drug users are none the wiser; they'll use anything to get high. So far, there are two deaths in Cincinnati and one in Des Moines where the victims' autopsies showed large amounts of the drug."

"That's just what we need," I said, "another fly in the ointment. Now we have to figure out if there's a drug dealer in the circus and if he's tied to Maria Garcia's death."

As I stood up to leave, Sheriff Remington said, "Keep me posted if you hear anything in your investigation."

"Likewise," I replied.

On the way home, I phoned the pseudo-detectives and brought them up to speed regarding the ominous trail of Carfentanil that seemed to be following the circus.

After arriving home, I cracked a cold one and sat on my deck wondering what our next move should be. Then it came to me. If you want to catch a big fish, you have to use the right bait. I picked up my cell phone and dialed an old familiar number.

The voice on the other end said, "Hello."

"Hello, right back at you," I said. "How are you, Kelly?"

"Good," Kelly Sanderson replied. "Jenni Durant and I just graduated from Michigan State, majoring in criminal justice, and Jenni and I have both been accepted into the Michigan State Police academy. We can't wait until we start."

"I have a proposition for you," I said. "Would you and Jenni like to start your police career doing some undercover work?"

"I know I speak for Jenni when I say we would love to," Kelly replied. "What do you have in mind?"

I explained the proposition to her. Since nobody in Cascadia knew either of them, they would be the perfect young people to enter The Timbers Bar and try to buy some drugs. If they could find the drug dealer, the pseudo-detectives and I could persuade them to tell us who else bought from them recently. There was a strong possibility we might have to skirt the law in our questioning techniques.

Because of the danger involved, we agreed the girls would have to be armed with new-age technology for their protection.

I checked my basement, where I was storing a recent shipment of surveillance gadgets I was eager to put into action. Sifting through packages of electronic eavesdropping equipment, I found what I was looking for. With the help of my wife, Barb, the gizmos were tested in our kitchen and the plan was ready to be implemented, sending the girls, Kelly and Jenni, into undercover action. Kelly Sanderson would carry a voice-activated keychain that could transmit up to thirty feet on The Timbers' bar table. Jenni Durant would be positioned in a booth using a fake smartphone camera that would videotape Kelly negotiating with the drug dealer. If Kelly was in danger, Jenni would call us on her cell phone and we'd charge through the front door.

~~~

Thursday Night

Armed with new technology and plenty of old-fashioned handguns, we made our way to The Timbers Bar. As we rehearsed, Jenni would enter and pretend to have trouble with her smartphone. She would be followed moments later by Kelly, who would make her way to the bar. After ample conversation and a little flirting, Kelly would ask the bartender if he knew who could get some drugs for her.

Both girls entered separately and took their prearranged positions. Leaning into the bartender, Kelly said, "I'm just home from college and my boyfriend wants me to pick up some coke." The bartender said, "Kid, I don't know what you're talking about."

He started to walk away when Kelly pulled a hundred dollar bill out of her pocket and slid it under her glass. She said, "Are you sure you don't know where I can get some coke?"

The bartender pointed to a long-haired man at the end of the bar and said, "You might try Dr. Feel-Good. He can get you anything you want."

Kelly looked down the end of the bar until she got Dr. Feel-Good's attention. She smiled, twirled her hair, and motioned for him to come over. The grungy-dressed man slowly worked his way down the bar. Kelly gave him a sheepish smile.

Dr. Feel-Good said, "Before I talk to you, I have to ask, 'Are you a cop?'"

"No," said Kelly.

Dr. Feel-Good ran his hand up Kelly's front and down her back, looking for hidden microphones. Then he started the conversation by saying, "My name is Dr. Feel-Good. That's all you need to know. What do you want? I can get you anything your little heart desires."

Kelly tried to play coy with him and said, "I'm a little nervous.

I had my own coke when I was at State, but I ran out. Can you get me good stuff? I heard that a woman died the other night. She overdosed on ecstasy. How do I know you aren't selling rat poison or dog deworming drugs?"

"Listen, bitch," said Dr. Feel-Good, "that broad must have taken too much. I told her sugar daddy not to give her all of it."

"Okay," said Kelly. "I guess I can trust you. Where do you have the coke?"

"Most of its kept with my stone friends," Dr. Feel-Good replied, "but some is out in my car. How much do you want?"

"How about five grams?" Kelly said.

"Fine. That will cost you $350."

Here's where Kelly set the bait.

"Are you kidding?" she said. "I only pay fifty bucks a gram at State. Get out of here."

Not wanting to lose a sale and a possible addict for months, Dr. Feel-Good said, "Okay, how's $300? That's $60 a gram. Take it or leave it."

"Okay," said Kelly, "but it better not be cut with anything. Let's go."

Dr. Feel-Good and Kelly walked out the door. That's the last thing Dr. Feel-Good did upright. He was met by a 2" x 4" right across the face, courtesy of yours truly. Falling to the ground, he tried to look up, but was met by a fist, courtesy of Tyler. His face was bleeding profusely as he murmured under his breath, "What do you want?"

I said, "Give us the name of the sugar daddy that left with Maria Garcia Monday night?"

"If I tell you, I'm dead," said Dr. Feel-Good. "So do what you want to me."

John Baldwin pulled him to his feet and dragged him over to the buck pole behind the bar. The pole was used during deer season to lure successful hunters in to show off their trophies and spend a few bucks inside the bar. It would make a dandy torture rack. I threw a rope over the buck pole and asked, "Are you sure you don't want to tell us who the sugar daddy was that bought the ecstasy for Maria? This is going to get pretty messy." I tied his hands and put duct tape over his mouth. Then I said, "I have to look away. This stuff really bothers me."

Placing the rope around his neck, we tied the other end to the bumper of our truck and started the engine. We all turned away so as not to witness the torture. Mark stepped into the driver's seat and started to pull the slack just enough so that the drug-dealer's tiptoes were barely touching the ground.

"All set here. Let her rip!" I shouted to Mark.

Dr. Feel-Good made a muffled sound that made it obvious we weren't kidding. Mark backed the truck up and unceremoniously dumped the sobbing drug-dealer on the ground.

"Dr. Feel-Good," I said, "I'm only going to ask this one time. Who was the sugar daddy you sold the ecstasy to Monday night?"

I tore the duct tape slowly from his mouth, so it would hurt as much as possible.

"Well, Dr. Feel-Good, what's it going to be?" I asked.

There was silence for a moment, and then he said, "It was Jeb Stalworth." We immediately dragged Dr. Feel-Good out of the dirt and laid him on the ground to catch his breath.

"That won't be able to be used in a court of law," I said, "but at least we know who we're dealing with."

For a moment, there was stunned disbelief. John broke the silence by saying, "I thought all along it would have been Bartle. Go figure."

"By the way," I said, "who are these stone friends of yours?"

"I'm definitely not telling you that," said Dr. Feel-Good. "You can hang me if you want, but I will take that to the grave."

Since we got the information we wanted, we released Dr. Feel-Good and threatened there would be terrible reprisals if he told anybody about our party at the buck pole. He nodded his head, stepped into his vehicle, and he drove away. When he felt he was far enough away, he shouted all the obscenities he knew.

"That's wasn't very friendly of him," said Ben. "After all, we helped cure his bowel problem. I think he's going to have to buy some new underwear."

We had more serious problems to deal with. Now that we knew who murdered Maria we had to prove it. I had another plan. I still wanted to know who Dr. Feel-Good's stone friends were. Maybe, we could shut the whole Midwest operation down.

Chapter Five

Friday Night

We now knew who had murdered Maria, but proving it was something else. When we reconvened at Geno's Pizzeria, this time we included Jenni Durant and Kelly Sanderson, who, hopefully, were going to play a big part in closing this case.

After the usual pizza and pitchers of beer, I proposed a toast. "Here's to Kelly and Jenni; our newest members of the pseudo-detectives. With their help, we can get justice for Maria Garcia." Everyone lifted a glass and thanked the young women for being a big part of the team.

After the toast, I remembered we had to solve this crime before the circus left Cascadia Sunday night.

"It does bother me that Dr. Feel-Good is still on the loose selling his drugs," John said. "Let's pay him a visit and shut him down permanently. Tyler and I also have a score to settle with the Gomez brothers. They tried to run us down a few days ago, and we found marijuana in their trailer. Somehow, we have to coax the Gomez brothers into selling marijuana to some undercover agents. I think I know just who fits that bill." He looked at Kelly and Jenni.

I said, "After we take care of Dr. Feel-Good, we can set up the Gomez brothers in the same way." We all nodded in agreement.

"I think I have a plan," I said, "but first, I'll have to stop at the bank and make a sizeable withdrawal."

Carolyn Raft excused herself to use the ladies' room. Upon returning, she was stopped by a man who asked, "May I buy you a drink?"

"No, thank you," Carolyn replied. "I'm with some friends."

"One little drink won't hurt," the man replied.

Carolyn looked him straight in the eye and said, "I said no and I mean it. Now let me pass."

The man grabbed her arm and said, "You don't think I'm good enough to drink with. Let me teach you a lesson." He reached into his pocket and pulled out a dagger. He was bringing it up to her throat when Rick Bonnetelli sprang into action, jumping over the bar counter and he grabbed the man's arm before the would-be murderer could carry out his threat. Tyler rushed to his damsel in distress, cold-cocking the would-be attacker. Tyler stepped on the assailant's arm and pulled the knife away. Tyler and Rick brought the man to his feet and Rick said, "I'll call the police."

"Let it go," said Carolyn. "We have enough on our plate to deal with."

Tyler shoved the man into a booth and said, "What's your name?"

The would-be mugger said, "I'm Renaldo, the knife thrower, and I'm with the circus. I apologize for my actions, and I thank you very much. If you don't mind, I'll leave, and allow me to give you some complimentary tickets for the circus."

"Don't bother," Tyler said. "If I see you again, it'll be too soon. Now get out."

Renaldo shuffled out the door, breathing a sigh of relief.

Upon exiting Geno's Pizzeria, Renaldo said to himself, that bitch and her boyfriend will regret the day they crossed him.

~~~

Back inside, Renaldo's friend, who had been sitting in the booth with him, smiled to himself. With all this excitement happening, he said to himself, this might be a good time to pay a visit to a local ATM.

Renaldo's booth partner had worked for Diebold years ago in Bogota, Columbia. He had been able to sneak out a crypto-processing chip from the factory that would allow the smartcard to bypass most ATM's metal-shielding layers on Diebold's crypto-processor chips.

The dark stranger stood and left the bar quietly without anyone noticing him.

He crossed the street and approached the local bank, pulling his hood up to cover most of his face as he stepped up to the ATM. He slipped his smartcard into the ATM slot, bypassed the PIN security code, and punched in "$10,000." The machine soon shot out hundreds of dollars as the stranger removed them as quickly as possible. After his hefty withdrawal, the stranger returned to his car, entered it, and the thief drove away.

~~~

Back in the bar, Tyler looked at Rick Bonnettelli and said, "Thanks. That could have been disastrous. You saved Carolyn's life, and we're really grateful."

"Don't mention it," Rick said.

Little did we know that altercation would only add to our problems.

We left Geno's Pizzeria and drove toward Cascadia. I looked at John and said, "Somehow, we have to shut that drug dealer down before another person falls victim to his drugs."

"We'll get 'em," said John. "Count on it."

When we arrived at The Timbers Bar, we recognized the drug dealer's truck. We huddled together behind our vehicle as I explained my plan. Since Dr. Feel-Good had not seen Jenni in our first escapade, we could use her to lure Dr. Feel-Good out with hopes of finding his stash of lethal drugs. We would have to send Jenni in without backup since Dr. Feel-Good had seen all of us in the sting.

"I can't order you to do this," I told Jenni, "but it might be our only way of closing his operation down. Try to have him take you to his stone people and his stash."

"No problem," said Jenni. "I'll tell him I'm in town and want to see if he's the real deal. If his heroin is pure, I'll call my contact and buy everything he has." It was risky, but we knew we had to do it.

I gave Jenni the money I had withdrawn from the bank. Hopefully, Dr. Feel-Good would be greedy enough to take the bait. We placed the few hundred dollars on top of the cut-up newspaper and placed it in her backpack.

Jenni exited the vehicle and entered The Timbers Bar. Dr. Feel-Good was busy doing his business, frequenting the bathroom with small-time addicts every few minutes. Jenni had to play it coy. She sat at the bar for hours until the bar emptied out. Then she approached Dr. Feel-Good and said, "I see you specialize in small-time druggies. I don't suppose you know of someone who can provide me with a large supply of heroin?"

"Listen, bitch," said Dr. Feel-Good. "I have all the heroin you want and more."

"I doubt if you have enough," said Jenni, playing hardball. "I want to move a lot since the college will be back in session soon, and my handler and I want to be ready. If you don't know of a large dealer, go away."

Dr. Feel-Good's blood pressure rose. Feeling insulted, he said, "If you're not a cop, I can load you up with all you can handle."

"Well, maybe, we can work something out," Jenni replied, "but I would have to test it first."

"Follow me," said Dr. Feel-Good.

They walked out of the bar and approached his vehicle.

"Wait a minute," said Jenni. "I have to get my test kit from my vehicle."

"Hurry up," said Dr. Feel-Good. "I don't have all day."

Jenni opened her car door and retrieved a small package. She returned with her heroin test kit and said, "If your heroin isn't pure, this test will show it."

"It will show the purity's just fine," Dr. Feel-Good replied.

"When this test comes in contact with heroin," Jenni explained, "the bottom layer will turn yellow or orange, depending on its purity."

"Open your jacket," said Dr. Feel-Good.

Jenni did as she was told. Dr. Feel-Good groped her, feeling for any wires or weapons. Once he was satisfied, he said, "Get in."

Watching from our vantage point, Kelly and I were relieved that we hadn't tried to plant a bug on Jenni, but it also meant we couldn't lose her. I had taken the liberty of planting a GPS tracking device on Dr. Feel-Good's car. Once Jenni and Dr. Feel-Good were in the vehicle, I tapped my cell phone on and turned on the Google Earth app. Just in case the GPS tracking device failed, I asked John and Tyler to drive toward Cascadia and wait there while also having Ben and Mark drive down M-95 the other way, and wait for further instructions. As we had hoped, after administering the drug test which proved the heroin was pure, Dr. Feel-Good and Jenni started driving toward Cascadia to a waiting John and Tyler.

Following from a distance, I contacted Mark and Ben to let them know Dr. Feel-Good and Jenni were driving in the other direction. After entering Cascadia and appearing to drive toward Emerald Heights, Dr. Feel-Good's lights were barely in the distant horizon as we allowed him to stay just enough ahead so as not to notice us. When we couldn't see him, we relied on the GPS app to follow at a safe distance. Unfortunately, Dr. Feel-Good turned into underbrush and was gone before I came upon the scene. Dr. Feel-Good and Jenni drove toward a dark undergrowth of bushes, which turned out to be an old mine shaft.

Jenni had the wherewithal to turn her cell phone on and put it on speaker. She shouted, "I guess nobody has been here at this mine shaft in ages. It's a good place to hide the dope." Hearing this, I phoned John and Tyler to follow me, but as I slowed down, Jenni and Dr. Feel-Good were nowhere to be found. We parked our vehicles and crawled through the underbrush, hoping it would lead us to Feel-Good's drug stash.

After parking the vehicles, I motioned for everyone to continue searching the underbrush for a possible road. I approached an open cavern and peered down the mine shaft, hoping not to see Jenni at the bottom. The pseudo-detectives knew enough to go into stealth mode and not make a sound because Jenni's life depended on their silence. We crawled through the tough underbrush, wondering how a vehicle could find a road in such a mass of foliage. We discovered another mine shaft, barely visible to the naked eye with all the overgrowth around it. The pseudo-detectives, led by John Baldwin, didn't miss a trick. We were right on Feel-Good's trail, and I knew we didn't have a second to lose.

~~~

Once inside the mine cabin, Dr. Feel-Good turned, grabbed Jenni's bag, and he tried to pry it away from her.

"Not a chance," Jenni said. "You don't get any money until I see the dope. I'll give you a peek, but that's it." She opened the bag, revealing the top of the real money, but not the cut-up paper underneath.

"Listen, bitch," Dr. Feel-Good said. "I get the money first or there's no deal. *Comprende*?"

Jenni tried to stall for time by saying, "I have to pee. I'm nervous as hell, and I don't trust you. What's to keep you from killing me after you get the money?"

Dr. Feel-Good thought for a moment and said, "I'll need you for my next buy. Besides, it's bad for business."

Jenni was trying to think of anything she could to stall for time, so she asked Dr. Feel-Good, "What's your real name?"

"What's it to you?"

"Just curious," she replied.

"Josh McQueen," he said.

"Where are you from?" Jenni asked.

"Nowhere in particular. I was born in New Orleans and grew up in my mother's whorehouse. I've been dealing since I was nine years old. What's with all the questions?"

"Nothing," said Jenni. "I just want to know a little bit about my supplier. Can you blame me?"

"Don't worry about me," said Dr. Feel-Good. "Just worry about you walking out of here alive if I don't get the money."

Jenni nodded and tried to stall for more time by starting to walk toward the door, but Dr. Feel-Good blocked her exit.

"I want to see all of the money now," he said, "or there will be no next time."

"I told you I have to pee," Jenni said.

"You're not going anywhere until I see the money," he replied, grabbing the bag and pushing Jenni down. When he started to unzip the bag, Jenny knew her life was in jeopardy; she jumped up, grabbed the bag, and she shouted, "No drugs; no money."

Dr. Feel-Good smiled and said, "You're a feisty bitch, aren't you? I could use someone like you to help run my operation."

"Not a chance," said Jenni. "I have my own gig at State, and I don't need a partner, just a temporary dealer until I get back to college."

"I can see that," said Dr. Feel-Good, "but don't push your luck."

We knew once Dr. Feel-Good saw that the money in Jenni's bag was mostly bogus, he would discard her quickly. We had to hurry or Jenni would be dead. I felt relieved when we saw the cabin door open, but the feeling was short lived. Kelly and I had approached the cabin, continuing to see Dr. Feel-Good's flashlight as we got everyone in place. Eventually, Dr. Feel-Good walked toward the mine shaft, dragging Jenni with him. Apparently, Dr. Feel-Good wanted to show Jenni he did have sufficient drugs to satisfy her needs. Now the question was could we rescue her before he realized she had a bag of mostly paper?

From the outside, we could see the drug dealer pull up a floor board and smile. We were able to hear him say, "I told you I had an unlimited supply of drugs."

Jenni smiled and said, "I guess you were right."

"Now for your half of the deal," said Dr. Feel-Good. "Let's go back into the mine cabin and see the money."

Jenni tried to stall, but to no avail. She repeated, "I really have to pee. We can finish the deal when I'm done. It's won't take long."

"I don't believe this," said Dr. Feel-Good. "Hurry up and let's finalize the deal. I got other customers back at The Timbers."

He allowed her to relieve herself in the bushes. Then he said as she emerged, "Are you finally ready?" Jenni didn't reply.

As Dr. Feel-Good and Jenni approached the cabin. I noticed there appeared to be lookouts perched down by the river. Dr. Feel-Good turned a light on inside. Then he re-emerged and motioned for Jenni to enter. We were apprehensive to move forward from fear of being seen by the men down by the water. The lookouts didn't move at all and appeared to be gazing into the river. Hearing a scream inside the cabin, we had to throw caution to the wind. Kelly and I rushed the cabin followed by the other pseudo-detectives. I broke down the door and saw Dr. Feel-Good with a death-grip on Jenni's throat. The bag was lying on the floor with the shredded paper strewn everywhere. I shouted, "Stop or I'll blow you away where you stand!"

Jenni was gasping for air when she reached back and threw Dr. Feel-Good over her shoulder onto the floor. Kelly took command of the situation as she strong-armed Dr. Feel-Good. "Go ahead; give me a reason to kill you!" Kelly shouted as she handcuffed him.

The other pseudo-detectives dived through the door collectively and enjoyed watching Kelly make her first unofficial arrest as Jenni pried up one of the floor boards and uncovered a cache of heroin and Carfentanil.

"I tried to stall as long as I could," said Jenni. "I'm glad you were close behind." We returned to the mineshaft shed, entered, pulled all the floorboards up, and we stared at the catch. We estimated it contained 70 kilograms of pure heroin worth over $2 million on the street.

I looked at Jenni and Kelly and said, "Don't let anybody tell you otherwise; you did great. We never would have bagged this dope dealer if you hadn't stepped up. I'll be sure to let the State Police Academy know how great you did."

"But you know," I added, "all this heroin just didn't come into the cabin by itself. Let's take Dr. Feel-Good out to his stone friends and see if any of them will save him from his destiny."

The pseudo-detectives and I dragged the bum out to the lake and proceeded to walk him into the water. "How long can you stand on your toes?" John asked him.

I told Jenni and Kelly to wait in the car in case this didn't end well. I didn't want to shackle the girls with a murder accusation before they even commenced their legal careers.

Dragging Dr. Feel-Good to the water, we could make out that the people we thought we had seen were actually rocks stacked on top of one another. Both Kelly and I smiled at each other for being fooled into thinking they could be people. Both Jenni and Kelly walked to one of our cars and waited.

Chapter Six

As we were persuading Dr. Feel-Good to share his information; the drug dealer lashed out, "I am in custody and I have rights that must be protected. If you harm one hair on my head, all of you will still be serving time when I am out on the street."

At this point, we were so sick of drug dealers intimidating our legal system that his threat fell on deaf ears. John and I hauled the sorry drug-pusher out to the middle of the water in order to allow it to enter his mouth and nostrils. Dr. Feel-Good had to stand on his tiptoes to prevent water from entering his mouth and nose. In between gasps for air, he called us every insult he could conjure up and promised we would be prosecuted to the fullest extent of the law. After a few minutes, self-preservation seemed to preoccupy him. John and I felt we should allow Mother Nature to persuade him to help justice prevail. Determined not to tell us the name of the main drug lord, Dr. Feel-Good began to succumb to the water. His gasping for air became less and less conspicuous. Finally, in his last gasp of air, I heard him gasp, "Henry Bartle." I pulled him out of the water and slapped him a few times to make sure he was not hallucinating. Now we had the local dealer and the middle man.

"Maybe Mark and I could re-question Dr. Feel-Good without witnesses," Ben suggested.

"I'll give you a few minutes," I said, "but then we have to get him to the sheriff's office."

The rest of us returned to our vehicles while hearing some intense interrogation going on. After a few minutes, Ben and Mark returned with a bleeding Dr. Feel-Good. His look of arrogance was long gone. Ben said, "This piece of garbage confirmed again that the ringmaster, Jeb Stalworth, was his contact man, and he also thought Bartle funded the whole operation.

"Now that we have Feel-Good taken care of," said John, "Tyler and I want to turn our attention to the two Gomez brothers."

John laid out his plan, which sounded strikingly easy. Jenni and Kelly would return to tomorrow night to The Timbers and wait for the circus to conclude its performance. The girls would try to entice the Gomez brothers to lure the girls back to their trailer in hopes of scoring through their supply of marijuana. We and the sheriff deputies would be waiting outside for the girls to signal us when the stash was uncovered. Jenni or Kelly would pull the shade down and raise it halfway up when the Gomez brothers had produced enough grass. Before we did that I wanted to pacify my conscience that had been bothering me.

Chapter Seven

The next morning, I called John and I said, "I think it would be a good idea to pay our respects to Javier Garcia. He's been through a lot, and he has to make sure his sister gets back to Galena, Mexico."

"I'd like to go with you," John said. Since there was only one mortuary in Cascadia, I thought it would be good place to start. Approaching the mortuary, we drove into the rear parking lot. Entering through the back door, we saw the mortician, Ted Fawnsly, and we walked up to him. I asked, "Could you tell me where I might find Javier Garcia? I know he's making preparations for his sister's body to be transported back to Mexico."

"As a matter of fact, he's in the basement paying his respects to his sister," Ted replied.

"Thanks."

John and I stepped through the door that led to the basement where the bodies and caskets were kept. We walked down the stairs and entered the backroom where we knew we'd find Javier. I hoped we wouldn't bother him too much. Upon opening the door, both John and I were surprised to see Javier placing something in his sister's casket. At first, I assumed it was a farewell letter, so I didn't think much of it, but then Javier reacted when he saw us. He tried to close the lid of the casket, but the bag opened and thousands of dollars spilled onto the floor. Both John and I unholstered our Glocks and aimed them at Javier. "You better have a good reason for having this money," I said.

"I am sending my savings back with her," Javier replied.

"I don't buy that for a minute," said John. "There was an ATM robbery last night, and I think you're the thief. Get your hands up where I can see them."

I picked up the money from the floor and said, "There must be over a hundred thousand dollars here."

"One hundred and fifty thousand dollars to be exact," said Javier. "I might as well tell you; every time we performed in a city, I took the opportunity to visit the closest ATM and borrow some money. I was going to ship the money back with my sister's body and retrieve it once we were back in Mexico."

"Smart, and it almost worked," I said, "but you dishonored your sister by doing this. We stopped to pay our respects to you, but now I'm not sorry we came." Javier was speechless.

I called 911 and Deputy Roads was there in minutes. Needless to say, the mortician, Ted Fawnsly, was surprised to see the commotion. We were bringing Javier out the front door when Deputy Roads met us at the entrance.

"Here's your ATM thief and the money," I told him as I handed the large bag to Deputy Roads.

Chapter Eight

That night, one by one, the performers entered the bar. Jenni and Kelly were only too happy to flirt with the men. When Carlos and Tomas Gomez made their appearance, the girls fawned all over the daredevils. The brothers couldn't believe their good fortune. It was their last night in town, and what better way to go out than with a party that would fulfill their fantasies.

Jenni began the flirtation with, "Kelly and I really want to party, but we don't have any dope to get it started."

Tomas Gomez said in fluent English, "I can fix that. Let's blow this place and go to our trailer. We have more grass there than you can imagine."

"I don't know," said Kelly. "I think I better be getting home."

"I can guarantee you a party you won't forget," Carlos Gomez replied. "We have enough weed to smoke until the sun comes up tomorrow."

Jenni and Kelly were surprised that both brothers spoke English, but the girls suppressed their astonishment.

"Let me talk to Kelly alone," said Jenni. "Maybe I can convince her."

"If you can persuade her to come with us," said Tomas, "we'll make it worth your while. Our grass is 100 percent and hasn't been cut at all."

"Let me see what I can do," Jenni said.

Jenni and Kelly retired to the ladies' room and waited a few minutes to increase the Gomez's anticipation. The girls emerged after a satisfactory time and pretended to be apprehensive about going with the Gomez brothers back to their trailer. But after the brothers promised them a night to remember, the girls relented.

"We'll follow you in our car," said Jenni.

"Try to keep up," Tomas replied. "We always like to drive fast."

When they arrived at the trailer, Tomas and Carlos were euphoric over their chances of scoring before leaving town. They exited their cars and proceeded to the Gomez trailer. Upon entering, Tomas said, "Make yourselves comfortable. I'll get the grass and be right back."

The girls sat down, hoping their backup was just outside.

Tomas emerged from the bedroom, smiling with a bag of grass. He started to roll a cigarette when suddenly he saw movement outside. Thinking it was a setup; he pulled an Uzi gun from behind the dresser and aimed it at the girls.

At that moment, John broke through the door, followed closely by Tyler. Tyler tackled Tomas before he could commence firing. Carlos reached behind the couch and pulled out a pump shotgun. He never got the gun up because John shot him dead. Tyler and Tomas continued to struggle over the Uzi until John called for Tyler to get out of the way. Tyler was finally able to roll over, and then Tomas never had a chance. John shot him twice in the chest. Both brothers lay motionless as Sheriff Remington and his deputies poured in.

"That was a close call," said Jenni.

"Yes, too close," Kelly added. "Jenni and I are having a pretty adventurous beginning to our police careers."

"You girls are going to make great cops," I said, entering the trailer. "You are both incredibly brave."

John and Tyler seconded that and shook the girls' hands.

Sheriff Remington said, "I can't believe everything that is happening with this circus."

"You haven't seen anything yet," I replied.

Boy, was I right.

~~~

Saturday Afternoon

The pressure was on since today was the last day the circus would be performing before it pulled up stakes and left the area. Our plan had to work. There was added pressure with the Gomez brothers being shot and killed the previous night, but we had to put our plan into action.

As we were driving to Cascadia, our optimism was hampered by the possibilities that could cause our plan to fail, but we had to persevere no matter how bad the odds were. We were running out of time, so the previous night while the Baldwins were taking care of the Gomez brothers, I had made a call to my old friend, John Crane. He was a crack private detective who used unorthodox methods to achieve his results. He had helped us last year solve a horrible kidnapping, and he had even saved our lives by killing a group of escaped convicts who were minutes from murdering us.

When contacted, Crane, also known as Man-Mountain (usually by me) answered in his usual gruff manner, "What do you want?"

"I miss you too, John," I said. "I need you. Can you be here in the morning? We're having a series of murders, and if we don't find out who is responsible, the person will leave town and we'll never see them again."

I continued to explain our dilemma. When I had finished, John Crane said, "What's in it for me?"

Thinking quickly, I replied, "My undying gratitude."

The phone went dead. Well, I tried.

~~~

The pseudo-detectives and I arrived at the circus in the afternoon. On the way, I explained I had called John Crane and asked for his help.

"Are you kidding?" Mark asked. "We don't need that overrated jarhead."

"Maybe not, but we're running out of time," I said. "We know Jeb Stalworth is the middle man and Henry Bartle is the main distributor. The methods we used to obtain the confession from Dr. Feel-Good might be plausible in a medieval court of justice, but the procedure we used to acquire it wouldn't be worth anything in a modern court. Somehow, we have to get the two men to confess to their crimes."

We pulled into the Cascadia circus parking lot. The crowd of spectators, mostly children, had their enthusiasm tempered by the torrential downpour now threatening to put the field under water. The big cats were edgy because of the weather, and attendants were diligent about keeping the children away from the cages because the commotion would only make the big cats more unpredictable and harder to control once the performance began.

To put our plan into operation Kelly and Jenni walked toward the owner's office with my directions firmly planted in their minds.

Kelly and Jenni knocked on the owner's office door, then stepped back, allowing him to open it if he was there. There was no response, so the girls knocked again, hoping he would respond to the second attempt. No response again. The girls retreated to our vehicle with defeat written all over their faces.

We exited our automobile and asked whether Henry Bartle could be found. After some confusion, we were informed there was a crisis with one of the big cats. Apparently, one lion had an infection that needed attention. We saw Bartle walking toward us, but I wasn't sure whether this was the time to spring the trap. The pseudo-detectives quickly disappeared from sight so as not to interfere with Kelly and Jenni's con game.

Bartle walked past the girls, not even paying attention to them. He was mumbling to himself in frustration. Kelly took it upon herself to step up to Bartle and say, "Excuse me, but are you the owner of this circus?"

"I've got a sick lion to deal with. I don't have time for chit-chat," said Bartle. "Go home."

Kelly and Jenni weren't going to give up that easily. "We could sure use a job," said Kelly. "We'll do anything you ask us to."

Bartle thought for a second and said, "If you really want a job, go and see if you can help the trainers take care of that sick lion. I'm sick of dealing with that problem." The young women scurried off to the lion cages, having no idea what they were going to do when they got there.

Part VI - The Lion of Michigamme

When Kelly and Jenni arrived at the lion's cage, Emil looked at them and said, "The lion, Chico, is very sick with pneumonia. Being mammals, lions are very susceptible to the same diseases we are. A veterinarian will have to be called, which means the USDA will have to be informed. Consequently, this might be the end of the line for Mr. Bartle's circus."

Jenni Durant called us on her cell phone and informed us of the perilous situation. The girls returned to the main office, realizing there was nothing they could do for Chico. The girls knocked on Bartle's trailer door and heard some mixed rumblings from inside. Bartle staggered to the door and invited them inside. Our plan called for the young women to gain his confidence and locate the drugs. That plan wasn't going to work. Jenni and Kelly could see Bartle was loading a rifle and drinking hard booze at the same time.

"Do either of you want a snort before I finish the bottle?" he asked.

The women declined the alcohol, but they were more worried about what he was going to do with the rifle. Bartle stepped toward the young women, leaned into them, and said, "I'm offering you a drink, and when someone offers you a drink, it's impolite to refuse. Now take a sip."

Jenni and Kelly pushed him away. Bartle staggered out of the trailer with Jenni and Kelly following close behind. Kelly called me on her cell phone and said, "You better come quickly. The old man is heading toward the big cats, and I think I know what he is going to do."

Before Bartle got to the cages, Jeb Stalworth joined him, carrying a pistol.

"You're definitely going to need help to control the cats," Stalworth told him. "They're getting worse every day. Old Emil can't keep them controlled anymore."

The five of us sprung out of our vehicle and raced toward the animal cages. Bartle approached Chico's cage, and using his key, opened the cage door. Stalworth moved around to the other side of the cage to get a better shot. Chico remained motionless as Bartle raised his rifle to fire. Bartle tried to take careful aim, but he was staggering so badly that he could hardly keep the rifle pointed at the cat. Before he could squeeze the trigger, Chico rose and jumped on Bartle, mauling him badly. Stalworth ran to his aid and tried to squeeze off a shot.

Fear is a funny thing when it completely takes over a person. There are stories that people only had to perform simple acts to survive, but because they were frozen in fear they were unable to move. Such was Stallworth's fate. He raised his pistol and just stared at the big cat.

Just then, the cat was pulled off Bartle and Chico was thrown to the ground. The big cat leaped up, but was knocked down again. John Crane, alias Man-Mountain, stood over Chico, staring him down. The big cat started to crawl toward the defenseless Stalworth. Chico, as sick as he was, could smell fear in the air. He took one look at Stalworth and started to lunge at him. John Crane shouted to Stalworth, "If you want to live, tell me who was responsible for Maria Garcia's death?"

Frozen with fear, Jeb Stalworth shouted, "It was Bartle all along. I had to go along if I wanted to keep my job."

Crane grabbed Chico from behind and wrapped his legs around the big cat's neck, keeping him at bay until Emil arrived and shot a tranquilizer dart into the cat.

Crane looked at Stalworth and demanded, "Can you prove it?"

"Yes," said Stalworth. "You'll find the drugs in Bartle's trailer."

Approaching with our pistols drawn, more assistants appeared and cajoled Chico back into his cage, and then they shut the cage door and locked the big cat inside. I called Sheriff Remington and informed him what had transpired.

Sheriff Remington said, "I'll send some deputies ASAP to arrest Stalworth and clean up the mess."

Shortly, his deputies were on the scene as was Carolyn Raft. It was a grisly spectacle to behold. After Bartle's body was removed, a veterinarian was summoned to administer an antibiotic for the cat's infection. The veterinarian said, "That will make the cat feel better for a while."

The other circus performers appeared out of nowhere, overwhelmed with the circumstances. Even Renaldo said to himself that he was lucky he hadn't tangled with this crew. I walked up to John Crane and said, "I knew you'd come."

"Don't flatter yourself," said Man-Mountain. "I knew you and your crew needed help. I understand the federal government has a reward for breaking this drug ring up. You know where to send the reward money." He disappeared into the crowd, and just like that, he was gone again.

We all looked at each other and smiled.

As the sheriff's cruiser drove away with Jeb Stalworth tucked safely in the backseat, I said to John, "We cleaned up this mess, and ironically, it was poetic justice. Since Bartle and Stalworth withheld treatment from the big cats, Chico got his revenge and truly was the *Lion on the Michigamme*."